She rested her **[ ]** of the detective **[ ]** in, dropping her voice to a whisper. "You understand that I don't always see evidence in the same way you do, Mr. Banning."

His green eyes filled with skepticism. "So I've heard."

"I don't dream this stuff up, Detective. I possess a psychic ability to sense things. When I put my mind to it, I can see things especially clearly. When I touch people or objects, I pick up emotions, memories—"

"You predict the future."

Kelsey bristled. "Look, Banning, do you want to know what I saw or not?" She waited for his prompt to continue. "I believe I've accidentally come across an object that has something to do with one of those prostitutes who've been murdered around Christmas and New Year's over the past decade."

"Nine murders in eleven years," he clarified. "Don't tell me you've found the murder weapon?"

"No. But it's something one of the victims touched. I'm sure of that."

"So you've found *some* object that *some*body touched, and you think it will solve the case for us?"

Mr. Uptight, Suit-'n'-Tie wasn't going to cut her a break, but she wasn't about to back down. Lives were at stake!

Dear Harlequin Intrigue Reader,

As we ring in a new year, we have another great month of mystery and suspense coupled with steamy passion.

Here are some juicy highlights from our six-book lineup:

• Julie Miller launches a new series, THE PRECINCT, beginning with *Partner-Protector*. These books revolve around the rugged Fourth Precinct lawmen of Kansas City whom you first fell in love with in the TAYLOR CLAN series!

• *Rocky Mountain Mystery* marks the beginning of Cassie Miles's riveting new trilogy, COLORADO CRIME CONSULTANTS, about a network of private citizens who volunteer their expertise in solving criminal investigations.

• Those popular TOP SECRET BABIES return to our lineup for the next *four* months!

• Gothic-inspired tales continue in our spine-tingling ECLIPSE promotion.

And don't forget to look for Debra Webb's special Signature Spotlight title this month: *Dying To Play*.

Hopefully we've whetted your appetite for January's thrilling lineup. And be sure to check back every month to satisfy your craving for outstanding suspense reading.

Enjoy!

Denise O'Sullivan
Senior Editor
Harlequin Intrigue

Julie Miller

THE PRECINCT

Partner—Protector

HARLEQUIN®

TORONTO • NEW YORK • LONDON
AMSTERDAM • PARIS • SYDNEY • HAMBURG
STOCKHOLM • ATHENS • TOKYO • MILAN • MADRID
PRAGUE • WARSAW • BUDAPEST • AUCKLAND

For Denise O'Sullivan.

I've worked with many people at Harlequin over the years,
but you've always been there—on the front line or in the background,
watching over me like a guardian angel.

We share a love for Intrigue and dark, tortured heroes. You answer my
rambling e-mails kindly and precisely. You don't see anything wrong with
my penchant for blowing up things and stabbing people <g>.
And you taught me the valuable lesson that it's all about the reader.

Thank you.

ISBN 0-373-22819-8

PARTNER-PROTECTOR

Copyright © 2005 by Julie Miller

www.eHarlequin.com

Printed in U.S.A.

ABOUT THE AUTHOR

Julie Miller attributes her passion for writing romance to all those fairy tales she read growing up, and shyness. Encouragement from her family to write down all those feelings she couldn't express became a love for the written word. She gets continued support from her fellow members of the Prairieland Romance Writers, where she serves as the resident "grammar goddess." This award-winning author and teacher has published several paranormal romances. Inspired by the likes of Agatha Christie and Encyclopedia Brown, Ms. Miller believes the only thing better than a good mystery is a good romance.

Born and raised in Missouri, she now lives in Nebraska with her husband, son and smiling guard dog, Maxie. Write to Julie at P.O. Box 5162, Grand Island, NE 68802-5162.

Books by Julie Miller

*The Taylor Clan
†The Precinct

CAST OF CHARACTERS

Detective Thomas Merle Banning—Once the rookie computer geek of the Fourth Precinct, brains, hard work and a couple of gunshot wounds had finally earned him some respect. So why was he being partnered with a psychic consultant to solve a cold-case murder? And why did somebody want her dead?

Kelsey Ryan—The Flake. With a nickname like that, how could anyone, especially the cops, believe she'd "seen" a grisly murder?

Rev. Ulysses Wingate—He runs a mission in downtown Kansas City for those in need.

Doc Siegel—Someone has to graduate at the bottom of the class.

Zero—A prince among pimps. Or so he claims. His girls might have a different opinion.

Rebecca Page—The crime beat reporter wants to finish the story her father never could.

Patrick Halliwell—He gave money to reputable causes. And some not so reputable.

Ed Watkins—He'd worked the Fourth Precinct for a lot of years.

Jezebel—Eleven years ago, she'd known how to show a man a good time. She'd paid for her expertise with her life.

Prologue

"I beg you. Please. Don't."

She backed away as far as she could go, giving a soft, startled yelp when she hit the hard, dark wall. Trapped.

Splinters of rough wood caught in her hair, scratched the bare skin of her shoulders. She crossed her arms in front of her, but there was no place to hide, no way to shield herself.

"I'm sorry. I didn't know there were rules."

But there were no words to placate the anger she saw, no words to assuage the hatred. She was cold. Shaking. Crying.

He was coming.

"Sorry about the gift, big boy." Fear dulled her reasoning, made her grasp at the first thought that flashed in her mind. "Big boy. You like that?" She reached out, but he wouldn't take her hand. She curled the rejected fingers into her fist and clutched it over her naked breast.

She tried to smile, but her lips quivered. The tears kept falling. The wall was cutting into her back and she was afraid.

"I can call you that. Big boy. I can do whatever you want."

Her breath caught in her chest and couldn't seem to get past her pounding heart. He didn't care. She'd laughed.

She shouldn't have laughed.

"Most men bring cash. I didn't understand. I'm surprised, that's all. It doesn't mean I don't like it. I can learn to appreciate it."

He caressed her face. She jerked her head to the side, hating his touch. Her cheek scraped against the unfinished wood. The pungent smells of cold and rot stung her nose. His finger traced a gentle path down her neck, over her breast. Such a loving caress. She nearly gagged.

She squeezed her eyes shut and tried to go to that distant place inside her head she always went when men touched her. But she couldn't find it. He was talking now. She couldn't make out the words. She was cold and shaking and naked and so afraid.

She had to make this right.

Her life depended on it.

She bit her lips to bring their color back. She lowered her arms to show him everything he'd come for. She dropped her voice to a husky pitch that had seduced before.

She looked up into his shadowed expression. "Just tell me what you want. Anything you want. I'll do it. No charge."

He reached into his pocket and pulled out a scarf. It was long and narrow, tattered as if it had come from an old woman's attic or a flea market. Its mustard-yellow trim and fuschia dots were the only colors that registered in the darkness.

Mustard and fuschia, with the hard wall cutting into her back and his nonsense words condemning her.

The damn thing was ugly. But she didn't look away.

She held her breath as he let it unfurl, shivered as the silk slid over her breasts.

"That's pretty," she lied. "Is that for me, too?"

Her entire body jerked at the exact moment she realized it wasn't another gift.

"No!"

Suddenly it was too dark to see anything, to know anything beyond the pain that clutched at her throat. She pounded her fists. She twisted. She fought.

Scratches flayed open as he shoved her brutally against the wall. Her hair tangled in the wood's coarse texture and ripped from her scalp.

As darkness closed in, fear dragged her down into its frigid grasp. Her screams gurgled in her throat. Her windpipe snapped. Starved for oxygen, her lungs imploded. Lights danced before her eyes. Her knees buckled. Blackness caved in all around her.

No more pain.

"Wake up! Wake up!"

Kelsey Ryan was clawing at her own throat when the voiceless words roused her from her nightmare.

Only, she knew it was no nightmare.

She snapped her eyes open and looked straight into two round, dark eyes, a black nose and a pair of paws on the pillow beside her. "Frosty?"

Real dog. Real time. Real world.

Not dead.

Kelsey grabbed the miniature poodle and sat up, hugging him tight, burying her nose in the soft mop of silver curls atop his head and inhaling his familiar scent. The rasp of his friendly tongue along her jaw and neck warmed the winter chill that clung to her skin.

"Did I scare you, sweetie?" She swiped her spiky bangs from her eyes and leaned over to turn on the lamp beside her bed. No wonder her faithful guardian had been so concerned. She'd trashed half her room this time. "Mama's sorry. I'm okay."

She kissed his furry head, then set him on the floor. Her reassurance was apparently all he needed to hear before trotting back to whatever chair or rug he'd deemed his bed for the night.

Kelsey untangled her legs from the wedge of sheets she'd thrashed between her legs and climbed out of bed. The late December deep freeze radiated from the polished wood floor through her stockinged feet. But even bundled in the gray sweats she wore for pajamas, she knew she wouldn't feel warm any time soon.

She righted the clock that had tipped over. Three-thirteen in the morning. Hopefully, she hadn't screamed out loud. Not that her retirement age neighbors paid her too much mind. As long as she kept her sidewalk shoveled in the winter and her yard trimmed in the summer, they seemed content to leave her alone in her cottage-style house in an old neighborhood on the north side of Kansas City.

Still, a random scream in the dark of night…

Wave after wave of shivers cascaded down Kelsey's spine. She squeezed her eyes shut tight and hugged herself, trying to block out the memories. But they wouldn't stop. She pursed her lips and breathed deeply, but the remembered terror wouldn't go away.

There'd been nothing *random* about what she'd sensed.

She'd felt that woman's pain.

She'd lived that woman's fear.

She'd seen that woman's death.

A crushing sense of destiny opened Kelsey's eyes. Something had triggered that episode. She had to find it.

Moving quickly now, she methodically put her room back in order. Her eyes burned with unshed tears as she waited for the inevitable attack.

Kelsey picked up the wad of blanket she'd kicked to the floor, and tucked in the sheet she'd ripped from the corner of the mattress. After retrieving the pillow she'd tossed against the wall, she picked up the dolls that had toppled over on the nightstand where she displayed them. She must have knocked them over when, barely awake, she'd reached for a tissue in the middle of the night.

One by one, she stood her little treasures up and re-arranged them. The porcelain-head doll her grand-mother had sewn such exquisite dresses for. The brocaded Beast doll she'd made herself with paints and thread and love. The fairy-tale princess—a Christmas present to herself—she'd found in an antique shop to go with him.

Kelsey picked up the princess by her narrow waist.

Cold. Fear. Pain. *"Help me!"* Death.

The same bombardment of words and images jerked through her.

She dropped the doll as if her fingers had been burned.

It lay on the bed now, a seemingly innocent package of old silk and beads and embroidery. She stared at it. Hard. Knowing what she must do. Hating it.

Gandalf the Grey hadn't dreaded touching the One Ring as much as she was loathe to touch that doll again. But she pulled the afghan from the foot of the bed and tossed it over the doll. Careful not to touch it directly, she carried it into the kitchen, dug the box it had come in out of the trash and carefully placed it inside.

Then, with every light in the kitchen blazing, she pulled out the phone book and looked up a number. The call could wait until morning, but there'd be fewer people around to laugh this time of night.

She knew that woman had been all alone. Wouldn't be missed.

Kelsey understood the feeling without having to see it in a dream or vision or impression.

That meant she was the only one who could help.

Conscience, and a promise to her grandmother said she must.

Pushing aside her own fears and stiffening her spine, Kelsey took a deep, fortifying breath and dialed.

"K.C.P.D. Crime Hot Line," a tired, bored voice answered.

Not for the first time in her life, Kelsey wondered why she'd been cursed.

"I'd like to report a murder."

Chapter One

"You're assigning me to The Flake?"

Detective Thomas Merle Banning stared across the office at his captain, Mitch Taylor. Nice back-to-work-after-Christmas present.

Yeah, right.

"Actually, I'm assigning her to you." The distinction wasn't any comfort. "You're the detective, she's the departmental consultant."

"She's the nutcase everybody jokes about in the coffee room."

"Nonetheless, she's expecting to meet with you later this morning."

How the hell had he gotten so lucky? He no longer had anything to prove, did he? His arrest record was solid, his aim good enough to earn a marksman's pin, his reports spotless down to the minutest detail. And no one who knew him—with two rare exceptions—dared call him nerdy Merle to his face anymore. He'd long since outgrown terms like *rookie* and *computer geek*.

But this smacked of some kind of practical joke or penance.

"Why don't you just shoot me now and put me out of

my misery?" He marched across the room in his determined, rolling stride and faced Mitch across his desk. "I thought you were putting me on the cold-case detail for the next few months while Ginny's on maternity leave."

"I am."

"Then put me on a desk. Let me work. Don't waste my time with this woman."

"This woman believes she's *seen* something that can help one of those cases."

With his regular partner, Ginny Rafferty-Taylor, assigned to extended bed rest for the last trimester of her pregnancy, Merle had already been taken off the active homicide investigation team and relegated to sorting through boxes of dead-end cases. He hadn't argued the reassignment because Captain Taylor had played to his ego, telling him he had a real knack for uncovering details others missed and patiently piecing together random clues to complete investigative puzzles.

But no amount of ego stroking was going to make this right. He worked with the smartest, prettiest, classiest woman on the planet. Not UFO-chasing, crystal-ball-reading, hocus-pocus crackpots. It was hard enough to lose Ginny. But to let another woman try to take her place as his partner?

Make that *departmental consultant.*

Merle scrubbed his palm across his clean-shaven jaw and shrugged. "The Flake?"

"She has a name." Captain Taylor's resonant voice reprimanded him like the father he'd lost so long ago. "Kelsey Ryan. She has a degree in criminal justice studies and teaches a course in psychic forensic science over at University of Missouri-Kansas City."

Psychic science? Wasn't that some kind of oxymoron? "What the hell is that? Since when does K.C.P.D. rely on psychobabble to solve cases? She's nothing but a PR nightmare. No one will take me seriously if she's attached to me. I'd rather work alone."

He pulled back the front of his tweed jacket and shoved his hands into the pockets of his khaki slacks, pacing the confines of the small office. The twinge in his right knee was more pronounced with the bitter temperatures plaguing the city these past few weeks. But pain was just something a mature man lived with. Banning had been on the force for seven years now, had been a detective for five. He'd long since outgrown his naive new kid on the block status.

Taking a couple of bullets that left his body scarred and his soul ancient beyond his twenty-nine years did that to a man.

In those seven years of service, he'd unholstered his weapon only twice while on duty. He'd been forced to kill a man each time.

Those were the kinds of odds that sobered a man's way of thinking. Made him understand the value of cold, hard facts and leaving nothing to chance.

That's why this made no sense.

He stopped and looked into his superior's sage brown eyes. "Why me, Captain?"

For such a big, robust man, Mitch Taylor was surprisingly gentle as he adjusted the framed picture of his wife and young son on the desk in front of him. When he sat down, Merle took the clue and eased into a chair on the opposite side. The old man wanted to talk, and Merle had learned it paid to listen to the veteran cop.

"One thing I've learned about you over the years, Banning, is that you're smart. You don't just learn from your books and computers, but from people. From mistakes and successes, your own and others'. I'm counting on the fact you might be willing to learn something from Ms. Ryan, too." The captain nodded toward the blind-covered windows that separated his office from the rows of desks and cubicles that formed the Fourth Precinct detective division. "I can name at least a half-dozen men out there who'd just brush her aside. But I can count on you to be gentleman enough not to laugh in her face when she tells her story."

Merle couldn't stop the sarcasm from bleeding into his voice. "You want me to work with her because my mother taught me good manners?"

"Someone has to talk to her. Take her statement, at the very least. If there's any credibility to what she has to say, I know you'll be fair."

The captain thought Kelsey Ryan was that important? Or was this more ego stroking to bribe him into taking a job nobody else wanted? He still wasn't about to accept this assignment wholeheartedly, but there was a certain wisdom in pleasing the boss. "All I have to do is take her statement?"

Captain Taylor nodded. "She claims she can help with the Holiday Hooker murders."

"Let me guess. She thinks she was a hooker in another life."

That one actually made the old man smile. "Don't dismiss her yet. We can't afford to alienate any citizen right now." He shoved this morning's *Kansas City Star* newspaper across the desk and pointed to a headline near the bottom of the front page.

K.C.P.D. No Closer To IDing Remains Of Infant Girl

"Ouch." The discovery of a baby Jane Doe's body in

one of the area landfills more than two months ago had galvanized the entire department from homicide to missing persons to traffic cops. Every man and woman on the force seemed to take it personally that that child had been killed. But even the special task force assigned to the investigation had been thus far unable to put together many leads.

"Ouch is right." Captain Taylor boxed up his emotions and set them aside the same way Merle had to. "The new commissioner, Shauna Cartwright, is desperate for some good press for a change. She's ordered us to pay attention to every report that comes in. And to solve some cases."

"So meeting with Kelsey Ryan would be doing a favor for the commissioner?"

"You'd be doing a favor for me."

"All right, then." It was enough that Mitch Taylor had asked him to do this. That the captain trusted he was the best man for the assignment—even if it was a lousy one. And hell, his hide was thick enough to withstand a little razzing from his peers.

Merle pushed to his feet, adjusting his jacket over the badge and gun clipped to his belt. "I'm off to make headlines for the department."

"Just make sure they're good ones."

"Yes, sir." Before leaving, Merle paused, exhaling caution on one overly curious breath. "How is Ginny doing?"

Mitch might have inside information on the petite blond detective. He was more than Ginny's boss. He was her cousin-in-law and her husband's best friend. They were all part of a big, happy family that Merle could hang out with and admire, but never truly be part of.

Mitch didn't know his secret. Didn't even question

Merle's interest. After all, it was perfectly normal for a cop to inquire about his partner's health and well-being. "She's fine. These last three months on total bed rest is driving her nuts, but Brett's keeping a close eye on her to make sure she does everything the doctor says." God, how that big brute loved his wife.

Just as Merle loved her.

But he was nothing more than Ginny's friend. The kid brother she'd never had. His feelings were anything but brotherly for his detective partner. But she loved somebody else.

Merle nodded, breathing through the pain with a smile, hiding much more than Mitch or anyone else would ever guess. "Give her my best when you see her."

"Why don't you stop by? She'd love to see you. Hell. According to Brett, she'd love to see anybody."

Merle laughed right along with him. "I'll do that."

The phone on Captain Taylor's desk rang. He put up one finger, ordering Merle not to leave quite yet. He picked up the receiver. "Yeah, Maggie?" His gaze shot to Merle's. The call had something to do with him. "I'll tell him."

Merle splayed his hands at his hips, waiting as the captain hung up the phone and stood. He tilted his chin ever so slightly to maintain eye contact with the bigger man. "What's up?"

Was that a smirk? The captain's barrel chest heaved with a sigh. "If nothing else, your flake is punctual. Maggie says Ms. Ryan just checked in. She's waiting for you at your desk."

Merle crossed to the blinds and peeked out, needing a moment to gather the gentlemanly composure Captain Taylor thought he had in such abundant supply. "You've got to be kidding."

He'd seen her in grainy black-and-white news photos, and in caricatures scribbled onto notepads. But nothing had prepared him for the real thing.

He saw her hair first. It stuck out from the crown in an explosion of short, flamboyant curls, with little wisps spiking around her ears and onto her cheekbones and neck. A sweep of bangs curled down over her forehead, flirting with her eyebrows and parting to one side as she pushed them off her face with the tips of her turquoise-gloved fingers.

But the gelled, pop-star style wasn't the most noticeable thing. It was the color. Red. Not copper. Not auburn. But a flashy, unnatural tint that reminded him of rubies and fire engines and flagging down ships.

A quick scan farther down her body indicated that subtlety just wasn't part of her vocabulary. Her knee-length, black-and-white checked coat hung open. A knitted scarf of bright turquoise draped around her neck and clashed with the electric-blue, snowman-patterned sweater she wore over a long denim skirt and clunky black lace-up boots.

Her cheeks and nose were flushed from the cold and wind outside. But instead of huddling her posture for warmth, she sat ramrod straight, shamelessly glancing all around the office and taking note of everybody's business.

But there was a sharpness to her light brown eyes that conveyed more than nosy curiosity. She was gauging distances, occupations, degrees of interest in her presence the way any con artist would upon entering a den of cops.

There was a hint of arrogance about her, a defiance that surprised him.

Kelsey Ryan didn't want to talk to him any more than he wanted to talk to her.

Merle frowned. He didn't know whether he felt relieved or insulted by that observation.

"Is something wrong?" asked Mitch.

Oh, yeah. But this was for the commissioner. For good press. For Captain Taylor. Out loud, Merle said the only thing he could. "No, sir."

He adjusted his tie as if donning a suit of armor.

Then he opened the door.

Brooks Brothers. Ten o'clock.

Kelsey kept her body facing straight ahead, but turned her eyes to watch the man approach.

Khaki slacks. Navy tweed blazer. Maroon silk tie. Dark blond hair cut too short for any strand to be out of place. Chiseled features cleanly shaven and devoid of humor. Trim, evenly-proportioned build from broad shoulders to slim hips. A coiled strength to his stride to hide the hitch in every step.

The little frisson of awareness that shimmied down her spine was inconsequential.

This guy was too neat. Too clean. Too buttoned down and under control to be open-minded at all.

Ho boy.

He was the worst kind of cop to tell her story to. Not that any of them in her limited experience had been gung ho about taking her talent seriously.

Still, that woman last night had been so alone.

For a few seconds last night, Kelsey had shared her stark, hopeless terror.

That woman had no one but Kelsey to help her. To remember.

As the detective neared the desk, she guessed him to be about six foot, maybe half a foot taller than herself. And despite the slight smile that touched the corners of his mouth, she didn't sense that he'd gotten any friendlier since stepping out of that office. Kelsey rose to meet him, instinctively clutching at the crystal pendant hanging beneath her sweater and camisole, warming her skin.

"Detective Banning?"

He nodded and extended his hand. "Ms. Ryan."

Since she still wore her turquoise gloves, she didn't hesitate to clasp his hand and exchange a polite, professional greeting. It might be the only civility she'd find here this morning.

"Have a seat." He gestured to the straight-backed chair beside his desk, then sat in his own chair and pivoted to face her. "So you found out something about the Holiday Hooker murders you'd like to report?"

Kelsey glanced down at the black leather backpack propped beside her chair and thought of the box with its well-wrapped doll tucked away inside. She wanted to hand over the tragic object with all its hate-filled psychic residue and get its poisonous influence out of her life.

But that would be disloyal to that sad, frightened woman whom she'd gotten to know so well in her last few seconds of existence.

Kelsey's grandmother had taught her to use her curse as a gift. Grandma Lucy Belle had said that by helping others who couldn't be helped in any other way, her inherited talent would feel less like a burden. Kelsey's grandmother had been so wise. So loving. She wouldn't disappoint the faith Lucy Belle had had in her.

Detective Banning was watching her with more politeness than patience when she looked up. Letting the calmness of the blue crystal pendant her grandmother had given her work its spell over her nerves, Kelsey took a deep breath. She rested her elbow on the corner of the detective's desk and leaned in, dropping her voice to a whisper. "You understand that I don't always see evidence in the same way you do, Mr. Banning."

His green eyes filled with skepticism. "So I've heard." He thumbed through some papers on his desk, but she had a feeling he wasn't reading any of them. "Captain Taylor tells me you had a dream about a murder last night, and called it in."

Kelsey sat back, disappointed, but not surprised by his misinformation.

"I don't dream this stuff up, Detective." She adopted her most succinct, teaching-the-uneducated voice and explained. "I possess a psychic ability to sense things. When I put my mind to it, or when my guard is down like it was last night, I can see things especially clearly. When I touch people or objects, I pick up emotions, memories—"

"You predict the future."

Kelsey bristled. "No. It doesn't work like that. I can't help you win the lottery. Sometimes I can sense what a person is thinking or feeling about the future, but that doesn't mean it's going to happen. I have better luck reading the residue of something that's already taken place in the past."

"Luck, huh?"

Poor choice of words. She'd set herself up for that one. "Look, Banning, do you want to know what I saw or not?"

He nodded, but she didn't see any glimmer of understanding lighting his eyes. "Okay. So you touched something last night, got a little freaky sensation and called the cops."

Crude and suggestive, but basically accurate. Kelsey decided to let the lesson drop and continued on. "I believe I've accidentally come across an object that has something to do with one of those prostitutes who've been murdered around Christmas and New Year's over the last decade."

"Nine murders in eleven years," he clarified. But he didn't ask about the object.

She nudged her backpack with her boot, grateful for all the layers separating her from the doll's frightening aura. "I don't know if this is something that belonged to one of the victims or to the killer."

His gaze dropped to the backpack, as well. "Don't tell me you found the murder weapon?"

"No. But it's something one of them touched. I'm sure of that."

"So you found *some* object that *some*body touched, and you think it will solve the case for us?"

Mr. Uptight Suit-'n-Tie wasn't going to give her a break. "Look, I don't presume to do your job. But since the murders haven't been solved yet, I assumed you might appreciate a little help. I'd like a chance to explain what I know."

He was already standing up by the time she finished her lecture. "So this could take a while, right? Why don't I get us some coffee. How do you take yours? Black? Cream or sugar?"

Kelsey tipped her gaze up to his, refusing to be so easily dismissed. "Both, please."

With a curt nod, he strode across the room. Kelsey watched him move. While she regrouped her tranquility and determination with some deep, even breathing, the analytical part of her mind strayed. She wondered if Detective Banning, with more control than grace in his movements, had one leg shorter than the other. And whether the stiffness of his right knee was the cause of his limp or the result of it.

She knew one way to find some answers.

But touching Merle Banning, skin to skin, wasn't an option she wanted to pursue. Hadn't she freaked out enough men over the years by holding hands or sharing a kiss?

Of course, she could always think about her disastrous relationship with Jeb if she ever needed a reminder about why she had no business getting involved with a man. His cruel jokes and abusive words should have been enough to kill any interest she might have in the male species.

Speaking of…

The distinctive sound of deep, male laughter diverted her attention to the break room. With the door propped open and windows forming the wall from waist to ceiling, she could see a short, bulky, uniformed officer resting his hip on the counter beside Banning and the coffeepot. Another blue-suited cop and a pair of plainclothes detectives sat at a table. Someone must have said something funny. Something teasing, something lowbrow, no doubt.

The stout officer's gaze connected with hers through the glass. Oh, no. His leering grin mocked her. As if a man with only four or five strings of hair to comb over his bald pate had any right to make fun of someone else. He took his leisurely time and finally turned his back to her. Maybe he didn't care that he'd been caught, or maybe he felt he'd already had the last laugh at her expense.

And was that…? Yes. Kelsey's stomach twisted into a self-conscious knot. Someone was singing an off-key rendition of the theme from *The Twilight Zone*.

Cute.

Not terribly original, but cute.

All the hurts and insults and accusations she'd endured throughout her life burned with a molten intensity in her veins. Some days, it seemed that defensive anger was the only thing that could keep her warm.

Today was one of those days.

She watched the interchange unfold in the break room without hearing the words. But she didn't need to. One didn't grow up different from everyone else without knowing when someone was calling you "The Flake" or "crazy" or "delusional." It was too easy for people to ridicule what they didn't understand. Most of the time she was patient with them, but not today. Not after what she'd seen and felt last night.

She'd been so cold. So scared.

She'd felt that woman's death.

Kelsey tugged her coat together at her neck and shivered inside, trying to hold on to her anger. But the fear was more powerful. She had to do something. She had to tell someone.

As if sensing her fight-or-flight instincts kicking in, Detective Banning turned. Green eyes met brown through the glass. For a few unguarded seconds, Kelsey held on to his gaze, wanting to answer the question there, wondering if she was imagining the concern.

With a blink, his gaze moved past her. Kelsey's

breath seeped out on a sigh. She felt strangely bereft, as if denied something precious almost within her reach.

Banning said something to one of the detectives at the table. The singing stopped amidst another round of laughter. To his credit, Banning wasn't laughing. A champion? He barely knew her. Just a nice guy, telling his buddies not to make fun where she could see them? Small consolation. Or was he embarrassed that they could see her sitting at his desk, linking them together, no matter how impersonally?

Jeb had been embarrassed.

Just like that, the anger was back. *Screw this.* There had to be someone else in this city she could talk to.

Kelsey stood, adjusted her skirt down to her calves. She slipped her backpack over one shoulder and started buttoning her coat as she zigzagged between the desks and headed straight for the bank of elevators that would take her back down to the street and out into the freezing cold.

"Hey!" She pretended she didn't recognize the voice, and that he wasn't calling to her. He'd be glad if she could slip out and never darken his desk again.

She had the elevator button in sight when a band of fingers closed around her arm, just above the elbow. Kelsey jumped.

"Whoa." Banning quickly released her, holding his hand up in surrender as she jerked around. She didn't bother with a *Don't touch me*. He probably got that idea loud and clear from her startled, chest-clutching reaction. "Where are you going? We're just getting started." He held up the two steaming plastic cups he balanced in his left hand. "Coffee?"

Kelsey stared at the cups for a senseless moment,

then tipped her chin to look up at him. "No, thank you, Mr. Banning. We're finished." Her voice sounded surprisingly succinct as she pushed it past the pounding pulse in her throat. "Hard as this might be for you to believe, my time is valuable. I'm here for a legitimate reason. I saw a woman murdered. I do not make up stories, and I will not be ridiculed by you, your friends or anybody else."

She spun toward the elevators, but he brushed past her in an eclectic whiff of wool and spice and overbrewed coffee to block her path. "Then let's get out of here."

Kelsey stopped short, lifting her gaze above his starched white collar and the jut of his chin. "Embarrassed to be seen with The Flake?"

He didn't deny the nickname or the embarrassment. But he did offer an unexpected argument. "Well, that hair does draw a lot of attention. I'm assuming it's not your natural color?"

Was that a serious question, or was he teasing her? The confusion was enough to defuse her temper. She simply explained the color choice. "I get good vibes from red."

"I always wondered why women dyed their hair. It's the vibes, huh?"

He thrust his wrist from the end of his sleeve and checked his watch. His jacket veed open, giving her a glimpse of the brass and blue enamel badge clipped to his belt beside the brown leather holster at his hip. The weapon inside was a sobering reminder that just because he was curious or teasing or polite, he was not her friend.

"You eat lunch?" he asked.

"On most days. I *am* human and do require sustenance."

He grinned, subtracting years from the serious set of his mouth. The unexpectedly sexy result was almost as disconcerting as when he'd grabbed her arm. "I meant, have you eaten lunch today?"

"Oh." Kelsey quickly gathered her composure. She had to think of Merle Banning as a cop, not a man. Certainly not an attractive one. "No. I haven't eaten since last night."

She hadn't had the appetite to stomach food.

"Well, since I require sustenance the same way you do, let's go grab a quick bite to eat. We can continue our conversation someplace without the audience." He nodded his head toward the break room. "Away from those yahoos."

Kelsey looked over shoulder and spotted the pudgy bald guy watching her again. Did he think he knew her? Should she know him? Being stared at like that, without any apology, like some sort of sideshow phenomenon, gave her the willies. The barrel-chested man, standing in the open doorway to the Captain's office and eyeing the interaction between her and Banning like some sort of watchful guardian didn't help, either. She quickly turned away.

She'd love to get out of here.

Kelsey nodded. "Okay. That's fine. I need to eat before my afternoon class, anyway."

"All right. Let me ditch these and we'll head out."

Kelsey refused to turn around to see where he dumped the coffee and retrieved his coat. That bald cop might still be staring at her. Well, he could look all he liked. She didn't have to give him the satisfaction of knowing how his unwanted attention rattled her.

Going out to lunch. That almost sounded like a date. But it wasn't. Kelsey knew better. Men didn't ask her out. Not ones who knew about her *talent*. Whether Merle Banning believed her or not, this would be a working lunch.

The weight of the bag on her shoulder multiplied with her resolute sigh, bearing down with the burden of so much more than that doll. She carried the memory of last night's murderous vision, the responsibility of her curse—along with the crippling knowledge that, more likely than not, she would always carry that burden alone.

Chapter Two

The Jukebox, just east of the Plaza in downtown Kansas City, was a 1950s-style soda fountain and burger joint, complete with twirling bar stools, vinyl booths and waitresses with handkerchiefs pinned beneath their name tags. The decor was airy and nostalgic, the food plain and simple. The clientele was mostly retirement-age patrons revisiting their high school years, and young families with kids on Christmas vacation looking for a fast meal served on a plate.

In short, the choice was more laid-back and less uptown than she'd expect Merle Banning to make.

Either he was trying to keep things fast and easy so he could be done with her as quickly as possible, or he'd purposely taken her to an out-of-the-way place so there'd be no chance of one of his cop buddies coming in and seeing him with her.

It wouldn't be the first time she'd been cast aside or hidden away.

At least the food was good. Hearty and filling. She couldn't exactly say her appetite had returned, but now that she was actually doing something about the doll and the dead woman, practicality had kicked in.

Her visions could be draining, physically, mentally and emotionally. She couldn't stop the headaches, and the emotions would always haunt her. But she could maintain her physical strength, keep her body healthy even when everything else in her life was royally screwed up.

Although the thermometer registered in the single digits outside and the graded snow stood thigh-high or taller along the edges of every street and sidewalk, she'd ordered a milk shake served with the chilled metal cup it had been blended in. In between bites of her steakburger with cheese, and thin, crunchy fries, she'd drunk and spooned her way through every last delicious drop.

She was paying for the indulgence, though. Even with the sleeves of her wool sweater pulled down to her knuckles, and her coat draped over her shoulders, she shivered with the pervasive chill that hadn't left her since she'd crawled out of bed last night. At this rate, she wouldn't be thawing out until summer. But she'd needed the reinforcing medicinal properties of chocolate and ice cream to sustain her.

Especially since Detective Banning's idea of lunchtime conversation was to question every detail about her account of the psychic impression she'd shared while they'd waited for their order to arrive.

"Like a log cabin?" he asked, picking up his last onion ring and popping it into his mouth. While he chewed, he pulled a paper napkin from the dispenser on the table and carefully wiped his hands.

Kelsey swallowed her impatience. While he was being Mr. Clean and acting politely interested, she was reliving the scratchy sensation of rough wood cutting into the skin on her back. "No. It was more like a building under construction—or one being torn down. The latter, I'm guessing, because of the smell."

He wadded up the napkin and tossed it onto his empty plate. "The smell?"

Of foreboding. The smell of dead bodies and buried secrets. But that sort of metaphorical description would surely elicit a laugh, so she stuck to more scientific facts.

"Rot. Decay. Like when the cold seeps in between the cracks and condenses. It turns moldy before it can evaporate. Slimy. This place was dark and horrible. She wasn't familiar with it. I'm sure it wasn't her regular place of business."

He responded by adjusting his tie unnecessarily. His straight nose and square face reflected few lines beyond the squint marks beside his eyes. But he dressed older than his youthful face might dictate, with affluent materials and a tailored fit to his clothes. He acted older than a man of twenty-nine or thirty. Conservative. Wary. Politely distant. He carried himself older, too. Not just in the slight limp he camouflaged with a quick, rolling gait, but the way he sat across from her—straight backed, never leaning in to show trust or acceptance, never lounging back to relax.

With her self-protective need to be constantly aware of the people around her, Kelsey couldn't help but notice other incongruent details about him.

Despite his relatively young age, Merle Banning's hands had seen something of life. They were clean and neatly taken care of, to be sure, but they were also nicked up with scars around the knuckles and callused enough to show hard physical labor of some kind. They moved with precise efficiency at every task, from opening the front door for her to cradling his mug of hot coffee.

He seemed unaware of her subtle perusal. Or perhaps her opinion just didn't matter to him.

"Those are pretty specific details for a crime you haven't really seen." He sipped his coffee, then frowned at the mug as if something about it didn't please him.

She had a good idea it was her report which didn't please him.

"But I have seen it," she insisted. "That doll triggered something. Either it's from the crime scene, or the victim touched it somewhere along the way. It carries her residue."

"Her DNA?" Banning's moss-colored eyes flared with mild interest.

"It's not that concrete, Detective. It's more of an imprint of her psyche, her consciousness. I can sense her thoughts and emotions. She was scared for her life. And I don't think she suspected the man who killed her had that kind of violence in him. Not toward her at any rate."

"You saw the man who did it?"

"No." She hadn't wanted to look that hard. She'd already felt death, she didn't need to look it in the eye, as well.

"Do you know who the woman was?"

"No."

"And you don't know where the murder took place."

Kelsey bristled at the challenge in his tone. "Apparently, you don't know the answers to any of those questions, either, Mr. Banning, or her murder wouldn't be relegated to the cold-case files."

His eyes narrowed at that one.

"I know this is more of a lead than you had twelve hours ago. I'm only trying to help." Kelsey clutched her coat more tightly around her and eyed the box she'd taken out of her backpack and slid across the table to him earlier. "I don't know if you'll find scientific evidence on the doll or not. But you're welcome to keep it and send it to a lab for analysis. I certainly don't want it anymore."

"That's generous of you, Ms. Ryan." His insincerity irritated her, and it didn't surprise her to hear him try to debunk her claim with a logical argument. "But unless you can tell me you picked that up at the murder scene, saw it used as a weapon or there's a written confession hidden inside, it's pretty useless to K.C.P.D."

She sat at attention, age-old defenses rising to the fore. Lucy Belle had tried to teach her to be patient with those who didn't understand. But she had a real problem with anyone who refused to even try. "I don't imagine these things, Detective. I know that's not the murder weapon. She was strangled with a long scarf."

He nodded as if he'd caught her in a lie. "Then you're conjuring dreams from facts you read in the newspaper and are using this doll as some sort of manifestation of them."

"No—"

He set down his mug with a precise thud. "Or you *were* at that crime scene and you're just now working up the nerve to report what you saw."

Kelsey gripped the edge of her seat to hold on to her temper. "I have no idea where the murder took place. That's why I tried to describe it to you in detail."

"Or perhaps you've been intentionally withholding evidence on a capital crime."

"Inten—?" She swallowed hard, then tapped out each sentence onto the table top. "I didn't get the impression until last night. I called right after. At three in the morning I called."

"Even if that doll was good for something, it's so far removed from the crime scene and so tainted, it'd be worthless now." He shoved the box back across the tabletop toward her. "So, no thanks."

Kelsey dodged to the side, avoiding the doll as if he'd fired his gun at her. "I didn't know it was evidence."

"I'm not sure if you need to get some professional help, or if you just need to get a life." He offered her an apologetic smile, arching one golden eyebrow and carving out a dimple at the side of his mouth, as if that would take the sting from his words. "But, plain and simple, Ms. Ryan, you're wasting my valuable time on this case."

With that, she stood up. She knocked her leather bag to the floor and spilled some of the contents. The curse she muttered was neither ladylike nor subdued. Watching her lipstick roll beneath the empty table across from them did nothing to improve her mood. This conversation was done as far as she was concerned. But so much for making a dignified, hasty exit and salvaging some semblance of her pride. Squatting down, she shoved her arms into the sleeves of her coat while she snatched up her lipstick, keys and a pen.

Detective Banning slid out of his seat to help her. She noted the tight set of his mouth as he knelt beside her, and idly wondered if his knee was giving him trouble. But Kelsey fought the sympathetic urge that would defuse her temper, grabbed the last item before he could reach it and shot to her feet. One coat sleeve caught at her elbow and tangled with the strap of her bag.

Banning rose more slowly, moving more deliberately, while she struggled to free herself. "I appreciate that you mean well and want to help, Ms. Ryan. The department always appreciates when a citizen steps forward."

When he latched on to her collar to try to help her, she shrugged that efficient hand away and dug inside her pack. Kelsey pulled a ten dollar bill out of her bag and threw it on the table. "There. That's for my burger and fries."

When she turned to leave, he blocked her path. He picked up the ten dollars and tried to hand it back to her. "Lunch is on me."

Too little, too late. "Oh, no. I insist. Heaven forbid I waste a moment of your precious time or a penny of your money, Detective. Forget the data I could have been evaluating at the lab or the class I should have been prepping for. And who's going to go home and let my dog out now? I have to be on campus in half an hour. This was a waste of *my* time, Mr. Banning."

He patted the air with a placating hand, trying to calm her before she created any more of a scene. "Keep your money. It's not a big deal. I'll have the department reimburse me if that'll make you feel better."

If Kelsey had kept hold of her temper, she would have seen it coming. She could have protected herself.

"Take it."

He grabbed her left hand, slapped the ten-dollar bill into her palm and curled her fingers down over it, holding her loose fist between his hands. Bare hands. Skin to skin contact.

Oh, hell.

The bombardment of sensations came fast and furious. The detective continued talking, apologizing, but she heard no words. It was nothing but a hum of noise in the background as her skin burned beneath his touch. Her chest constricted and a flood of images flashed through her mind like movie clips spinning faster and faster, flying off their reel.

Banning, lying broken on the ground. So much blood. So much pain.

A tiny blond woman at the altar in a wedding gown. Longing. Sadness. Regret.

The explosion of a gun, firing over and over at a shadowy target. Such anger. Such determination.

The musky scent of sweat. Exertion. Banning's muscles straining, harder and harder. A determined mind pushing the body beyond its limits.

A little boy at a funeral, squeezing his mother's hand. Confusion. Grief.

T. Merle Banning, typed on a document, and a pencil, scratching out the first name. Gouging out a memory. Erasing shame.

It was the shame that got to her. Washed over her like a bucket of icy water. The emotion inside her—her own emotion—woke her, breaking the spell.

She jerked her hand away. "Let go of me."

Still disoriented, she saw broad shoulders and a forceful chin swim in front of her eyes. Years of rote training reminded her to reach into her pockets for her gloves and quickly pull them on.

"Ms. Ryan?" She forced herself to breathe, in through her nose, out through her mouth. "Are you all right?"

Firm, gentle hands closed around her shoulders. The twin spots of warmth shocked her back to reality. She lifted her gaze past the sensuous male line of Detective Banning's mouth to read the concern etched beside his alert, assessing eyes. A frisson of energy that was neither psychic nor temper sparked along her nerve endings. He really was a good-looking man—in a buttoned-down, just-the-facts-ma'am kind of way.

This is wrong.

Kelsey wiggled her shoulders and shook herself free from his grasp, heeding the warning voice from her conscience. "Get your hands off me, T."

Without his touch she felt cold. Even colder than she'd been before the psychic impression had fully left her.

The chill was nothing new to her. Nor was Detective Banning's instant withdrawal. How many other people had she freaked out with her talent? How many others would scoff at her knowledge of things a normal person wouldn't know? He spread his hands out to either side of her, in plain sight. "Did you just call me *T*?"

"Isn't that your name? T-something Banning?" She set her bag on the tabletop so she could tie her scarf and button her coat with some degree of grace and then get out of there. "Merle's your middle name."

"The T's for Thomas. But nobody calls me that. And I did not tell you that was my name."

Kelsey simply turned her face and glared, daring him to put two and two together to come up with the right explanation for her knowledge of his secret. But that wasn't a leap of faith he was willing to make.

"I don't know where you did your snooping, lady. But this game isn't funny anymore. I've done my duty." He pulled another ten from his wallet and laid it with hers, leaving the waitress a huge tip. Then he was slipping into his long, camel-hair coat and limping toward the exit, robbing her of the glory of walking out on him. "Have a good day, Ms. Ryan. Drive safely."

Kelsey stared at the worn-out box he'd left on the table behind him.

How had this gotten personal? How had she gone from ultracaution to trading barbs with T. Merle Banning and letting her emotions rule her? Lesson one in Grandma Lucy Belle's book of down-home advice was keep your eyes focused on the goal. Kelsey's goal had been to help that poor woman. To give a forgotten murder victim a chance to find justice.

This meeting wasn't about her, or justifying her gift, or making sense of the tumble of emotions Detective Banning stirred inside her.

Ashamed that she'd let old wounds get the better of her, Kelsey took a deep breath, grabbed the doll box and hustled after Banning, beating him to the glassed-in lobby before he could open the outer door. She planted herself squarely in his path and pleaded her case one last time. "I don't know who that woman was. I know she was naked. She was in some falling-down, ramshackle building. I know that man strangled her. She thought the scarf was payment. A gift. Maybe the doll, too." She held it out. He didn't take it. "I don't know. Putting that all together makes me think she's one of your hookers."

He pulled back the front of his coat and jacket, propping his hands on his hips and exposing his gun and badge. "Your point?"

She got the message. But she refused to be put off.

"I have a degree in criminal justice studies, Detective. I know police procedure. You didn't ask me any probative questions. You spent this entire interview trying to get me to admit I'm a fraud. You didn't write down a damn thing I told you in that notebook of yours. And now you're going back to your office to have a good laugh with your buddies at my expense."

"I wouldn't—"

"You're not the first cop to think I'm crazy. In fact, you're more close minded than most. If you want scientific facts, you find that building. You check out the store where I bought this doll. You interview the man who sold it to me. The doll's the key if you want to use it." She shoved the box into the middle of his chest and backed out the door into the icy winter chill. "*Now* we're done."

T? MERLE SAT at his desk—tie loose, collar unbuttoned, sleeves rolled to the elbow. He looked as if he'd been working all afternoon, but it was an illusion. That crazy fake redhead had gotten under his skin and disrupted his concentration by saying one stupid letter!

How did she know about his past? Who had she been talking to? Could she be the disgruntled relative of one of the investors his father had cheated and abandoned twenty years ago? If so, it had to be the cleverest way he'd come up against yet for one of his father's victims to take a strip of retribution out of his hide.

Merle stared at the data on the computer screen, seeing nothing but the capital *T*s jump out at him. "How the hell…?"

Thomas Banning was the name he'd given up years ago, when he was just a boy. He'd given it up because Thomas was his father's name. His mother stopped using it and had taken to calling him by his middle name.

Thomas had been a curse at his house.

Merle wasn't much better. Merle was an old man's name. A nerd's name. Sometimes even a girl's name. It was a name that invited teasing on elementary playgrounds and in junior high locker rooms. It was a name that high-school girls giggled at and college professors mispronounced.

It never quite fit. Yet he'd been stuck with it.

The only time he tolerated *Merle* without a hint of

resentment was on his mother's lips or in his partner Ginny's sweet, succinct voice.

Thomas Merle Banning, Jr.

That was his name.

But he couldn't use it.

She'd come close. Too damn irritatingly close.

Merle tossed his pen onto the open file in front of him and sank back into his chair with a heavy sigh. He rubbed his fingers back and forth across his chin and jaw, and tried to sort out his thoughts. He wasn't just feeling defensive or distracted here. He had a good dose of guilt working on him, too.

The fact that Kelsey Ryan had somehow uncovered his first initial bothered him almost as much as the fact she knew he'd only been humoring her by taking her to lunch and asking a few questions. Technically, he'd obeyed Captain Taylor's request, but he hadn't really done his job.

Flake or not, he should have listened to her story, thanked her, then sent her on her way. Not voiced his opinion of her dubious "vision," get her pissed and then let her storm off without so much as a thank-you or apology.

But she'd pushed his buttons. Not just the this-feels-like-a-practical-joke button. The computer geek desk jockey wants to see some action? Let him interview the wacko. Sergeant Watkins and the other guys he'd met in the break room that morning seemed to find it terribly amusing that The Flake had been assigned to him.

She looked like an overdecorated Christmas tree, said one. Take her to a New Year's Eve party and use that hair to light off fireworks, said another. Sergeant Watkins had been even more direct. *"I'm surprised the doctors let that looney out."*

For some reason, though, Merle hadn't felt like laughing. Their crude jokes and unapologetic stares had triggered the chivalric streak inside him. He outranked the blue suits and could shut them up with a command. And he'd earned enough respect from his fellow detectives for them to honor his request to let it drop.

He hadn't laughed because Kelsey Ryan had gotten to something deeper inside him. Maybe he saw a little of that skinny, four-eyed kid he used to be in her. The kid whose daddy had stuck a gun in his mouth and killed himself because he couldn't repay the funds he'd embezzled or face the consequences of his actions. He'd been the kid who hid behind books and rebuilt computers so he couldn't hear the teasing.

He'd outgrown the skinny phase, graduated valedictorian and had his pick of colleges. He and his mother, Moira, had worked for years to rebuild the estate that had been decimated by his father's debt, so he had a little money to his name. He'd become a cop after earning the first of two degrees, and had made detective on his first application. He'd made his share of mistakes along the way, but he'd solved crimes. He'd taken bullets and killed men in the line of duty.

Thomas Merle Banning, Jr. wasn't anybody's victim anymore.

But he'd never forget what it felt like.

And he'd never fail to recognize it in someone else.

Kelsey Ryan had been hurt somewhere along the way in her life. Now she dyed her hair and lost her temper and put on airs because she didn't want anyone to see how much she hurt.

Merle nudged the beat-up shoe box sitting on the corner of his desk. He might not believe her story about the doll triggering visions of murder. But he should have believed her intentions. A woman like that wouldn't knowingly set herself up to be ridiculed. She wouldn't take that risk unless she believed what she was saying.

It wasn't all that long ago that he'd worked his tail off to get someone to listen to his ideas, to take him seriously. To give him a chance to prove his worth to the world.

Mitch Taylor had given him that chance.

He'd be a hypocrite if he didn't offer Kelsey Ryan that same chance.

Merle pulled the box closer and read the name of the defunct local shoe company imprinted in faded green letters on the box. Clearly, the doll wasn't in its original packaging. Flipping over the lid of the box, Merle poked at the multicolored afghan wrapped around the doll inside and wondered who had knitted it. Probably Kelsey herself, judging by the rainbow palette of colors. He pulled out the bundle and unwrapped it on his desk.

He had to believe she really thought there was some kind of answer here.

Merle peeled back a layer of worn newsprint, taking a moment to check the faded date. *December 24, 1994.*

"The day before Christmas."

He frowned as the encyclopedia of random facts he carried around inside his head tried to tell him something. Slipping on his wire-frame glasses, he scrolled through the data on the computer screen until he found the first victim in the file—a Jane Doe prostitute the original investigators had dubbed Jezebel.

He scanned the information, then rechecked the wadded paper around the doll. He checked the computer again. "Gotta be a coincidence."

Jezebel's strangled, nude body had been discovered in an alley the day *after* Christmas.

1994.

Merle sat straighter in his chair, pulled a pair of plastic gloves from the bottom drawer and put them on.

Most coincidences could be explained away by facts.

Beneath the old newsprint he found a layer of tissue paper wrapped around the doll. The doll itself looked like some sort of collectible, with a face and body crafted of wire and silk and stuffing. It had feathery golden hair and wore an embroidered gown trimmed in beads of glass and mother-of-pearl. Pretty nice handiwork.

Pretty nice gift for someone back in 1994.

Probably given to someone the very same day Jezebel was murdered. His brain hovered around the information, absorbing what he read on the screen and saw in the box, trying to make a plausible connection.

"Taking up a new hobby?"

Merle glanced up at the deep, laughter-filled voice, and watched the Odd Couple of the Fourth Precinct—Josh Taylor and A. J. Rodriguez—stroll past to the pair of desks beside his.

"Right. I'm into playing with dolls now." Pulling off his glasses, Merle shook his head. "I'm trying to figure out if this is evidence or just a bad joke."

Josh—a big, blond goofball who was always into everybody's business—dumped his coat in his chair and propped his hip on the corner of his desk. "I heard you got the honor of dealing with The Flake this morning. Does that have anything to do with her?"

"She brought it in. Said she had a vision—" he held up his hand and corrected himself the way she'd corrected him "—excuse me, a *psychic impression,* of one of the Holiday Hooker murders. She said this doll was the key to interpreting that impression."

"Cool." Josh, Captain Taylor's youngest cousin, was nothing if not direct. "You buy what she said?"

"Claiming she was inside the victim's skin, feeling her pain and terror as she was being murdered? No." He smoothed the newsprint between his plastic-gloved fingers. "But the date on this packaging matches the time frame of the first death. It's as good as anything else I have to go on. Which isn't much."

"Might be worth checking out." A. J. never said much. But then, the dark-haired, compactly built detective didn't have to. Merle had quickly learned that with his instincts and street smarts, and an eerie patience that allowed him to sit back and let the other guy show his hand first, A. J. didn't need to waste time with idle words. He waited until he had something to say. And then smart people listened.

If he thought this was a lead worth pursuing…

Merle had already made his decision. But it was nice to know he had some backup on his opinion. "If you gents will excuse me?"

He flipped through the pages of his notebook, reluctantly accepting that his dealings with Kelsey Ryan hadn't ended. Locating the cell number she'd given him, he punched it in. As he waited through several rings, he worked to adjust his attitude. This wasn't just another crazy trip into la-la land; it was an opportunity to make amends and ease his conscience. An opportunity to do the job Captain Taylor expected of him. Maybe he could find a few answers along the way, as well.

"Hello?" The soft, almost timid voice at the other end of the line surprised him. But Merle recognized the subtle hint of a southern Missouri twang from their lunchtime conversation.

"Ms. Ryan? This is Detective Banning at the Fourth Precinct."

He could hear her bristling up, donning that huffy, self-protective shield she wore. He could also hear the honks and hums of traffic moving in the background. "Detective."

So much for conversational pleasantries. He didn't suppose he'd earned any friendly overtures, so he kept his tone as businesslike and impersonal as hers. "I was calling to ask for the name of the shop where you bought the doll. Looks like there might be some loose ends I can follow up on, after all."

"Too late, Banning. I'm a step ahead of you. I already talked to Mr. Meisner at the Westport Antique Mall where I bought it, and he said he purchased the doll from The Underground. That's a pawnshop over on 10th Street off of Broadway. I'm on my way there right now to find out where *they* got it."

"You what?" Every muscle in Merle's body clenched.

Broadway and 10th was smack in the middle of no-man's land, nestled between the new construction around the Bartle Convention Center and the reclamation of downtown. Merle checked his watch and wished he could look out a window. By four-thirty this late in December, the sun would already be fading. Legitimate businesses would be closing soon and, despite the winter chill, less legitimate entrepreneurs would be crawling out of their cubbyholes to open shop. The people who actually lived in the neighborhood didn't always welcome strangers, especially ones who asked a lot of questions. And he had a feeling she wouldn't be shy about asking.

Merle was already buttoning his collar and rolling down his sleeves. "You cannot go into that neighborhood by yourself. Especially after dark."

"It's okay, Detective Banning. The danger's all in my imagination. Remember?"

Click.

She hung up on him?

He was trying to protect her butt and she hung up on him?

Merle shot to his feet. Unfamiliar frissons of anger mixed with a chilling pulse beat of concern. He grabbed his jacket off the back of his chair and shoved things into his pockets.

"Problem?" asked Josh, looking up from his desk. He had A. J.'s attention, too.

"Yeah." His problem was about five and a half feet of mouthy redhead who thought she could goad him into working with her. "This temporary partner thing isn't working out."

"You've got a new partner?"

"I've got a departmental consultant who doesn't know when to quit." He jerked the knot of his tie up to his collar. "If I don't show up for work tomorrow, tell the captain I gave my all for a little good press."

Josh and A. J. laughed as he shrugged into his coat and dashed to the elevators. Kelsey Ryan might know the how-to's on following up leads, but she didn't know squat about surviving out on the streets.

He intended to get her home, safe and sound, and then get her out of his hair.

Chapter Three

The Underground was a subterranean curiosity shop with grimy, street-level windows and the eye-watering odor of cat urine hanging in the air.

Despite the stench, Kelsey had spotted only one scraggly-tailed Siamese darting between the narrow aisles that had been crammed with more trash than treasures. She cringed at the possibility that the dearth of visible cats might have something to do with the collection of three boa constrictors that the proprietors—who'd introduced themselves as Mort and Edgar—kept on display in a glass case behind the cash register.

The place was dimly lit, probably to hide the fact it couldn't meet health code or fire safety standards. Not to mention ASPCA regs. The steps leading down to the basement entrance door were lined with sooty snow that absorbed rather than reflected the light from the cold, fading sun and the street lamp on the curb above them.

It was the sort of place where that woman had been killed. Filthy. Cold. Dark. Damp. And not a friend in sight.

Only, the smells were different here. And the room she'd seen had been empty, not a wall-to-wall display of lewd posters and broken furniture and exotic trinkets.

But this was where the trail had led her. If she could locate the doll's original owner, she might be able to track down a murderer, turn him in to the police and put that poor woman's psychic energy to rest.

But so far, her interrogation skills had done little more than earn sneers of contempt and trigger a banter of inside jokes between the two men. Kelsey was dying to take a deep breath to steady her nerves. But that might result in gagging or fainting, and she was already at enough of a disadvantage as it was.

"The doll?" She tried to get them back on track. "Do you have a record of who pawned it? Can you remember anything about the person who brought it in?"

"Do I look like I know 'bout dolls?" Mort was a middle-aged man of indiscriminate heritage, yellow teeth and Oriental tattoos on every exposed region of his thin, wiry body. "I see what people bring me and if I like it, I buy it. If they don't come back for it, I sell it. That's what we do here, honey. Buy and sell." He licked his lips in a way that could have been suggestive, or could simply have been a means to circulate the brown tobacco juice she glimpsed on his tongue. "We're not much for talking."

Kelsey looked away and swallowed hard, struggling to salvage her courage and keep her stomach down where it belonged. She glanced up at Mort's partner. "What about you? Can you tell me anything more about the doll?"

Edgar was a defensive-lineman-size black man with shoulder-length corn rows and a fascination for shiny objects. Like the blue crystal pendant she wore around her neck.

He stared at the thimble-size crystal teardrop with a

greedy interest that seemed to take in more than just the silver chain and handcrafted mount. She fought the urge to breathe hard, fearing that moving any female body parts would be seen as an invitation she didn't want to give.

"Well?" she prompted, sounding tougher than she felt. "Edgar? Mort?"

The two men wouldn't even talk to her unless she bought something or paid them for their time. She was pretty sure she didn't want to touch anything in the shop or take it into her home. And since she didn't carry large sums of cash with her, she'd unhooked the amber bracelet she wore and offered it as a bribe for information.

The yellow beads had gotten her an introduction and confirmation that the doll had indeed been purchased here over a month ago by Mr. Meisner. But Mort had settled in behind the register, claiming amnesia regarding the doll's history before that. With her bracelet stretched around the span of his knuckles, Edgar sidled up beside her in front of the counter, invading her personal space with his cheap cologne and curious hands.

The big man's answer was to pick up the crystal in his meaty palm, letting his fingers slide with loathsome familiarity against her breasts. Kelsey flinched, unable to shake the feeling of violation. Panic poured into her veins, leaving the desperate need to bolt in its wake. Even through her coat and the layers of clothing she wore, the brief touch had felt as if he'd fondled bare skin.

Kelsey breathed hard, clinging to rational thought. Her breasts heaved. Edgar noticed.

Ho, boy.

This was a mistake. This was such a mistake. What the hell had she been trying to prove by coming here? Worse, who had she been trying to prove herself to? She didn't want to even consider that answer. She'd sacrifice the bracelet as payment for her foolishness, cut her losses and run. She'd deal with her guilt at letting down that helpless woman later—when she felt a little less helpless herself.

She quickly made her excuses and pulled the chain from Edgar's hand. "It's after five. You need to close. I'd better be going."

He snatched it back, closing his fist around the crystal and blotting out the protection it gave her. With a tiny push to her sternum, he backed her against the counter. "Give you fifty bucks for this," he offered, flashing a diamond-studded gold tooth in the middle of his leering smile. "A hundred if you let me take it off you myself."

He was already reaching behind her neck for the clasp when she jerked her grandmother's pendant from his grasp and swatted his hand away. "It's not for sale."

Neither was she.

She tucked the pendant back inside her coat and prayed that her guardian angel, Grandma Lucy Belle, would keep her angry and focused instead of afraid. Since she clearly wasn't going to wrestle her way past a man like Edgar, she'd have to rely on brainpower to get out of this mess. Kelsey tipped her chin defiantly and countered his offer. "I have a coin purse with a collection of different crystals and polished sicun stones in my bag. I'll let you choose three of them if you tell me everything you know about that doll."

Pretty bold move considering she should be negotiating her escape rather than making a plea for more information. Or just running like hell and driving as far away as fast as she could.

Edgar seemed to actually consider the deal. But as

her hopes rose in one direction, she neglected to pay close enough attention to the other. Mort moved with surprising speed for a man who'd been too tired to get up when she'd first walked into the place. He reached across the counter and jerked her bag off her shoulder. "Pretty stones, huh?"

"Hey!" Instinctively, Kelsey spun around to retrieve it. Edgar grabbed her arm and yanked her back to her place. Her elbow smacked against the counter. "Ow!" Tingles of pain and numbness radiated toward her fingers.

"Let him look."

She twisted inside Edgar's bruising grip. "Give that back." Mort grinned an ugly smile. "I'll scream."

"Who's gonna hear ya, honey?" Mort took his sweet time unzipping the bag and rifling through her things, fouling the items he touched. "What else you got in here that's worth trading for?"

"Stop that." She switched her attention back to Edgar, who'd palmed her hip with his heavy hand and dipped his nose to sniff her hair.

"It ought to smell like strawberries with a color like that."

Kelsey braced her hand beneath his chin and shoved, wishing he'd go back to being interested in shiny things. "Get away from me."

"That's not very nice." He whipped his chin beyond her reach and pinned the attacking arm behind her back, wrenching her shoulder in its socket. His chest and hips pressed against her as he leaned in closer and sniffed some more.

"Oooh!" She grunted a frustrated protest and fought his hold on her. They were amused by her struggles now. Oh, to be seven feet tall and built like a tank and break every one of his grubby, grabby fingers. "Let go!"

Thank God she'd stuffed her keys into her pocket. At least she'd be able to drive away from this place and get straight into a shower to hose off the ick. *If* she could free herself.

If she could get away right now, she'd just run. She didn't have much money in her wallet. Still, her credit cards? Irreplaceable pictures of Frosty and Lucy Belle?

Kelsey couldn't stand it. She twisted around, freed her arm, jammed her elbow into Edgar's gut and made one last valiant lunge for her backpack. "Give me my bag!"

But Edgar threw his body into hers, sandwiching her between his big, bulgy belly and the counter. "I don't think so, honey."

She rammed the heel of her boot down onto his instep and punched at his Adam's apple. "Get away from me!"

The jingle of the bell over the front door interrupted his foul-mouthed curse of pain.

"You heard the lady. Move away."

Edgar twisted her arm, anchoring her in place. Mort shot to his feet.

"I wouldn't."

She knew that voice. Crisp and biting, low-pitched and not to be messed with.

"T." She whispered a sigh of relief.

"Who the hell's gonna make…" Edgar's challenge faded into a startled gasp when he turned around and got a good look at the man standing behind him.

Kelsey saw him, too.

Her heart beat faster, though she didn't know whether to run into his arms or back away. This was a whole new side to T. Merle Banning she hadn't seen before.

And there was definitely nothing bookish, buttoned down or Brooks Brothers about him anymore.

DETECTIVE BANNING wasn't as big as Edgar, didn't fit the smarmy surroundings as well as Mort. But he had their attention. Kelsey's, too.

He'd brought the cold in with him, and the raw temperature clung to his clothes and his attitude. Standing there, with his feet braced apart, he planted his black-gloved hands at his waist, spreading open his coat and jacket. The badge, the gun and the tough facade—the survivor who'd beaten death and heartbreak and whatever the world dared throw at him—were all in plain view.

"Detective Banning," she uttered with more force, worried about how much of that displeased look was directed at her.

"Sorry, Detective," Edgar apologized, covering his backside rather than sounding sincere. His grip on her was rapidly cutting off the circulation down to her wrist and hand. "I didn't know the cops were paying us a visit this evening."

Mort shoved his stool back and circled around the counter. "You're jumpin' our case? She's the one who came in here buggin' us. Said she had some crystals and rocks to trade, but have we seen 'em?"

"Easy, friend." Banning's sharp-eyed gaze seemed to take in both men at once. "Better sit back down. But keep your hands up top where I can see them."

Mort took a moment to weigh his options. He looked at the gun, at Kelsey, back at Banning. Then, with a shrug, he slowly returned to his seat. "We didn't know she was with you," he grumbled. "This is just a misunderstanding. If she'd have said she was working with

K.C.P.D., we would have answered her questions. We're all into cooperation here, Officer."

"Yeah. Cooperation," Edgar echoed.

Kelsey didn't trust the conciliatory mood for one second. Neither did Banning. He extended his hand toward her and crooked his fingers. "You'd better step over here with me."

The instant Edgar released her, Kelsey spun around and grabbed her purse, her gaze snared by Mort's accusatory leer. She gathered the things he'd scattered across the counter and backed away toward Banning. When she felt his hand at the small of her back she jumped. She was even more startled when he laced their gloved fingers together and pulled her to his side, claiming a proprietary ownership the other men took note of.

"Hey, we didn't know it was like that with you and her." Edgar rattled off a hasty explanation. "She came on to me first, asking all those questions."

Yeah, right.

Mort tried to shift the blame, as well. "You ought to keep a tighter rein on her, Detective. A pretty girl like that doesn't usually come into our part of town unless she's willing to, um, do a little business."

Banning's shoulders broadened. "I trust you won't make that mistake again."

"No, sir."

"No, sir."

Kelsey savored a few moments of blessed reprieve, her deep breaths dragging in the clean scents of cold and wind from Banning's wool coat. He held her hand as if he had every right, as if they were more than adversarial colleagues. As if there wasn't anything freakishly wrong with a man wanting to hold her hand.

But there was.

Kelsey's fleeting sense of security rushed out on a weary sigh. They both wore gloves, muting her ability to sense anything, but there had been too many times when an accidental brush or an intentional clasp had triggered insights people didn't want to share. She'd lived through too many humiliating rejections and out-right attacks to delude herself into thinking she could ever have a normal relationship with a man.

Protecting herself from wayward desires, Kelsey moved a step away from the sense of security Banning provided and subtly tugged against his possessive claim. She was only asking for trouble if she thought snuggling up to his strong shoulder would give her the peace she'd craved for so long.

But he tightened his grip around hers, refusing to let go. "Do you have everything?"

He glanced her way, warning her to play along. The silent threat seemed to indicate that Mort and Edgar weren't the only danger in the room she'd have to deal with if she refused.

With the slightest of nods, Kelsey wiggled her fingers into a more comfortable position and held on, trying to remember how she'd acted when she thought she'd been in love with Jeb. Before she'd understood his cruel game. Before she realized she couldn't wink or cuddle or kiss or drop her guard—or hold hands—as other women did when they gave their heart to a man.

Her rueful gaze slipped to the amber bracelet still twisted around Edgar's fingers. But she'd foolishly agreed to the trade. "I just want to go."

"Then we'll be on our way." Kelsey dutifully followed as he backed toward the door. But he paused a moment before stepping outside. "By the way—" His friendly grin seemed to put Mort and Edgar on as tight a guard as his authoritative voice had. "Did you answer Ms. Ryan's questions?"

Mort warned Edgar to keep his mouth shut. "We answered enough."

Banning considered the lie, then concluded the conversation. "The three of us will talk later," he promised. "Right now I'm going to take the lady home."

The two looked less than thrilled that their dealings with Merle Banning weren't over. "Later works for me. You, Edgar?"

"Later's good."

The detective left her at the door and crossed the length of the shop in long, purposeful strides that gave little indication of his limp. He pulled the amber beads from Edgar's unresisting fingers. "I'll take that." He gave the two men a curt nod. "Gentlemen."

Kelsey opened the door, anxious to make a hasty exit and regroup after her dismal foray into criminal investigation. The winter air blasted her as if she was standing in front of an open freezer. She squinted her eyes and turned her face from the biting wind that swirled down the concrete stairwell leading to The Underground.

But she held the door and waited until Banning was outside with her before pulling her knit cap out of her coat pocket. However, she never got a chance to put it on. As soon as he'd shut the door behind them, he had his hands on her waist, turning her and half lifting, half pushing her up the stairs ahead of him.

"Hey." It wasn't much of a protest. She was as anxious to get out of there as he seemed to be.

"Where are you parked?"

"In the next block. Across from the mission."

He scanned a hundred and eighty degrees up and down the street as they stepped out onto the sidewalk. Dusk had fallen and the street lamps had come on, igniting tiny sparkles of light in the drifts of snow that clung to bumpers of parked vehicles and lined windowsills and doorways. "Good. That's not far from my car."

Without breaking stride, he switched his grip to her arm to hurry her alongside him at his pace. Kelsey dug in her heels and jerked her arm free. "I've been manhandled enough for one day, thank you very much. At least let me get bundled up. It's freezing out here."

"Make it fast." Banning stopped a couple of steps past her and turned to face her. "Are you hurt? Did you get all your stuff back?"

"I'm fine. Maybe a little grossed out, but fine." His concern, though slightly delayed, was appreciated. She dangled the bracelet and smiled her gratitude as she hooked it over her wrist beneath the black-and-white cuff of her coat. "Thanks to you, everything's accounted for."

Though he pulled his jacket shut, he made no move to button his coat. To give him easy access to his gun? To let the wind bulk up his coat to give him a bigger, broader silhouette? Because he was impervious to the cold, biting wind?

Her first impression of Detective Banning was that he looked more at home in an office or behind a computer. But seeing him so hard and not to be messed with downstairs in the Underground, and watching him now on full, guarded alert as the nighttime crowd filtered onto the streets, made her think there was a lot more to T than first impressions might indicate. She sensed it had something to do with that limp, and those scattered images she'd seen from his past.

Banning was smart, complicated, conflicted—and very impatient, judging by the tiny white clouds that formed in front of his face and dissipated with every heated breath.

"Today?" he urged her.

Knowing she owed him for saving her dignity, if not her very life, Kelsey worked quickly, pulling her turquoise cap down over her ears and tying her scarf high around her neck. She inhaled deeply, welcoming the damp air that crystallized inside her nose and cleared the odor of Mort and Edgar's shop from her sinuses.

"I guess I got in a little over my head."

"You think?"

She let his sarcasm slide off into the dusting of new snow beneath her feet. "They know more than they told me. It's just a matter of convincing them to talk."

His panning gaze finally stopped on her. "Did you read that in your crystal ball?"

More hocus-pocus insults? "I told you, I don't—"

"Time to move, sweetheart." He wasn't in the mood to listen to any argument or explanation or even a thank-you. Snatching her by the arm above her elbow, he pulled her into double time beside him. "I distinctly told you not to come down here by yourself."

Apparently, resistance was futile. His grasp might be gentle, but it wasn't budging. "Well, you weren't going to talk to them."

"You don't know that."

She glared at his stern profile—the square jaw, the straight nose, the grim expression. "If Mort and Edgar were on your to-do list, why didn't you say something?"

"Did you give me a chance?" They halted at the intersection to let traffic roll past. "As I recall, I was sitting at my desk, trying to piece together some information from that box you gave me—"

"You were?" Kelsey was stunned.

"—when you hung up on me. Look around you. You decided to go on a scavenger hunt in one of the most dangerous parts of town. Alone. Unarmed. Clueless." He inclined his head toward a short, muscular black man standing catter corner from them. Dressed in leather from head to toe, and wearing enough gold jewelry to start his own store, the man stared back without apology. "That's Zero, one of the local pimps. He's already secreted away his girls because he's heard there's a new cop in the neighborhood. I imagine your two friends down in The Underground started making calls as soon as I was out the door."

"I didn't think this was going to be a cakewalk, Detective. But I do know a little about self-defense."

A girl didn't grow up as different as she was without learning how to defend herself on the playground, in a barroom, or—like that last night with Jeb—in the bedroom.

"Yeah, I saw you gettin' your licks in on the big guy. But what if they both decided to go after you?" He glanced down at her. "Could you take them both?"

"Probably not." She conceded his point, but still tried to make her own. "But I was just going to a pawnshop to ask shopkeepers a few questions. It wasn't like I was trying to track down drug dealers."

Banning's laugh made wispy clouds in the air. "Are you kidding? You didn't smell the pot down there?"

Pot? Good grief. Kelsey hung her head and wished the light would change so she could get to her car and get away from Mr. Know-it-all. "That would explain the Eau de Cat that made my eyes water. It was to cover up the smell of marijuana."

"Exactly. And those murders you're so anxious to help K.C.P.D. solve? The nine dead women were all found in this part of town."

She lifted her chin and squared her shoulders, accepting the blame for her impulsive choice. "I get the idea. I'm sorry. I shouldn't have tried to do this on my own. Bad things happen around here."

"I'll say. My partner got shot just a couple of blocks down the road."

The stark announcement, combined with the sudden distance in his focus, reached past her own feelings of remorse. No wonder it had been so important for him to keep even someone he considered a nuisance like her safe.

"I'm sorry." Her instinct was to reach out and offer comfort. But Kelsey curled her fingers into her palm and held them at her side. She didn't have to be a psychic to know that her touch wasn't the one he'd want. "Did he…?"

"*She*…recovered after a few months of rest and rehabilitation. I took out the shooter myself. It was an ambush. The other two perps got away, but were eventually killed at another crime scene."

"How horrible."

"She's on maternity leave now. That's why I'm temporarily working solo." Kelsey heard the first hint of softness in his tone when Banning mentioned his partner. "That's why I'm stuck with this old case."

That's why I'm stuck with you.

Kelsey could imagine the unspoken line. And there wouldn't be any softness when he talked about her.

"I'm glad she's all right."

A man wearing a plastic trash bag on his head beneath a faded red Chiefs cap jostled past as the light changed. Kelsey stumbled into Banning just as he stepped off the curb. With his fingers still wrapped around her upper arm, he easily righted her. But the bump was enough to throw him off stride and he came down wrong on his right foot.

"Son of a bitch."

Banning's fingers clenched on her arm. Standing perfectly still, he grit his teeth hard enough to make a pulse leap along the line of his jaw as he worked his way through the pain. This time, she did offer help. She clutched a fistful of his jacket and steadied her hand against his chest, ready to take his weight and guide him back to the sidewalk when he was ready to move. "Is it your knee?"

He nodded. "Cold weather doesn't help. Damn thing isn't as flexible as it used…" His breath stopped up and the tenor of his voice changed. "How do you know about my knee?"

"I've seen you limp. You hide it pretty well, but the stiffness is still there."

He covered her hand with his and pried it from the front of his jacket, warily keeping her in his sights as if he didn't trust that that was all she'd seen.

A half dozen more people shuffled past them. A horn honked. The light had changed. Banning tugged on her hand to get them out of the street. "C'mon. We need to keep moving."

He walked just as quickly as he had before, though his rocking gait was more pronounced. "What does your car look like?" he asked.

"It's a red Saturn."

He led her around a group of homeless people, mostly men, lining up against the gray stone facade of the Wingate Humanitarian Mission to get inside for the promise of a hot dinner. The painted sign beside the double front doors offered meals, free medical service three days a week, plus counseling, religious services, adult literacy classes and overnight lodging. A smaller, handwritten note beside the billboard, however, warned the would-be patrons that the beds were full, medical supplies were limited and that classes had been suspended until a new teacher could be hired.

Kelsey's compassion slowed her pace. "Those poor people."

It was the bitterest part of a bad winter, and they lived on the street alongside dope dealers, pimps and prostitutes. Now, apparently, their one place of refuge was short on funds and volunteers. She looked into the eyes of some of the men standing in line. Dullness stared back.

"Those poor people know more about surviving out here than you do. At least they have the sense to get off the street when the sun goes down."

Kelsey had stopped walking. Had the woman whose death she'd seen lived like this? Just trying to stay alive from one day to the next? Had that cold, pitiless room been her home, after all? Had the doll been pawned for a meal? Had she sold her body just to survive?

Could that faceless man with the cruel hands be one of these men?

Compassion stayed with her, but fear tempered it. Kelsey hugged her arms around her waist, feeling the chill more deeply than she had a minute ago.

She scanned the line now, looking for some spark of

recognition from her nightmarish impression. She studied the twenty-some men lined up from the building's cornerstone to the front steps where a charismatic man with a deeply receding hairline and salt and pepper beard shook each man's hand and greeted him by name before inviting him inside.

She stared harder. Something about the hands…

"Kelsey." She started at the hand on her shoulder, and realized he'd been calling her name. She blinked her focus back to blond hair and green eyes and that insistent tone. "You sure you parked on this block?"

"Yes, I… It's…" Kelsey pointed to the street, then turned completely around. *Ho boy.* She'd had one of those rare, distracted moments when she could actually understand her flaky nickname. They'd gone too far. Banning fell into step beside her as they retraced their footsteps. "Who's that man in the doorway?"

"Reverend Ulysses Wingate. He's been running the mission for the past fifteen years or so. Your car?"

"I parked right—" she stopped "—here."

A souped-up black Cadillac sat in the space where her little red car should be. For a moment, she felt lightheaded, as shock drained the blood inside her. Just as quickly, temper fired her pulse. She threw her hands out in front of her. "Where's my car?"

"You're kidding, right?"

"No. I parked it right here. I'm positive."

He pulled off his glove and touched the hood of the car. "Still warm."

That meant it hadn't been there long. That meant her car had been stolen. "I locked it. I always lock it. I still have the keys in my pocket. With all these people around, do you think anyone saw anything?"

Banning's glare didn't leave her much hope of a positive response. But he already had his cell phone out and had called to report the theft. He verified that there was no meter to run out, no reason to be towed. He relayed her license plate number as well as their current location.

"Are you always this much trouble to work with?" he asked, waiting for a response from the dispatcher.

"No." Huddling inside her coat, she'd never missed her grandmother's wisdom more than she did at that very moment. "Sometimes it's worse."

Chapter Four

"I'll pass the word around to B and C shift." Ed Watkins adjusted his flat blue cap low on his forehead and shrugged. "But if her car was stolen between four and five o'clock, then that thing's already been taken to one of the local chop shops and stripped down for parts. It's after six now. We're not gonna find it."

Merle listened to the sergeant's report with half an ear and jotted the appropriate notes. This was pointless. His knee ached, his glasses had fogged up, and he hadn't made any progress on either the stolen car or the murdered prostitutes. About the only thing he had succeeded in doing was keeping Kelsey Ryan safe from her own misguided intentions.

Which could turn into a full-time job at the rate things were going.

After walking into The Underground and finding her fighting off the advances of a man twice her size while that sleazeball Mort rifled through her things, Merle knew that keeping her in one piece would be no small accomplishment. Thank God he had come after her. The whole neighborhood had probably seen that red hair and plaid coat coming a mile away and pegged her as an easy mark.

He liked the idea of Kelsey Ryan's car being the convenient victim of a stolen parts ring only marginally better than the idea that someone had followed her, known that was her car and had taken it to leave her deliberately stranded in no-man's land.

And despite the glimpses of strength he'd seen in her, Merle got the idea that there was something vulnerable, well guarded and almost shy hidden inside her. She could talk tough all she wanted. But men like Mort and Edgar, Zero—and an unknown killer—would chew her up and spit her out before she ever knew what hit her.

After verifying the time on his watch, Merle took off his glasses and put them away. He'd sent Kelsey inside the mission almost an hour ago to get warmed up and out of range of Watkins's lame jokes about The Flake losing track of her own car.

Once she'd finally quit arguing with him, she stood there shivering, her face pale except for the color whipped into her cheeks and tip of her nose by the wind. She'd tilted up her chin in a show of courage that didn't quite fire up those fawn-colored eyes as the sergeant asked several routine questions of her. Frustrated as Merle was with her, he didn't want to have to deal with shock on top of everything else. So he'd ignored her protests, introduced her to Reverend Wingate and sent her inside the building for safekeeping.

But there was little more he could do for her. From the time Kelsey had left her car to when they were back outside after visiting The Underground, this block of Kansas City had apparently been deserted. No one he'd interviewed had seen a thing. He didn't think any of them were blind. A few might be crazy. But smart money said that someone had them too intimidated to admit anything to an outsider. Especially a cop.

Not even Sergeant Watkins, who was the regular patrol officer assigned to this neighborhood, could get anything out of potential witnesses beyond having seen a red car parked in front of the mission. But no one had seen anyone hanging around the car; no one had seen a break-in; no one had seen the red car drive away.

If those were the kinds of responses earlier investigators had gotten on the Holiday Hooker murders, it was no wonder the case was never solved. He wanted to find out who had that kind of power. Who could make an entire neighborhood close ranks and keep their mouths shut?

Who would have the courage to break that silence?

It annoyed him that he found himself glancing over his shoulder to the double doors where Kelsey Ryan had disappeared inside the mission.

"Hey, Detective." Merle pulled his attention back to the short, pudgy cop, who didn't seem to be as affected by the subzero windchill as anyone else on the street. Watkins pulled down the cuffs of his shearling-lined uniform jacket and rested his elbows on his gun butt and utility belt. The fifty-something cop's posture sagged, and he looked tired. But then, it was the end of his shift. "You want me to file the report or are you gonna do it?"

"I called it in. I'll handle the paperwork." Merle closed his notebook and stuffed it and his pen back inside his jacket pocket. "How long have you been working this neighborhood, Watkins?"

"Twenty years. Outlasted three partners and two wives along the way."

Maybe it wasn't just the long day that made him

seem so weary. "Twenty years, huh? So you were walking this beat back when each of those prostitutes was killed."

Watkins laughed, but it sounded more like a curse. "I was even on duty when four of the bodies were found and helped work the scenes. Never gets any easier. Always the same—naked, not a mark on 'em except the bruises around the neck, eyes open and terrified. A frozen body's a gruesome sight. You'd think nine deaths would've put 'em out of business by now."

He patted his thick waist and let his dark eyes drift across the street to a couple of women, woefully underdressed for the weather. One wore short shorts and thigh-high boots, the other a miniskirt that didn't quite cover the top of her stockings.

The heated discussion between the tall black woman and the petite blonde snagged Merle's curiosity, as well. "You know them?"

"The tall one calls herself Cleopatra. Blondie goes by Monique." Watkins's dough-boy face creased with sadness. "Life's tough for the gals who work around these parts. I don't cotton to them making a living that way. But nobody ought to have to die like that."

"No. They shouldn't." Banning had seen the crime scene photos. The nine women had all been killed in an interior location, then dumped in alleyways and Dumpsters within a two-mile radius of the mission. There'd been no pattern in the victims' racial backgrounds or physical characteristics. Their profession and a man who wanted them dead seemed to be the only thing they had in common.

The image of Kelsey Ryan shoving that box into the middle of his chest and daring him to ask questions flashed across his mind. Hell. Why not ask? What other leads did he have? "Say, Watkins—Ed—did you ever find a doll at any of the crime scenes?"

This time, the laugh was real. "A doll? Are you kidding? The first one we found—Jezebel was her street name—had a gold cross in her hand. You know, a charm on the end of a chain. None of the others I saw had even that much on 'em."

"I read that the original investigators checked out Reverend Wingate because of that cross."

"Yep." Watkins hunched his shoulders against the cold and glanced over at the argument across the street that had just gone up about ten decibels in volume.

"You don't want to do that!" the tall woman shouted, traipsing after the shorter one. The blond woman was crying. "You know what he'll do." It wasn't an argument so much as one person trying to convince the other to heed her warning.

Merle turned back to the sergeant's story. "The preacher didn't know anything about the necklace. He had an airtight alibi, too. Jezebel was killed Christmas morning. Ulysses was running services in the mission all day."

"With plenty of witnesses, I suppose."

"Enough to clear his name. I'm not sure we ever had a solid suspect after that. And then, well, you know." He shrugged. "These aren't the people the city really cares about. They want us to find out who killed that baby girl from the landfill, not nine hookers."

Merle definitely had his work cut out for him.

All of a sudden, Watkins perked up, like a dog with a fresh bone to gnaw on. "Hey, is that what The Flake's helpin' you with? Diggin' up ghosts of old homicides? The new commissioner must be desperate."

Knowing that Kelsey's alleged psychic abilities and hit-and-miss successes in helping out had earned her that nickname throughout K.C.P.D. was nothing new. He'd even used that name himself on more than one occasion. But tonight, hearing it said out loud like a joke in Watkins's insulting tone, the word *Flake* grated against his ears and bristled along the back of Merle's neck.

"I'd appreciate it if you'd address her as Ms. Ryan."

Watkins scoffed. "You're not buying into that sideshow of hers, are you? Sometimes women claim they have something extra like that—to pull you in. But it's only real on TV shows and sci-fi."

He might not believe she could read things and pull clues out of thin air, but he believed in treating her with respect. He'd promised Captain Taylor. His mother would have his hide if he didn't. And it felt like the right thing to do.

"She's an official departmental consultant," he explained, suspecting logic wouldn't override Sergeant Watkins's good-ol'-boy opinions. But an order from a higher authority would. "If Captain Taylor wants me to work with her on this, I'm going to do it. Now, I wouldn't think of insulting your partner, Ed. So I expect the same courtesy from you."

"Fine. Whatever." He leaned in and whispered in a tone that reminded Banning of a veteran cop getting his gibes in on a rookie. "At least I know my partner's not gonna fly off into la-la land and leave me hangin'."

Merle's hands curled into fists at his sides, but he never got the chance to question the need to wipe that condescending smirk off Watkins's face.

"Monique!"

The petite, blond prostitute dashed into the street.

Her friend followed a few steps, but a truck drove past and she retreated back to the curb.

"Officer? Can I talk to you a minute?" Monique ran right up to Merle and Ed. She swiped her teary eyes with the back of her hand and latched on to Merle's sleeve. "I want to report a missing person."

She reeked of perfume and cigarette smoke, and her long, painted nails dug into his arm. But he was more concerned about how young she looked beneath her runny mascara. "How old are you?" Merle asked. "Are you all right?"

She shook her head frantically, choking back a sob. "This isn't about me. My roommate, Delilah, hasn't come home for a couple of days. She got roughed up before Christmas by one of her johns, um…" She swallowed hard, catching herself. "I mean, her boyfriend. She checked into the mission to spend the night, so she could see the doctor. And—"

"Can you tell me her real name?" Merle asked. "Her *boyfriend's* name?"

"Susan Cooper. I don't know the guy's name. We just call him Mr. H. I've seen him in the paper."

"What does she look—"

"Now, Monique, what do you wanna worry these fine gentlemen for?" A man's hands, with at least one ring on each finger, closed around Monique's quaking shoulders and pried her loose. Merle raised his gaze to dark brown eyes and a fake smile. Zero.

"We were having a conversation."

Zero wrapped his heavy arm around Monique and pulled her to his side. It might have passed for a supportive embrace if he couldn't read the fear in her downcast eyes. A glance across the street told him Cleopatra didn't seem any more thrilled that Zero had joined the conversation. The stocky black man's slick drawl betrayed nothing but friendly confidence. "These men have a job to do, honey. We can't be pestering them. Right, Detective? Sergeant?"

Maybe too friendly. Too confident.

Clearly, Zero and Ed Watkins were well acquainted with each other.

Monique whimpered in his embrace. "I just wanted to ask about Delilah."

"I told you she went on vacation to see her little boy." He winked at Merle, indicating Monique might be the one with the problem. "Delilah's boy lives with foster parents. She went to spend Christmas with him."

Merle's protective hackles rose in full force, but Ed stepped in first. "I'll handle this, Detective Banning." He laid a hand on both Zero's and Monique's arms and turned them back toward the street. "Why don't you go inside and find your partner. Ms. Ryan," he added with all the sincerity of a rat. "I'll keep an eye and ear out for her car and let you know if I find anything."

Then he turned his back on Merle to escort the pimp and prostitute across the street. Fine. This was Watkins's beat. Those were his people. If he had his own way of dealing with them, Merle wouldn't step on his toes.

But he made a mental note to check the missing persons list when he reported for work in the morning.

MERLE STOOD in the main hallway of the Wingate Humanitarian Mission to unbutton his coat and shed his gloves. It saddened him to see the steady stream of destitute people filing in to the main dining room, checking in for a blanket or pillow or winter coat, and signing up for appointments with the doctor tomorrow.

His stomach twisted into the knot of guilt he'd carried with him for so many years. Were any of these people victims of his father's selfish game? Had he cheated them out of a life savings? Put a low-rent apartment building out of business? Cost a job? Ruined a retirement?

Chances were that after twenty years, these people were victims of other circumstances, some of their own doing, some at society's mercy. But he still felt the need to atone for the sins of his father. He still felt compelled to make their world better. Safer. More secure.

"Detective Banning." The Reverend Ulysses Wingate chose that moment to step out of his office and greet Merle with a hearty handshake. "Did you finally decide to come inside and warm yourself? Any luck with the stolen car? I'm sure sorry about that. If I'd been at the door sooner, I might have seen something. But we don't open for dinner until five each night. And the staff usually works in their offices or the kitchen until then. Not a very observant group, I'm afraid."

Merle couldn't help but grin at the cosmic irony. Atone for his father's sins? Then, voilà, he's shaking hands with the minister? He waved aside the reverend's apology; he'd earn his redemption another way. "Don't worry about it. Looks like you've got your hands full here. K.C.P.D. will handle the theft."

"I'm sure they'll do a fine job."

"Have you seen Ms. Ryan? The redhead I came in with?"

"I put her to work. Well, she volunteered and I didn't say no." He slapped Merle on the shoulder with a blustery laugh. "The Lord loves a volunteer." Reverend Wingate led him over to the dining hall, and keeping one hand on his shoulder, pointed across the long rows of tables and chairs. "She's over in the soup line, servin' the rolls for dinner. We've got plenty tonight if you want to share a plate."

Merle spotted Kelsey behind the glass-and-stainless-steel cafeteria counter. She wore plastic gloves to pick rolls from the giant basket in front of her and hand them over the partition to the people going through the line. She exchanged words and a smile with each guest and seemed peculiarly energized for a woman who claimed to see murders.

He realized the reverend was waiting for an answer. "Maybe a cup of coffee."

"Help yourself. I have to go do some paperwork. End of the month, end of the year—it's always a mess to add up the donations and government funding and expenditures." He pointed a stubby finger into the air. "The Good Book says that the Lord will provide." Then he poked Merle in the chest with that same finger. "But not if I don't get everything turned over to the accountant first. Enjoy."

Reverend Wingate was still amused with himself as he walked down the hall to retrieve a folder from the lodging check-in. He stopped twice along the way to chat with someone in line as if he or she was an old friend, and reminded all of them who were staying the night to sign in. Briefly, Merle recalled the cold-case reports he'd read and Sergeant Watkins's comments. Ulysses Wingate seemed far removed from a man who would murder a prostitute—strip her naked, wrap a scarf tight around her throat and watch the life snuffed out of her eyes.

But he'd seen and heard stranger things. All of the

murders had happened around his mission. Just because Ulysses Wingate had an alibi for one murder eleven years ago didn't mean Merle was going to scratch him off his list of suspects. Tomorrow morning he was going to pull that cross necklace out of the evidence box and see if he could trace it back to Wingate or the mission.

The reverend might be innocent of murder. But logic said the cross and the mission location was too big a connection to ignore.

If he wanted morning to get here, though, he'd better get today over with. Using the reverend's joke as a reminder to put in some money to pay for his cup of coffee, Merle stepped into the dining hall. He didn't want to take Kelsey away from her job before everyone was served, but he ached to put an end to the long day, go home, put his knee up with some ice and get some sleep.

Trouble was, the longer he stood there, the less he seemed to mind the wait.

Kelsey Ryan was fascinating to watch when she wasn't talking psychobabble and trying to save the world.

A hair net tamed her wild hairstyle and muted the color, giving her face a chance to shine. She had quite a smile when she decided to use it, and the warmth of the kitchen and all these bodies in one room flushed her skin with a peachy glow. Without her bulky black-and-white coat to camouflage her, he got a better idea of her womanly shape.

Everything about his ideal woman—Ginny Rafferty-Taylor—was delicate and petite. Two words he couldn't apply to Kelsey Ryan. She was taller than Ginny. More voluptuously built. He saw nothing overtly sexy in Ginny. She was smart, beautiful, vulnerable—a woman to cherish.

But Kelsey's full breasts pushed at the snowmen on her sweater every time she breathed or laughed. She stood with her hands at her waist, emphasizing the lush swell of her hips. Ginny was tough enough to make an excellent homicide detective—but she was all lady, all understatement, all femininity, through and through.

Kelsey was earthier, louder, brighter. She was more impulsive, more temperamental. She was, well…more.

Funny how his accelerated pulse rate and heated, itchy skin seemed to take note of the differences.

An elderly man with a walker tapped Merle on the arm and asked him to give him some more room to pass. Surprised at how long he'd stood there spying on Kelsey, Merle excused himself and quickly stepped to the side. The older man thanked him and scooted past.

But the interchange in the doorway was enough to snag Kelsey's attention behind the counter. Brown eyes met green across the huge, noisy room, questioning his presence, his interest. Just as quickly, those soft eyes switched focus back to a man at the counter. Kelsey handed the man a roll, asked him something about the weather and smiled.

Merle Banning wanted that smile.

But he didn't suppose he'd done anything yet to deserve one.

Maybe it would be best if he stuck to business and good manners and positive press for the department, and forgot anything his misfiring hormones and lonesome heart were asking him to do.

After stuffing five dollars into the locked wooden donations box beside the door, Merle put his money clip back in his pocket and made his way toward the serving counter. Bypassing the offer of a tray, he grabbed a ceramic mug and filled it with hot, black coffee. He waited his turn until the line thinned and he stood in front of Kelsey. It hurt the ego to note her smile had vanished again.

"You don't have good news for me," she stated, instead of offering a cheery *"Enjoy your meal"* the way she had to the three men ahead of him.

Merle shook his head. "Sergeant Watkins thinks your car is already being broken down for parts. You'll need to call your insurance agent in the morning. I'll have a report ready for you to turn in with the claim by the end of the day."

"Thanks. I guess."

"I wish I could do more. I'll at least offer you a ride home once you're done here."

She inhaled deeply, as if she had to debate the pros and cons of the practical offer. Merle shamelessly watched the snowmen dance across the front of her sweater and decided then and there that no matter how much his knee hurt him, he was definitely taking a cold shower tonight and washing these crazy thoughts of attraction out of his system.

"I suppose that's okay." Ah. Lukewarm approval. His ego was definitely taking it in the shorts tonight. "I promised I'd help with clean-up, though. It might be another hour or so before I can leave."

Thoughts of atonement kicked in, along with a modicum of surrendering to the inevitable. Merle smiled even if Kelsey wouldn't. He set his coffee on the counter and took off his coat. The tie and top button of his shirt went next. "I'm off the clock. Worked my way through high school washing dishes. Just point me to the kitchen."

T. MERLE BANNING had actually rolled up his sleeves, manned the sprayer, scraped plates and helped the mission's volunteer staff clean hundreds of dishes.

Not quite so uptight and buttoned-down as you thought, hmm?

Kelsey could almost hear her grandmother's voice saying *I told you so* in her head.

Despite his handsome face and down-home charm, her grandmother had never liked Jeb Adams. She'd gone to her grave warning Kelsey to dump the man whom, for a few insane weeks, she'd actually agreed to marry. Fortunately, she'd finally come to her senses and realized her grandmother was right about the man who'd *loved* her with such vicious words.

But Kelsey had a feeling Lucy Belle would like T. Kelsey did.

It was stupid. It was pointless. But she did.

How could she not have feelings for a man who saved her life, risked dishpan hands and looked at her across a crowded room as if he actually enjoyed the view?

True, it was the same man who thought she was a fraud and a pain in the butt.

But the tenuous feelings were still there.

Ho boy.

She'd needed to work at the mission tonight. She was still raw with guilt at accomplishing nothing to help the women she'd seen murdered. She'd made a mess of things. And then someone had had the gall to steal her car and leave her stranded with no way to escape to the sanctuary of her home.

Before her day got any worse, she'd needed to do

something good. She'd needed to make a difference in somebody's life.

Amazingly enough, T hadn't chewed her out for being selfish or making him wait. Instead, he'd rolled up his sleeves and joined her.

Now he was waiting patiently for her, holding her coat while she dried her hands and gathered her things.

Jeb had never been patient about anything.

"Yuck." Kelsey's long turquoise scarf had slid off its hook and landed on the tile floor where the staff had mopped. She picked it up by one grungy end and watched grayish water drip off the other.

"Problem?"

"Nothing a little dish soap won't fix." She hurried to one of the sinks and rinsed it, twisting it carefully when she was done so the wool wouldn't stretch out of shape.

Banning stood beside her by the time she was done and grimaced in sympathy. "Probably wouldn't be a problem if it didn't feel like twenty below outside." He snapped his fingers with an idea. "I know. Reverend Wingate has a box out in the hallway where they were handing out blankets. It was full of coats, hats, gloves, that kind of thing. I'll bet we can find you a replacement scarf there."

He stepped aside to let her lead the way. "Do you think he'd mind if I took one?"

"From what I can tell, for the right donation, he'll let you have anything in the building."

Kelsey let her guard slip a little and laughed at the joke. "I thought that hair net did a lot for me. I've got ten bucks left in my purse. You think he'd let me have it for that?"

Banning reached out and combed his fingers through

the hair on top of her head, mussing the curls and pulling one spiky strand straight beside her ear. "I'd pass on that. If you're going to have hair this bold, you don't want to hide it."

From the width of his grin to his brief, teasing touch, Kelsey knew that had only been a friendly gesture—as if they were comrades of sorts. But to feel a man's hand in her hair... The familiarity... Her breath seemed to catch in her chest and her cheeks felt feverish with heat.

It was the third time that day he'd touched her. Without hesitation. Giving her money. Claiming her hand. Teasing her. As if he thought she was normal.

Normal.

Sheesh. That doused her body's silly reaction to his touch.

She was so far from normal that Detective Logic would never believe it. He just thought she was crazy.

"I'm warning you, Ulysses. I can do better than this dump."

Kelsey stopped at the raised voices from the open doorway to Reverend Wingate's office. A tall, skinny man with stringy brown hair pulled back into a ponytail stood with his hand on the knob, either ready to make a dramatic entrance or beat a hasty retreat.

"You've threatened me before. To no avail." The calmer voice inside belonged to Reverend Wingate. "Halliwell will come through. He always does. Besides, you know you won't find a job anywhere else."

"This isn't a job, it's a sentence. You get me the money," the skinny man warned, his knuckles white around the doorknob from squeezing it so tight. "Or this hell-hole will be short a doctor as well as a teacher."

Skinny Man spun around, nearly crashing into Kelsey. T grabbed her by the arm and dragged her back a step, saving her from a collision. "Watch it," he warned.

The other man spared a wild-eyed glance at Banning, then dropped his gaze to Kelsey, raking his eyes up and down her body. His bleary inspection missed nothing and left her feeling as violated as Edgar's touch had back at The Underground. He stood there for only a second, but stared long enough and hard enough that T drifted up beside her, subtly positioning himself between her and those eyes.

"Can we help you?" T asked, moving even closer.

Kelsey didn't mind. She curled her fingers into the sleeve of T's jacket and held on. There was such anger, such contempt in that man's gaunt face—an eerie recognition in those black eyes she couldn't put a name to—that it frightened her.

"Get the hell out of my way." He finally moved, knocking shoulders with T as he strode down the hallway and out the front door.

"Doc?" Reverend Wingate's voice grew louder. "Doc!" *Doc?* "Great bedside manner," she cracked.

Banning watched him all the way to the door.

Neither of them laughed.

When the reverend popped through the doorway, he looked like the wrath of God. As soon as he saw Kelsey standing there with Banning, though, his bearded face creased into a smile. "Headin' out?"

"Sorry." Kelsey apologized for eavesdropping. "We didn't mean to interrupt."

"Not a problem. That's Doc Siegel. He's what passes for a medical professional around here—if I can keep him sober long enough. Which wouldn't be tonight."

She didn't see the humor in it that Ulysses did. "Would you believe he first walked in here as one of the homeless men off the street? Had a degree, had a life. Lost it all in the bottom of a bottle. That was more than ten years ago. Now he helps me run the place. But forget him. He'll have to sleep that temper off. What can I do for you?"

Kelsey released her death grip on T's jacket and held up her soggy bundle of turquoise wool. "I got my scarf wet and was wondering if I could buy one from your coat box over there."

"Take what you need. If you want to leave something, just put it in the box. Everything's a freewill donation around here."

Except, apparently, Doc Siegel's time and expertise.

"Thanks, Reverend."

"No. Thank you." He stuck out his hand to shake hers. It had taken a lot of years of training and discipline not to automatically extend her hand and risk skin-to-skin contact. "We appreciate your help tonight. Both of you. Anytime you want to stop back by, we'd love to have you. Especially around the holidays when volunteers are in short supply."

"Thanks," T answered, questioning her hesitation. "We might take you up on that."

The men shook hands first, giving her the time she needed to pull on her right glove. By the time they had finished, she was ready to take his hand.

He thumbed over his shoulder to his office. "Well, back to the books. You two help yourself to whatever you need. Good night."

"Good night, Reverend."

He closed the door behind him with an almost noiseless click, giving no indication of the argument they'd just witnessed.

"Let's get going." T's purposeful sigh enervated them both.

Kelsey nodded and reached for her coat. Instead of handing it to her, T held it open and waited for her to slip her arms inside. After only a brief internal debate, she turned and let him help her on with it, allowing herself to be pampered in a way she wasn't accustomed to.

"Thanks. Just give me a second to grab a scarf."

After putting her money into the donations box, Kelsey knelt beside the deep wooden box and dug in. She'd forgotten to put on her left glove, but the sensations she received were mild and easy to block out. Good feelings mostly. Relief at getting rid of an item. Gratitude that the item offered warmth. The contented pride of having done a good deed. She rifled through parkas and ball caps, mittens and umbrellas. Her fingers brushed across nubby wool and smooth nylon and…

Oh, hell.

It hit her hard and fast, before she could pull away. Before she could throw up any walls and stop the nightmare from coming.

A woman screaming. No, dying to scream. A choking sound gurgled in her own throat.

No. Just dying.

She was back in that horrible place. Back in the damp, black, rotting smell. The wall cut into her back. The air chilled her naked body down to the bone. Her lungs burned, starved for oxygen. She scratched at that dark face, clawed at her own throat.

But the hands were too strong. The man was too big. The scarf was too tight.

They should have been gentle hands. Kind hands. *Why?*

Her head felt like lead and toppled to the side. Her legs went limp.

He lay her on the floor beside the other tiny body and the darkness rushed in until there was nothing left but the sounds in her ear. The deep, angry chant.

"Abi in malam rem." Over and over, fading into the darkness. *"Matrona. Abi in malam rem."*

"Kelsey?" She heard her own name from far away. Outside the darkness. "Kelsey?"

Her left hand was on fire.

"Kelsey!"

She jerked her mind back to the present. Jerked herself to her feet. She threw the fire from her hand and stumbled back into a warm, solid wall.

"Whoa. What the hell's going on?" Strong arms folded around her stomach and chest, holding her close to that wall. "Kels?"

Not a wall at all. But a man. Living, breathing. Real.

"T?" She spun around in his arms and buried her face against his chest. "Oh, God. T."

"I don't know why the hell you call me that." That crisp, articulate voice was clearer now, close to her ear. She reached behind him and linked her hands behind his back, inhaling the clean smells of wool and winter and man, desperately trying to absorb his abundant heat. He rubbed slow, soothing circles against her back until she stopped shaking. She hadn't even realized how her body trembled with the aftershocks of reliving that horrible scene. "What happened? Is there a snake hiding in the bottom of that box? A mousetrap get ya? C'mon, Kels, you have to talk to me."

Snake? Mousetrap?

Of course. Detective Banning would be looking for a logical explanation for her bizarre behavior.

But for her, the only explanation was the truth. Taking a deep, resigned breath, she left the temporary security she felt and leaned back against his arms.

"I got mascara on your coat," she remarked, wiping at the black smudges. That meant she'd been crying. She hadn't known that, either. But scrubbing the wool between her gloved fingers was a simple detail to focus on while she hid that nightmare beneath a thin veil of conscious thought and placed herself back in the empty hallway of the Wingate Mission.

"Kelsey," he urged gently. "You just cried out as if you'd been attacked. Are you hurt? What happened?"

He still hadn't released her. He would soon enough.

She looked up into that moss-colored gaze so he could read the sincerity in her own eyes. "I had another psychic impression about Jezebel's murder. I saw more this time. I heard words."

His eyes went cold and his hands stilled their massage. She braced herself for the chill to return when he let her go and backed away. "Don't play that game with me. If you've got facts to share, fine. Tell me. But don't wrap it up in all this drama. I can't take a man to court because of some daydream you make up about him." He counted off the requirements on his fingers. "I need facts to arrest a man. Facts to convict him. Facts to keep him from killing anybody else."

Kelsey turned around and looked at the scattered pile of clothes, lying in the box, on the floor and over the edge in between. She didn't have to take one step closer to identify the item that had triggered the impression. She didn't have to touch it again to remember the overwhelming terror that had imprinted itself on that cloth. She recognized it from before. Faded and frayed now, but no less vivid in her mind.

A long yellow scarf with fuschia polka dots.

With both gloves on, she picked up the long ream of worn silk and held it out to him.

"Here's your fact."

"An old scarf?"

"The murder weapon."

When he wouldn't take it, she draped it over his shoulder and marched out the door. "Kelsey. Kelsey!"

She heard his hurried, uneven footsteps on the planked floor behind her, but she had the door closed before he could stop her. The cold, clear air took her breath away, but she didn't stop to button her coat. Overlapping the placket in front of her, she hugged it shut, bent her head into the north wind and hurried down the steps.

"Kelsey, stop." He caught up with her halfway down the block and limped along beside her. "Where are you going?"

"Home."

"It's minus twelve frickin' degrees out here. My car's parked across the street. I said I'd drive."

"No, thank you. I'll find a cab."

"There are no taxis in this part of town at this time of night."

She put her hand out beside her, refusing to listen. "I'm not going to be any more of an imposition on you than I already have been. If I can't find a cab, I'll take a bus or I'll walk."

"Don't be ridiculous."

"You already think I am."

He muttered a curse beside her. "Was this the scarf used on Jezebel or all nine victims?"

Kelsey's steps faltered and slowed. She hadn't expected him to ask a question about the murder. "I don't know. He used it on somebody. I'm only getting images of one death." She spotted a distinctive yellow car speeding through the intersection more than a block away. She ran toward it and waved. "Taxi!"

It disappeared before she reached the curb.

"What was the scarf doing at the mission?" he called after her.

Was he really interested in her ideas, or was he just using the questions to slow her down? "I don't know. But the mission seems to be a lightning rod for this case. Too many leads keep bringing me back to this neighborhood. Maybe it was just a convenient place to stash it. Hundreds of people go in and out of there every day."

"Would it kill you to slow down? You're not going to find a taxi."

She stopped and faced him. "Is this slow enough? I just want to get home. Not that you care, but I usually get nasty headaches after I have an impression that strong."

She spun around and hunched her shoulders in defense against his arguments and the wind.

"I care. I just—"

"—don't believe me. Woo. Hoo." She twirled her finger around in the air. "Your compassion overwhelms me."

"Dammit, Kelsey." He grabbed her arm, but she shook him off. He grabbed her again, tugged her to a halt and turned her around. "We can either walk until your butt freezes and my knee gives out, or you can let me drive you home."

She couldn't resist looking at his knee. Why couldn't she just stay mad? Why couldn't she just walk away? Why did she have to care that he was in pain? "Is it really hurting?"

"Probably like your nasty headache."

As guilt and compassion dissipated her temper, her gaze fell to the strip of yellow and fuschia hanging from his coat pocket. "I thought you didn't believe."

"That you see things? I don't know." He finally eased his hold on her shoulders. "That you know something about those murders? I intend to find out."

Chapter Five

Kelsey had to admit that practicality and logic kept her a lot warmer than stubbornness and hurt feelings.

Once inside T's boxy black Jeep Cherokee, he'd cranked up the heat and offered her a lap blanket, which quickly thawed her fingers and toes and warmed her chilled body.

She wasn't the only one feeling the effects of winter and a long day on her feet. The late-night drive through the streets of Kansas City's business district into an old Italian neighborhood near the City Market passed by in relative silence. The quiet journey allowed Kelsey plenty of time to study T. At every stoplight and every long stretch of straight road, he slipped his right hand down to his knee and rubbed it through the khaki slacks he wore.

She was guessing now that his limp was a chronic injury, aggravated by cold weather and running after her. His hands worked methodically, efficiently, just like that logical brain of his. There was no wasted motion there. Everything was planned, precise.

The same way he'd taken her hand, the same way he'd played with her hair, the same way he'd held her in his arms and comforted her—even when he refused to understand why she was afraid. He tried her patience with his old-fashioned, inflexible ways. But that same, staunch approach to life had also made her feel safe. And warm.

Merle Banning had warmed her with his eyes, his hands, his body, his words and his consideration all day long. It had been far too long since any man—since anyone—had been able to chase away the chill she lived with every day of her life.

If only she could find a way to fit into a logical world.

Then maybe she could feel warm—and secure—every day.

"Turn here," she instructed, when they reached her street. "It's the fourth house on the left. The little gray stone cottage."

"Quaint," he commented as he turned into the driveway. He nodded toward her front porch. "You should have left a light on."

She pulled her keys out of the side pocket of her backpack purse where she'd zipped them in. "I didn't plan on being gone so long. Thanks for helping out at the mission tonight. You didn't have to do that."

"Neither did you."

Shrugging aside the compliment, she folded up the lap blanket and set it behind the seat. "I guess I thought I'd find the answers I needed this afternoon. Then I could just give you a phone call and be out of your hair." It had taken longer than she'd anticipated, but it was time to make good on her word. She opened the door and stepped down. "I appreciate the ride home. I'll call you tomorrow about the stolen-car report. Good night."

Summoning a decent smile, she closed the door behind her.

She hadn't taken two steps when the engine died and T was climbing out on his side. He met her in front of the Jeep.

"What are you doing?" she asked.

He brushed his fingers against the small of her back and turned her toward the house. "Walking you to the door."

"I know the way."

"It's dark. It's late. Humor me." In other words, *you won't get rid of me until I do this.*

With a reluctant nod, Kelsey led the way up to the porch. The instant she opened the storm door, the barking started. Insistent, high-pitched, guarding-the-territory barking. Kelsey grinned and inserted her key into the dead-bolt lock.

"You've got a guard dog?" T asked, holding the storm door open.

"Of sorts." She unlocked the doorknob next. "Are you afraid of dogs?"

"Only the ones that attack me. Look…" He put his hand on her wrist when she would have opened the door. His steadying sigh filled the air between them with a cloud of warm air. When the cloud had dissipated, the moon in the clear sky above them offered enough light for her to see the frown crinkling the corners of his eyes. "I'm sorry this hasn't been a better day for you."

"You didn't steal my car."

"I'm not talking about that." He glanced at the door, considering the barking still coming from the other side. Whatever he wanted to say, ultimately, it was more important to him than silencing the ferocious noisemaker.

"I'm sorry I was such a jerk today." He put up a hand

to deny her protest. "I'll admit, I'm pretty much a skeptic about psychic powers. If they really exist, and they can read criminal minds and the clues they leave behind, then we should be able to solve every crime on the book. At least we'd know who to go after."

"We're not infallible. Sometimes we get bombarded with so many images and emotions, we can't pick out what's useful and what's not."

He pressed a leather-gloved finger to her lips. "Let me finish."

Her breath caught behind the gentle caress, but she warned herself not to read anything personal into it. She simply nodded her acquiescence.

He pulled his finger away and reached for her hand. The slim turquoise glove seemed to disappear inside his larger black one. "It wasn't very gentlemanly of me to make fun of you or discount what you believe to be true. I didn't take you seriously when I should have. My mother raised me better than that."

Kelsey decided sight unseen that she liked his mother. Mrs. Banning had done a fine job with her son.

"If I'd paid better attention to what you were trying to say earlier today, you wouldn't have gone to The Underground. That creep wouldn't have put his hands all over you and you wouldn't have had your car stolen."

"Neither of those things were your fault."

"I let my emotions rule my head today, and I don't know why. It was just like I was a rookie all over again. I should have done better by you."

"I didn't see anything rookielike about you today. Despite dealing with my impulses—which I'm sure were not choices you would have made—you were large and in charge and completely in control, as far as I could see."

His earnest expression relaxed into a grin. "Then you don't *see* as well as you think, Ms. Ryan. I think you just helped a skeptic prove his point."

She was either going to burst into tears or hug him if he went any further with his apology.

Kelsey laughed out loud instead and knocked on the door to get the dog's attention. "Frosty. Cool it. It's me." The barking stopped, but was quickly replaced by eager scratching at the door. "He's very protective."

"I can see why he needs to be."

Standing on her front porch, trading apologies and teasing, felt silly. Intimate. Wonderful.

T made her forget for just a few moments that relationships didn't work with her. He made her think that a man might actually want to spend time with her. He made her think…oh, hell. She was tired of thinking. "Would you like to come in for a cup of coffee?"

"What, no herbal teas?" he joked.

Kelsey made a face. "Have you ever tasted the stuff?"

"Sure." He shrugged as if he couldn't find any reason to say no. "Coffee would be nice."

Coffee *was* nice. They sipped the warm, rich java and wasted an hour doing nothing more than getting acquainted and pretending they could actually get along. But the coffee was getting cold. The hour was growing late.

Reality had to happen sometime.

After insisting he get a share of the home-baked cookies she'd set out on the table for her and T, Frosty had settled at Kelsey's feet for a snooze. But the instant she got up to carry their mugs to the sink, the dog was on his feet, following her every step. He followed her into the living room to retrieve T's coat and gloves from the couch. He followed her to the front door to hand them over to T. Her miniature silver bear of a dog allowed T to scratch his ears, but managed to keep himself squarely positioned between Kelsey and T.

So, no chance of a good-night kiss. Not that T would be thinking along those lines. Not that she should.

She should just be happy they'd reached a truce.

T grinned as he pulled on his coat. "He's a good guard dog. Makes a lot of noise when someone's outside the house and stays right by your side. He's a good little alarm system."

The poodle seemed to think T was a decent guy, too, as long as he had cookies and tummy rubs to share. But once the food and petting was gone, his allegiance was clear. "He stays close because he knows I'll spoil him."

T shrugged as he buttoned his coat and pulled on his gloves. "I thought familiars were cats."

He was just asking a curious question. More fodder for that fact-oriented brain of his. But Kelsey bristled, anyway. "Witches have familiars, Detective. I'm not a witch."

Jeb had called her that. And worse.

"Uh, oh. Back to *Detective,* huh? I was just getting used to T."

The truce had ended.

She didn't know why she was suddenly so irritated with him. Or why she was making the comparison. In one, long crazy day, T. Merle Banning had already shown more kindness than Jeb Adams had in the six months she'd dated him. Still, it hurt that she was feeling something more, wanting something more, than any man could ever want from her.

God, she was lonely. And all she had were nightmares and a dog to keep her company.

"I'm just tired." She excused her testy reaction. "You must be, too."

"Sure. But I was just commenting on how close the two of you are. I imagine he's good to have around. You probably don't worry about touching him, do you?"

He'd noticed her reluctance to touch unknown objects and people with her bare hands? He probably thought it was just some eccentric phobia she had. He couldn't understand that her fear of crowds and skimpy summer clothing were matters of mental survival and emotional security to her. She couldn't protect herself 24/7 from every person in every environment. So she limited her exposure where she could. She kept to herself. She wore her gloves and pretended she didn't need human contact like everybody else.

But an explanation like that would blow his logical thinking right out of the water.

"Frosty's a pet. A damn good one." She reached around him to flip on the porch light and open the door. The perpetual blast of winter was a welcome wake-up call to her fairy-tale thinking. "Good night, Detective. I need to get to bed. I have a lot to do tomorrow."

He opened the storm door, but seemed oddly reluctant to leave. "You won't go into the mission neighborhood by yourself again, will you? I promise I'm going to do some more investigating myself. Please leave it to me."

She'd make no such promise. That dying woman's terror would haunt her until she found answers. And the sooner she found them, the sooner she could say goodbye to Merle Banning and these crazy, foolish longings he stirred in her. She could go back to her safe, lonely existence. "I'll try to limit my search to daylight hours. Good night."

He stopped the door with his hand. "It's too dangerous."

"I'm not your responsibility." She held on to her side of the door and pushed.

"Every citizen in this town is my responsibility."

"Fine. Go be rude to one of them."

"I already apologized—"

"Your words mean nothing to me, Detective." The resistance on the other side of the door suddenly stopped. "Now go away. Good night." The door clicked shut and she fastened the dead bolt.

Kelsey held her breath for an endless moment until the outside door slammed shut. She jumped back, startled, and stared at the reinforced steel that kept the outside world from getting to her.

That kept the outside world from ever finding her.

Once the Jeep had pulled out of her driveway, the house was quiet. Morosely quiet except for the rattle of the wind against her windows.

Before, she'd always found the quiet soothing. The solitude a blessing.

But not tonight.

She'd invited the outside world into her home tonight.

She'd let T. Merle Banning into her life.

And now he was gone.

She turned her back to the door, sank to the floor and cuddled a willing Frosty in her lap.

She'd gotten her wish, hadn't she?

She was finally alone.

WHAT THE HELL had happened last night?

And why was he still thinking about it this morning?

Merle pushed the elevator button that would take him to the top floor of the historic Peabody Building.

Ginny shared the loft condominium with her entrepreneurial husband—and the building's renovator—Brett Taylor.

He stuffed the manila envelope he carried under his arm to peel off his gloves and unbutton his coat. He'd been dreading this visit for several weeks. Not that he ever dreaded spending time with his partner. But jealousy and unrequited feelings were hard things to live with for as long as he had. It hurt inside to see her at home with Brett—to see her so obviously in love and so happy.

She deserved it. She'd lost her entire family and had been so closed off before meeting Brett. All work. She didn't even know how to play. But Brett Taylor had changed her life.

Merle had somehow hoped that he'd be the man to change it.

Now she was pregnant and on leave. Despite an open invitation to pay a visit, he'd put this off because he'd known she'd be even happier. And he'd miss what he didn't have even more.

Until last night.

Until Kelsey Ryan wreaked havoc on his orderly life.

Now, instead of obsessing over a woman he couldn't have, he'd spent the night obsessing about a woman who drove him crazy.

One minute he'd been all relaxed, sitting in Kelsey's homey, intimate kitchen. The coffee hit the spot, the cookies were delicious, the conversation stimulating and the woman sitting across from him was beautiful in a way he'd never considered before.

It was the sort of evening he'd always pictured with Ginny. Only, Merle was having a hard time picturing the petite blonde sitting across from him, a dog practically in her lap, laughing out loud at that goofy story he'd told about starting a fire in his dorm room when he'd tried to soup up his computer without upgrading the electrical outlet in the wall.

But Kelsey had laughed. She'd talked about collecting dolls and Santa Clauses and quilts and magnets. She'd talked about her grandmother with love and pride. She'd asked intelligent questions, offered insightful opinions. She'd dubbed him with that goofy letter that seemed to fit when she said it, that made him feel as if he was more than just his father's namesake. That he was his own man.

He'd been thinking about sampling a good-night kiss and thought he was getting the message that she was, too. Then, bam! She was pushing him out the door, igniting his temper and throwing a very real fear of God into him because he knew that, despite every warning, she was going to go off on some other fool errand today that would put her in harm's way.

Having her car stolen was bad enough. He knew the victim of any crime felt a certain sense of violation and vulnerability. He had an unsettling feeling in his gut that that theft had been more about sending a message than making a profit. But Kelsey refused to see the danger. Who knew what Mort and Edgar, or Zero, or even that Doc Siegel would do to a nosy, pseudo detective who asked too many questions in the wrong part of town?

He knew.

That meant he had to hustle his sore leg and get some answers to piece together these murders before she got in too deep with her crazy notions and couldn't get out. She *was* his responsibility, dammit, even if she didn't want to be. Captain Taylor had assigned her to him. His conscience and something a lot less tangible inside him demanded that he keep her safe.

"Your words mean nothing to me, Detective."

Then, by God, he was going to do it some other way.

After his unceremonious departure, he'd driven straight to the precinct office. Most of the night shift worked on the streets or out of satellite stations, so the place was relatively deserted. That was fine. He wasn't much in the mood for company.

He'd spent a couple of hours on the Internet, reading up on the claims of psychic phenomena and how to debunk them. He'd been left with more doubts than before. Some so-called psychics claimed they could read minds or see the future. Kelsey herself had said that was impossible for her. Others simply picked up on positive or negative vibes in the air. Some went into trances; others used crystals to channel or deflect energy.

Like one so-called expert he'd found, Kelsey claimed she had to touch the object or person in order to see anything. Did that mean she got impressions from every single thing she touched? Twenty-four hours a day? Talk about sensory overload. Talk about invasion of privacy. Had she read anything about him?

T, she called him. *Merle's your middle name.*

The headache had set in about then, throbbing in synchronous time with his knee. What else did she think she knew about him?

And if he believed she knew things about him, could he believe she knew about those murders?

Or was she still just The Flake he had to save from her own misguided intentions?

Frustrated with more questions than answers, he'd

turned off his computer and focused on something more tangible. He'd bagged up the doll and its box and labeled it. Then, against his best logical judgment, he'd bagged the yellow scarf, as well. He prepped both packages for Mac Taylor and his team of forensic scientists.

He doubted either one would provide DNA, a fingerprint or a fiber match to lead him to a murderer. But he was guessing, at the very least, he could find a clue to prove there was something funny going on down in The Underground curiosity shop. Drugs. Fencing stolen objects. Maybe he could even get a warrant and remove that danger from Kelsey's path.

Beyond that? Hell. He'd been working the Kelsey Ryan problem all night long. He hadn't gotten beyond anything yet.

The elevator dinged to announce the top floor. Merle got off, pressed the buzzer to Ginny's loft and waited. She was sitting in a wheelchair when she opened the door, but she looked gorgeous.

"Hey, partner."

"Ginny."

"Banning to the rescue." She greeted him with a hug and a smile and ushered him in. "Please, come break up the monotony before I'm forced to play another game of solitaire. Brett's stopping by the library on his way home for lunch to bring me some books I ordered. But I've already read everything else in the condo."

"I could have picked them up for you."

"I know. But he likes to check on me, anyway. If I give him an assignment, I feel less guilty about taking him away from work just to plump pillows and talk to me."

Merle took off his coat and followed her into the sunny, airy living room. Its cool palette of colors complemented Ginny's silver-blond hair and ice-blue maternity jogging suit. "You two are really getting this place fixed up."

She nodded. "About all we have left is the mural I'm painting in the baby's room. But the doctor says I can only be up for a couple of hours each day, so it's taking a while."

He nodded toward her round belly. "And everything's going okay with the baby?"

Hugging her arms around her precious cargo, Ginny smiled. "Just fine."

"And you?"

"Even better." Ginny parked her chair beside the coffee table and invited him to sit on the sofa opposite her. "But enough about me. Stimulate my brain. Please. Tell me what you're working on. I heard Mitch assigned you to the cold-case files."

Merle nodded, settling himself on the couch. She wasn't going to like this. "I'm working the Holiday Hooker murders."

That sobered her smile. Ginny had been shot, nearly killed, the last time the department had investigated a lead on the case. It had turned out to be a false lead, a heinous ruse to draw members of the Taylor family into a deadly ambush. But she'd survived. She was stronger for it. Her marriage was stronger for it.

And the man who'd fired the shot was dead.

By Merle's own hand.

The pall that settled between them lasted for less than a minute. Ginny quirked one perfect, silvery brow. "So why did you want to come see me?"

He handed her the manila envelope. "What do you know about doll collecting?"

"Not much. But I can find out. What do you need?"

In a few brief minutes, Merle had showed her the scanned photos of the doll Kelsey had brought in and explained Kelsey's claims about the doll being the key to the first murder, maybe all the murders. Ginny grabbed her sketch pad and jotted notes while Merle talked. He related every factual detail he could, from their first meeting at the precinct office to her bizarre dismissal at her house last night.

By the time he'd finished, he was pacing the room. Ginny was doodling pictures on her sketch pad and hiding an amused smile.

He stopped when he saw that grin. "What?"

"You sure seem to have an awful lot to say about Ms. Ryan."

"Of course, I do. She's my partner." He put up his hands, reassuring Ginny of her place. "Temporary partner. Nothing more."

"Mmm-hmm." Ginny nodded, apparently seeing something in this scenario he didn't. "I'm just getting some vibes from you. You're pretty agitated this morning."

Vibes was a Kelsey word, not something he'd expect Ginny to use. "Look. If you do sense anything between me and Kelsey, it's just friction. She's not the easiest person to work with. She's not nearly grounded enough to suit me."

Ginny threw up her hands in surrender. "You don't have to marry her. But it's nice to see you finally notice someone. That's all."

"I'm not interested. Believe me, she's not my type." He had to say it. "You know I go for cool, Nordic blondes."

Ginny smiled indulgently, if a bit sadly. She knew

about his crush, and appreciated that he'd never acted on it. Still, it had to feel awkward at times to share this deep, abiding friendship and professional relationship, and know he had feelings for her she would never return. As usual, when the awkwardness surfaced, one of them had to change the subject and keep things light and teasing. "So she's not a blonde?"

Merle shook his head, picturing that trendy, rock-star hair. "Try glow-in-the-dark redhead. She's about this tall." He tapped his chin. "A little on the round side. With soft brown eyes. Big, like doe eyes, but lighter in color."

Ginny's smile had gone Mona Lisa again. Now what?

"In the six years that you and I have been partners, Kelsey Ryan is the first woman you've noticed. The first woman you could quote eye color and statistics on who wasn't a suspect. I find that very interesting."

"She drives me nuts, that's all," he insisted. "Makes my job harder than it needs to be."

Ginny simply looked at him.

Hell. Merle blew a frustrated sigh between tight lips.

Very interesting indeed.

THIS DAY JUST KEPT getting better and better.

The afternoon sun couldn't seem to reach the shadowy corners of the alley that ran beside the Wingate Mission. Too bad the sunshine couldn't work as efficiently as word of mouth on the streets apparently did. Merle had been in his Jeep on the way to question Mort and Edgar at The Underground when he'd gotten the call about the nude body buried among the bags of trash.

Only two blocks away and it seemed as if half of Kansas City had already beaten him to the crime scene.

"Oh, God! Delilah? No!" Monique, the petite blond prostitute, screamed and sobbed in her friend Cleopatra's arms. "Delilah!"

A camera flashed and Merle had to blink and look away.

Hell. He didn't suppose he needed to ask for an identification of the body now. He draped the blanket back over the brunette woman's frozen, distorted face, cursed his stiff knee and pushed to his feet.

He first turned to the lanky brunette who clicked off half a dozen more pictures before he could position himself between her and the body. "You can't be here, ma'am."

The woman held up the plastic ID card hanging from a strap around her neck. "I'm Rebecca Page. I work the crime beat for the *Kansas City Star*." She angled her head to peek around his shoulder. "Looks like you've got another Holiday Hooker murder."

"We don't know anything yet, Ms. Page." He touched her elbow and pointed toward the street. "I'm going to have to ask you to leave."

She resisted when he nudged. "I hear K.C.P.D.'s brought in a psychic because you haven't made any progress on this case in over a decade and you're desperate for answers. Has she found something? Stirred things up? Do you think that's why the killer has struck again?"

How did she know about Kelsey? Or was she fishing for confirmation of a guess? Merle bit his tongue and tried to remember Rebecca Page was a lady. "I can't answer any of those questions right now."

"My father covered the first murder eleven years ago when he was at the paper. Now I've got the job and I'm going to finish the story he never could. Can you tell me anything?"

He shook his head. "I can tell you that all you're doing right now is contaminating my crime scene. You'll have to write your father's story some other day in some other place. So if you don't mind?" He pointed to the end of the alley.

"You haven't heard the last of me."

He'd bet not. Not the way his day was going.

With a determined huff, Rebecca Page strode out to the street where she started snapping photos of the gathering crowd and official vehicles.

The two hookers and the press weren't the only curious onlookers who had gathered to see what the fuss of police cars with flashing red-and-white lights was all about. There were easily ten people loitering in the alley, with a dozen more back on the sidewalk trying to get a peek.

"Hey, can we clear this scene?" One of the uniformed officers immediately spoke to the homeless trio huddled around a refrigerator box they didn't want to leave.

Tragic as it was, this homicide might be the break he needed to solve nine other deaths—if the scene hadn't already been contaminated beyond usefulness.

Merle looked straight at Ed Watkins, slouching in his weary pose at the end of the alley, and gave him a direct order. "I want tape blocking off this entire alleyway and every entrance in or out of these side buildings. Think you can handle that?"

The sergeant gave a fake salute. "Yes. Sir."

Merle waited until he disappeared around the corner, taking most of the gawkers with him. He himself stepped aside as the CSI team came in to snap photos and mark potential evidence.

This was one call he hadn't wanted to take. It was the call that turned his cold case into an active investigation. The call that turned him back into a full-fledged homicide detective.

Another dead prostitute. Estimated time of death? Five days ago. Christmas Day.

Happy holidays.

Turning off his disgust at the violent waste of a human life, he turned on his logic and went to work. He caught up with Monique and Cleopatra as they exited the alley. He helped the young blonde find a seat on the mission's front steps and offered her his handkerchief.

"I take it that's your roommate, Susan Cooper?"

Monique buried her face in his handkerchief, blew her nose, then nodded.

"I'm sorry. I'm sure you two were close."

"I knew something bad had happened to her. No matter what Zero said. Delilah would have called to tell me about visiting her son if she could. If she couldn't come back and tell me herself, that is. She loved that little boy so much. And now he's all alone."

She gasped a huge sob, then cried for several more minutes while Cleopatra comforted her.

"You said he was with a foster family," Merle reminded her. "I'm sure he's being taken care of."

"I know." She sniffed again. "Delilah always thought it best that he was with a real family."

Cleopatra agreed. "She was trying to earn enough money so she could walk away from all this. Get a respectable job. Maybe get her boy back then. She never wanted him around this place."

Maybe Susan Cooper had known how her life might turn out. Merle just hoped her son was too young to understand what losing a parent to a tragic death meant. He hoped he was too young to have to choose between the grief and guilt and shame that Merle had battled with for so long.

But he couldn't deal with any emotions right now. He pulled out his notepad and went to work. "You said she checked into the mission before Christmas?"

Monique nodded. "She needed to see the doctor. Didn't know if she had a broken wrist or if it was just sprained. Mr. H. had been a good…friend…of hers for about a year. But he picked her up that last night, and then…"

Cleopatra finished when the tears struck again. "She came up to the room real late that night. And she was all beat-up. The two of us, we took her to see Doc Siegel. He wrapped up her wrist, tended some cuts and put her to bed in his office because the mission was already full for the night. That was the last time we saw her."

"Alive." Monique lifted her face to Merle. With most of her makeup cried off, he could see the fat lip that had been disguised with extra lipstick. A quick visual sweep revealed the bruises on her wrists.

"Looks like somebody roughed you up some, too." He had a good idea who the abuser might be. "Who did that to you? One of your boyfriends?" He could play their euphemistic game, too.

He'd love to pack up these two women and take them someplace safe. Someplace where they didn't have to sell their bodies and lose their souls in order to survive. He'd love to arrest Zero and put him permanently out of business.

But he wasn't working vice this afternoon. He had ten homicide cases to deal with. Right now that meant overlooking one set of crimes so he could earn their trust and get whatever help they could give to solve another.

Maybe Susan Cooper had found her way home before she'd been beaten. Maybe someone she trusted had been waiting for her.

Merle heard the chains jangle an instant before he saw the black leather out of the corner of his eye. He rose to meet the devil head-on.

"Ladies, ladies." Zero waltzed up and held out his bejeweled fingers to Monique and Cleopatra. "What did I tell you about gettin' in this gentleman's way? 'Specially, now. We gotta let him do his work."

Merle intervened before either woman could go with him. "I'm having a conversation with them, Zero. Not with you."

"Dat's cool. I just don't want them to be a problem. They're both gonna be real emotional right now. I don't know if you can trust anything they say."

"Zero—"

Cleopatra's protest was silenced with a single glance.

Merle never looked away from the man he suspected abused his own girls. "You don't have to go with him, ladies."

Monique patted his arm as she walked down the stairs to stand beside Zero. "Yeah, we do." The black man put out his arms and hugged a woman to each side. Merle would give anything at that moment to toss his badge aside and punch that smug, victorious grin off Zero's face. "He keeps us safe. If we do what he says, he'll make sure nothin' happens to us like what happened to Delilah."

"He doesn't have a very reliable track record, ladies."

Zero's smile thinned. "What are you talkin' about?"

"In the past eleven years, nine of your girls that you *promised* to keep safe have ended up dead. Did they all not do what you told them to?" He glanced at the blank expressions on Monique and Cleopatra's faces. "You sure you trust those statistics?"

"That ain't right." The first hint of temper flickered in Zero's dark eyes. "That first one, the one all over the TV and in the papers—that Jezebel—wasn't my responsibility. I let her walk the turf out of the goodness of my heart because she had nowhere else to go." Zero had a heart? "I offered to take her in, but she kept insistin' she was only temporary here. I can't protect what's not mine."

Apparently, no one else had protected her, either. Jezebel's time in the mission district had been more temporary than she'd ever expected.

Backtracking a step from his anger, Merle remembered the case at hand. "But Delilah was your responsibility. Did she disobey you, Zero? That last night, when she was beaten—did you fail to keep her safe? Or didn't she do what you told her to?"

He took a step closer, putting him almost nose to nose with the pimp. "Did you see Delilah that last night before Christmas?"

Zero's arms flinched around the two women. From the corner of his eye, Merle saw them drop their gazes to the sidewalk. They wanted to be somewhere else but were too afraid to leave. Merle shut down his compassion. He never blinked. He wanted an answer.

"She was goin' to visit her boy," Zero insisted.

"Try again."

The two men dueled it out visually.

"Is this off the record?" Zero finally asked.

"No."

A long moment passed before Zero dismissed the girls, then stepped over to a relatively secluded spot near the mission's front door. The tough guy was still there in the talk, but not in the eyes. "Mr. H. came to pick up Delilah Christmas Eve, just like he did every other Friday night. In a limo. Treated her like a goddess. Made her forget who she was. Who she belonged to."

"She wanted to leave you?"

"I got no problem with my girls movin' on, as long as they pay what they owe me first." No doubt it was some exorbitant fee. "Mr. H. had that kind of money. She was gonna ask him for it."

"Did she get it?"

"Yeah." Zero glanced around as if he expected somebody else to be listening in. "She came home with the cash and paid me. But she was all busted up, just like the girls said. And she was on the bus. Usually, Mr. H. drives her home. The last time I saw her, she was on her way to the doc's."

"Did Mr. H. have contact with any of the other victims over the years?"

"Maybe."

"Zero."

Eventually, the pimp nodded. "He's a regular customer. Has been for a lot of years. But I don't keep records. So I couldn't say for sure he knew all of 'em."

"You have a name for this Mr. H.?"

"I can do better than that." He pointed a gold-clad finger at the mission door. "He's in there right now, talking to Reverend Wingate about donatin' money to the mission."

Chapter Six

Patrick Halliwell was not your garden-variety john. The widowed, seventy-year-old, self-made millionaire had a full head of bright white hair, deeply tanned skin, a Southern gentleman's accent—and a solid alibi for Susan Cooper's murder.

Of course. *Why should anything about this case be easy?* Merle thought. But out loud he remained civil.

"Thanks," he told the airline rep who'd given him the information. "If I need anything else I'll call."

Merle disconnected the phone, hooked it back on his belt and turned his attention back to the evening's rush-hour traffic. He exhaled an impatient sigh, feeling the same congestion inside his head.

This morning, he'd had next to nothing to go on to solve the murders. By four-thirty, he had suspects with the opportunity to do the crimes, others with the means to kill. He could even rationalize a few motives. But nobody matched up on all three counts to warrant any kind of arrest. Preliminary reports from CSI indicated no usable fingerprints or foreign DNA on the body. Nothing added up.

Patrick Halliwell had been in Tampa visiting his

daughter and grandchildren over the Christmas holiday. The airline had the records to prove he'd left KCI at 10:37 p.m. on December 24—hours before Delilah had come home on the bus with cuts and a sprained wrist. He'd returned on the twenty-eighth.

With his lawyer present to oversee a hundred-thousand-dollar donation to the mission, Halliwell had sat in Ulysses Wingate's office and claimed Delilah was his mistress, whom he showered with gifts and money—not payment for services rendered. He'd never laid a hand on her, he claimed. Except in love. He'd given Merle his alibi, showed him his unblemished knuckles, wished him luck and left. His attorney had lingered back just long enough to inform Merle that he'd need to go through him if he came up with any more questions for Mr. Halliwell.

But the man hadn't cried, hadn't hollered, hadn't seemed upset beyond a generic *"That's too bad,"* when he was informed of his so-called mistress's death.

Ulysses Wingate was another story.

The jovial minister heard the news and collapsed into the chair behind his desk. Bemoaning the loss of *"another child to the violence,"* he'd put his hands together and prayed. His eyes were rimmed with unshed tears by the time he had finished and offered to see to Delilah's service and burial. Merle had promised to put him in touch with the right people for his generous offer, and obliquely wondered why Patrick Halliwell, who claimed to have a more personal relationship with the deceased, hadn't offered the same.

"No sense at all." Merle's voice echoed inside the Jeep. He needed something about all this to make sense. And soon.

Ten murders in the mission district in eleven years.

With a morbid laugh, Merle wondered why the killer had skipped the year after Jezebel's death. The murderer hadn't been willing or able to kill again for two years—then he'd turned the crime into an annual holiday tradition.

Why? Where was the motive? What was the connection?

He didn't know which lead to follow. He didn't know which way to turn.

So, of course, he was driving out Volker Boulevard to the University of Missouri of Kansas City to visit the psychology department.

Where Kelsey Ryan worked.

"Hey, Merle." Dr. Rachel Livesay-Taylor, professor of psychology and Josh Taylor's wife, greeted Merle with a serene smile. Resting one hand on her pregnant belly, she rose to meet him in the suite of offices outside the psych lab. "Good to see you again. Did you have a good Christmas?"

Sure. Before he'd become so entrenched in cold-case files and murder investigations. "Mom and I had a nice, quiet day together." Probably nothing like the loving free-for-all of getting the entire Taylor family in one place for the holidays. "And you?"

"It was the biggest family get-together that I have ever been to. I loved it, even though I had to skip out early to catch a nap." He listened politely for a couple of minutes while she recounted the antics and excitement of her one-year-old daughter, and the matching antics and excitement of her eternally young husband, Josh. But Rachel was smart enough to know that he hadn't stopped by just to chat about the mutual friends they shared in the Taylor clan. "What can I help you with?"

"I'm here to see Kelsey Ryan. She said she worked late in the lab on Tuesdays and Thursdays."

Rachel nodded. "She's here. Is she expecting you?"

"I doubt it." He wasn't quite sure he could explain what had drawn him here at the end of his shift. Talk about things not making sense. "It's police business."

"Oh." With a detective for a husband, she understood the gravity of that statement and quickly pointed down a hallway lined with individual meeting rooms. "She's in the back running an experiment. I'll take you to her."

Merle shrugged off an uncomfortable tingle of familiarity as he followed Rachel down the hallway. The rooms he passed reminded him more of the precinct offices rather than the halls of higher learning. The individual offices were small, like an interrogation room, and every other one had a one-way mirror like the look-at room where witnesses were brought in to look at lineups of suspects.

Rachel put up her hand to stop him and quietly whispered. "We'd better wait here a few minutes until she's done so we don't interrupt."

That unsettling discomfort returned when he looked into the last room on the right. Something deep inside Merle's gut burned. Kelsey wasn't conducting an experiment.

She was the guinea pig that the young man in a lab coat was experimenting on.

"Looks like she's taking a lie detector test." He kept his voice as low as Rachel's.

Kelsey sat on one side of a long table, with wires and eletrodes hooked up to her temples and wrists, to her nape under the fringe of red hair and running inside her bright gold sweater, presumably to monitor her heart.

The wires ran across the table and disappeared behind a screen that blocked her view of the man sitting at the table across from her. A computer sat to one side and a large printer whirred away, logging something on graph paper with a bouncing needle.

"It's a similar concept," Rachel explained. "Checking physical reactions to mental stimuli. Our grad student is testing brain waves and other body functions as Kelsey runs through various cerebral exercises. The goal is to find out if psychics use more of their brains than the rest of us, or if those intuitive powers are just the mind working in a different way."

"Do you believe she has psychic abilities?"

Rachel smiled, taking a graceful out to the question. "It's not my experiment."

Merle stepped closer to the glass, wishing it would bring him closer to understanding Kelsey's claims and whether she really did possess some kind of gift he could trust.

Right now she just looked on guard, he thought, reading the stiff set of her shoulders. Like yesterday in the precinct office, she was hyperaware of her surroundings. Her eyes darted to every piece of equipment and back to the blocking screen. She knew more about what was going on than that kid running the equipment did.

The beginnings of a smile tipped the corners of his mouth. That kid was in trouble if he thought he was going to trip up Kelsey Ryan.

"Here." Rachel pushed a button on the wall beside him, activating an intercom system. "We can listen in."

"Try it now," the grad student ordered.

Kelsey's posture shook with a minute tremor as she tried to control her reaction. Temper? Fatigue? "I'm not telepathic, Randy. For the last time, I can't tell you what you're thinking."

"Can you tell me what's on the cards I've chosen?" Was the kid trying to get her riled up?

"No. I can only read the imprint of what's on the cards themselves." Merle splayed his fingers against the wall and dug in the tips, as if he could reach through the wood and plaster to get to her and…and what? Pat her on the back and say relax? Offer his arms as some kind of safe zone to snuggle up against, like the way she had last night at the mission when she freaked out over that damn scarf? "And I have to touch them to do that."

"All right, then." Randy stood and dealt six cards, facedown, on the table in front of her. He sat back down and pushed a button. "One more round. Hold up each card and tell me what you *see.*"

Was that what happened to her? Pick up a doll, see a murder? Pick up a scarf and see the murder weapon? Illogical. Impossible.

Right?

She picked up the first card and held it so that Randy alone could see the picture. Kelsey had blunt-tipped, sinewy, piano-player fingers. Graceful and adept. Merle realized he hadn't really noticed her hands before because she always wore gloves or kept them wrapped around a mug or glass. But she had beautiful hands.

"House," she stated, handing the card to Randy.

He nodded and revealed her guess was correct. He marked something on the printout. "Go on."

Kelsey picked up the remaining cards in rapid succession and handed them to Randy. "Rainbow. Cat. Car. Feather." She picked up the last one and gasped.

"Kels…?" Merle almost cried out.

Her cheeks blanched, then fired with bright pink spots of color. She flicked the card over the divider and slumped back in her chair. "Very funny. What are you, in junior high?"

What? What had he done to her?

Randy grinned in smug triumph. "For the recording, you have to tell me what it is you see."

"A lewd picture of a naked man. I hardly think you can include that in your thesis."

"Can he do that?" Merle snapped the question.

"I wanted to throw in a picture of something you hadn't seen before," Randy explained. "So I could rule out the predictability of any pattern in your readings."

Rachel had stiffened beside him, not liking what she saw, either. "I see his reasoning, but his choice wasn't terribly ethical. You talk to Kelsey. I'll take care of him."

Rachel pushed the second intercom button. "Randy. It's Dr. Livesay." The instant Randy's attention shifted to the window, Kelsey started ripping the plastic electrodes from her skin and tossing them on the table. "Get your things. I want to see you in my office. Now. Kelsey, you have a visitor."

"Me?"

Her face flushed with surprise, and she stopped with one hand cupping the side of her breast and the other stuck inside her sweater, fishing for that last electrode. Though the sweater was a bulky knit, adorned with sequins, she'd pulled it taut in such a way that there was no mistaking the proud abundance of that breast.

Something hot and instinctive pooled behind the zipper of his slacks.

What was he, in junior high?

Hell. Randy had noticed it, too.

With a rush of something embarrassingly territorial and completely inappropriate for a woman who was supposed to be a co-worker, Merle opened the door and invited himself in. "It's me, Kels."

"T." She froze.

Randy looked more surprised than Kelsey. Merle narrowed his gaze and encouraged the grad student to move a little faster. *Yeah, T's here, buddy. Quit gawkin' and go away.*

Kelsey quickly dropped her hands and let the sweater bag down over her figure. She clutched the center of her sweater, holding tight to something in the layers underneath. Randy gathered his stuff, slid Merle an apologetic look and disappeared out the door.

"Does he always—?"

"What are you doing—?"

They chimed in together and fell silent at the same time.

Kelsey buried her hands in the pockets of her jeans, giving Merle the perverse desire to want to see them again. She took a deep breath and he found himself watching with greedy curiosity instead of thinking of what he needed to say.

She came to her senses first. "What are you doing here?"

Okay, this would be tricky. "I've, um, been doing some research on psychics and how they work." He didn't give her time to get defensive. "I thought it might be best to get firsthand knowledge from an expert."

"You don't believe in me." Her eyes were wide, hurt. But she advanced as if getting angry gave her strength. "You just want to catch me in some lie."

"I need to ask questions. That's what I do. That's what I need...to do." He threw out his hands, not sure if he was surrendering or beseeching her. He couldn't control his emotions; his hormones had taken on a life of their own, and the damn case kept getting more complicated instead of clearer. "Meet me halfway here. I'd like to find some concrete answers to something today."

She tilted her head back and frowned. "T, what happened?"

Maybe she was a little telepathic, or maybe he looked as whipped as he felt. He pulled back his coat and jacket and braced his hands at his waist, near his gun and badge, reminding her he was a cop…reminding himself he was here on business. And not very pleasant business at that.

"Another dead body was found this morning in the mission's trash. A prostitute. Strangled. Probably killed Christmas Day. Our serial murder case has been upgraded to an active homicide."

He watched the emotions play across her face. Shock. Grief. Anger. Futility. Sadness. She crossed the room until she stood right in front of him. Her lush mouth parted on a sympathetic breath. "I'm so sorry."

She reached out to touch him and…

She stopped.

Her outstretched hands froze between them, mere inches from his own. He didn't move his hands from his belt. He couldn't make the choice for her. But, damn it all, he wanted her to touch him.

He'd never had anybody reach in far enough to ease the raw emotions he buried beneath all his practicality and logic.

"Why can't you touch me?" Pointing it out made her withdraw completely. She curled her fingers into her palms, then tucked both hands safely out of reach beneath her arms. No way. If he was going to open up his mind to the possibilities, then she was going to help him understand. "Does it hurt? Do experiments like he was conducting hurt you?" She glanced up at that one. "These are things I need to know."

"I've had people make fun of me and doubt me before." She squirmed in her boots and dropped her gaze to the middle of his chest. "That hurts."

He hadn't considered the emotional impact of being ridiculed. But he understood it. In spades. That inexplicable tension that had been building inside him throughout the day eased a bit by her just opening up a little and sharing that.

"I need your help, Kelsey. I've got too many suspects and not enough clues. But I need to know how this works. I need to know how you work." He dipped his head to make contact with those soft brown eyes and urge her to read the sincerity he hadn't felt before. "I need to know how to work with you."

Her eyes locked on to his, humbling him with their shaky trust.

"You may not like what I can do." She pulled out her hands and wiggled her fingers in an elegant warm-up of some kind. She tried to smile. "Other men have run for the hills and laughed in my face and called me every freaky name in the book."

"I'm not other men."

His quiet statement hung like a vow in the air between them, and it seemed to give her the confidence she needed.

She bravely moved closer and started fiddling with his tie. Then his jacket and coat. Her graceful, balletic fingers smoothed the silk and wool, gathered it together, bundled him up with tender care.

He wanted to take hold of her hands now, press them flat against his chest, explore their contours the way she was exploring him. But he hesitated. He didn't want to do anything to stop the lesson or make her doubt his professional curiosity—and a need that was far more personal than it should have been.

"Your mother gave you this coat. The two of you are incredibly close." He bit down on the urge to demand how she knew that, but then he realized she *was* trying to explain. "She picked it out and wrapped it with loving hands. There are other images I get from the coat, but fainter. Maybe something from the people who made it. Or the salesclerk."

Kelsey swept her hands up across his shoulders. T had to rock back on his heels to keep from doing the natural thing and wrapping his arms around her to complete the embrace.

She grinned and giggled like a kid.

"What?"

She patted his shoulders and pulled away. But the sass in her voice made the loss of contact easier to accept. "Your mother doesn't think you dress warmly enough."

"You don't have to be a psychic to know a mother thinks that when she gives you a wool coat for Christmas."

Kelsey planted her hands on her hips and challenged him. "Your mother is about five foot four and has silvering blond hair that she pulls back into a bun. She never has been able to get you to button your coat. She bought you long underwear, too. It's still in a package at the bottom of one of your drawers."

"You got all that by touching my coat?"

She nodded. "I was concentrating. If I put my mind

to it, if I don't restrict myself in any way, I can sense almost anything that's come into contact with an object."

"So if you touch a person, skin to skin—"

"The reception, if you will, is more direct. So the impressions are, too." All of a sudden, her smile vanished. She hugged her arms around her waist and latched on to that item beneath her sweater. The lesson was over. "You don't want me to touch the body, do you?"

"Too much to ask, huh?"

She shivered and turned away. "That's not even funny."

"What's under your sweater?" he asked, not considering the more interesting responses to that question until he'd said it out loud. He cooled his jets with a determined breath and went on. "You keep clutching at something. What is it?"

She rubbed at the pink mark on her temple where the electrode had been, and he wondered if she was getting one of those "nasty" headaches she'd mentioned last night, or if his questions just made her uncomfortable. But after a moment, Kelsey touched the long silver chain around her neck and pulled out a necklace. At the end of the chain, he saw a pale blue, teardrop-shaped crystal in the palm of her hand.

Caressing the silver filigree work holding the crystal, she held it up for him to inspect. "This was a gift from my grandmother—jewelry making was a hobby of hers. I inherited my *gift* from her. I never knew my parents. Apparently, 'Daddy' was some sort of traveling musician who got my mother pregnant and left. My mother didn't survive childbirth. Lucy Belle—" the pipe-smoking grandmother from the Ozarks she'd talked about last night "—raised me. Taught me how to use my talent. Taught me that if I used it to help others, it wouldn't feel like such a burden."

"I can see why the necklace would have such meaning for you."

"It's more than sentimental value. Go on."

With Kelsey's permission, he touched the pendant. The blue prism glowed with heat beneath his fingertip. "It's warm. But that's from body heat, right?"

"It's always warm. Even when I'm not, which seems to be most of my life. I believe it has the power to control the impulses I receive."

"Crystals?" Like from-another-planet religious cults?

She closed the pendant in her fist and pulled away, sensing his skepticism. "Let me put it in layman's terms you can understand. This pendant, this symbol of the greatest love I've ever known in my life, protects me. If I focus on it, it sharpens my perception. If I touch it, it dampens the input I receive and diffuses it. Like the gloves I wear."

He tried to understand. "So, when you get stressed out—like when persistent detectives ask a lot of nosy questions or claim you're a fraud—you use that pendant to ground yourself. To center yourself back in a calmer place."

"Basically."

"Yoga or tai chi would do the same thing for you."

She shook her head, but she was smiling. "You asked me how I worked. And, for the record, I don't mind your nosy questions. It's people who have all the answers already who get on my nerves."

He almost laughed. "Well, then, you and I should get along really well this evening. Because I don't seem to have answers to anything."

"This evening?" Kelsey tucked her necklace back inside her sweater. She picked up her checkered coat and black leather backpack, holding them in front of her, shielding herself when she faced him again. "Is something going on?"

He plucked her coat from her hands, shook it open and held it out to help her put it on. "Last night, you indicated that you intended to go back to the mission district to try to find some more clues to the Jezebel mystery."

Kelsey paused with one arm in her coat. A-ha. He only needed the gift of deductive reasoning skills to figure out that she'd probably intended to go back to no-man's land once she got off work. By herself.

"I've decided I don't have a problem with that. I could use someone else to take a look at things, hopefully point me in the right direction, maybe catch something I've missed. But you're going to go with an escort."

She shrugged into the other sleeve of her coat and started bundling up. "It almost sounds as if you're asking me out."

On a date? He hadn't thought that far ahead. Though now that he considered it, the idea wasn't...no, wait. "I'm taking you to a murder scene."

She laughed and headed for the door. "I've had worse dates than that. Believe me."

"T, LOOK AT THIS." Kelsey sank down onto the couch in Ulysses Wingate's office and flipped through more pages in the dusty, leatherbound volume she'd pulled off the bookshelves.

Since he loved a volunteer, Reverend Wingate had

been delighted to see Kelsey and her detective friend back on his doorstep. They'd missed the opportunity to serve dinner, but in a big place like this, there was always cleaning to do. The residents who spent the night were responsible for keeping their quarters neat, but there was no staff who went into the offices.

T had been quick to offer their services, and in minutes Ulysses had loaded them up with dust rags, a vacuum and trash bags. He'd left them in his office and gone out to greet and preach to his evening guests.

Turning off the vacuum, T brushed the inevitable dirt off his gray slacks and sat beside her. "Did you find something?"

"It's last year's record of overnight guests."

At T's request, she wore only one glove, in the hopes that something at the mission would speak to her and point his investigation in a helpful direction. Technically, without a warrant, he couldn't search through anything except the trash. But she had freer rein to explore. The books on the shelves she'd been dusting had spoken volumes.

"Here." She turned to one of the last pages in the handwritten log book. Closing her eyes, she laid her fingers on the page and let the sensations wash over her. "There are a lot of sad stories here."

"I imagine homelessness has its own set of fears and stresses." She nodded, tuning out the garble of images and emotions, and focusing on the strongest, saddest voice. "You're on December twenty-fourth."

T's announcement startled her. She clenched her fingers back into her fist and opened her eyes. "Is that important?"

"Delilah spent the night at the mission on December

twenty-fourth." T leaned in closer to look over her shoulder and read the list of names on the page. Though the lemony-chemical scent of furniture polish clung to his shirt, Kelsey didn't mind the way his arm curled behind her back on the couch, or the way his golden scruffed jaw hovered so close to her cheek.

She was overwhelmed by the heat the man generated. Even without touching him, she felt his warmth flowing into her—a pervasive, comforting warmth, almost erotic in the thoroughness with which it moved throughout her body.

"Son of a bitch."

Kelsey jumped at the curse, the hazy mood of sexual awareness broken by the sudden alertness in his posture. She turned her focus back to the book. "What is it?"

He pointed to an entry. "Sally Lattimer. She was last year's holiday victim. Spent the night here Christmas Eve."

"Do you think there's a pattern?" She shifted the book to his lap and started to rise. "Do you want me to check the others?"

"No. I want to get a warrant, make it official."

A tug on her hand pulled her back to her seat. It was the hand with the glove, so she shouldn't have received any sort of image. But the warmth she'd sensed just by sitting close to him intensified. His grip was sure, strong—confident—around hers. Maybe that's what she'd noticed. He didn't seem to mind holding her hand. Jeb had gone straight from *no touching* to *let's make out.* She liked easing into things. She liked T's patience and willingness to learn and adapt.

She liked T.

"Good work." He smiled and closed the book. He was talking all business and facts now, but she didn't mind. He still hadn't released her. "Everything points to the Wingate mission. Somebody who lives nearby, who's stayed here, or who works here knows about those murders. Maybe more than one person. But something's keeping them from talking."

"They probably see the mission as a haven—the one bright spot of hope in this neighborhood. Your potential witnesses might not be talking because they don't want to jeopardize that."

He nodded, conceding the possibility. Adjusting his grip, T laced his fingers with hers and pulled her hand into his lap. For a moment, he seemed to study the meld of his long, dexterous fingers wrapped against her shorter, turquoise-covered wool ones. "Or it could be something more sinister. Our killer might have a hold over these people we don't know about yet."

"Like blackmail?"

"Blackmail. Intimidation."

His green eyes hooded and dropped their focus to her lips. That same, inexplicable heat seemed to rush to her mouth. She pressed her lips together, unused to the tingling rise in temperature. They felt parched and needy. Her tongue darted out to lick between them. But she found no relief. T watched the subtle movements. His eyes dilated and darkened, as if he found something fascinating about her mouth.

Instead of closing the distance, Detective Brainiac was still trying to talk. But the tone of his words was a hazy seduction against her ears. "That's another reason why I don't want you snooping around here on your own. The neighborhood's dangerous enough." Had she drifted closer? Or was he finally angling his mouth toward hers. "But one man, in particular, is more dangerous still."

Kelsey braced her hand against his shoulder, and more warmth trickled in through her bare skin. But that's all it was. Warmth. And awareness. And a hot, needy desire to connect with this man. "I'll be careful."

"You promise?" He came closer.

"I promise."

His breath mingled with hers. The warmth of him caressed her face. She moved her fingertips to the firm line of his jaw, to guide him...

She saw the pretty blond woman at the altar again, sensed T's regret.

Just as his lips brushed against hers, Kelsey slipped her fingers between their mouths and stopped the kiss before it ever happened. She blinked her eyes open and pushed away, taking the imprint of his confusion, his curiosity, his bitterness and his desire with her.

"I'm sorry." She stood and put the distance of the room between them, hiding how much she wanted that kiss, hating how jealous she was of a woman she'd never even met. "I shouldn't have let...I know we're here to work."

T was on his feet, coming after her. "Kelsey. I'm not complaining. I can keep it strictly professional if that's what you want. But I thought there was a mutual thing there. Was I wrong?"

Another woman. A lost love. He might have a passing interest in Kelsey; he might even be willing to be her friend. But his feelings were tied to someone else.

She crossed behind the reverend's desk and kept it between them. "You must care about her very much."

"Who?"

"The blond woman in the wedding dress."

T planted his hands at his waist and stared at her. Hard. She couldn't blame him. She shouldn't know these things, but she did.

"Let me get this straight. While I'm putting myself on the line, taking a risk on something that is completely out of character for me—you're sitting over there, reading my mind? Getting bent out of shape over some hallucination you think you see inside my head?"

"You asked me how I work. This is it. I wanted to kiss you. But she was so clear, so beautiful. I can't read minds," she insisted. "So how do I know you weren't thinking of her, when you were stuck kissing me?" Kelsey hugged herself, felt through her sweater until she could grasp Lucy Belle's pendant in her hand.

His gaze flicked down and took note. "Yeah, you'd better hold on to that. If you're going to get inside my head and mess around, you need to get the message straight. That blonde is Ginny Rafferty-Taylor, my partner. We've worked together at K.C.P.D. for six years."

"But you love her."

Everything in the room went still. She couldn't even hear herself breathe. After several endless moments, T nodded. Though what he was agreeing to, she couldn't tell.

"I thought you told me you could only see things in the past." His voice was crisp, but subdued. "Ginny's married. She's having a baby. She's in love with someone else. Ginny's in the past."

"Your feelings for her aren't."

The grinding of the doorknob was Kelsey's cue that this conversation was over. The door swung open and Ulysses Wingate blew in. "Good evening, boys and girls. My gosh, I can see the woodwork in here again. You can sure smell the clean."

He'd blustered his way halfway across the room before he realized that Kelsey still stood behind his desk, and T wasn't moving much faster. He stopped at the seating area and looked down at the log book on the coffee table before lifting his concerned gaze. "Is there a problem?"

T had unplugged the vacuum and was winding up the cord. That was his answer.

Ulysses looked to Kelsey. "You know I'm a good listener if you two need to work something out. I've done couples therapy before."

Kelsey finally roused herself. "There's no problem, Reverend." She grabbed her dust rag and headed for the kitchen. "And we're not a couple."

Chapter Seven

"Ow!"

Kelsey dropped the shards of the glass that had shattered around her hand into the sink and thrust her fingers under the running water. She muttered a few choicer words beneath her breath as she inspected the damage. One edge of the glass had cut straight through the plastic glove she wore and opened a gash across her last two fingers.

"Not good. Not good at all."

She glanced around for some assistance, but most of the staff were out in the dining room taking a coffee break, including T, who was slyly asking more of those never-ending questions of his. The industrial dishwasher was already running, so her shouts wouldn't be heard over the crunch of gears and roar of water.

It wouldn't be the first time she'd had to fend for herself. And, judging by the outcome of the camaraderie-turned-passion-turned-unspannable-gulf she'd shared with T in the office, it wouldn't be the last time she'd have to function all by herself, either.

Kelsey breathed slowly, in and out, keeping her mind off the pain and distracting herself from the steady seep of blood. That was goal one. Stop the bleeding. Holding her hand up above shoulder level, she found a dry dish towel and wrapped it tightly around her fingers. Then she spared a few moments to toss the biggest pieces of the glass into the trash and rinse The Flakes and splinters down the drain.

Goal two? She needed some antiseptic and a bandage. A big one. The blood had already soaked through to the outer layers of the towel.

"Wait a minute." Duh.

Doctor Siegel had an office, down the hall from Reverend Wingate. If a medical doctor didn't have gauze and tape on hand, then she really was in trouble.

The hallway was deserted when Kelsey stepped out. The reverend had locked himself in his office to work on his New Year's sermon, the staff was either in the dining room or outside smoking, and tonight's residents had already gone upstairs to their beds.

Kelsey's low-heeled boots clicked along the dark marble floor as she walked past the office, the check-in window and the chapel and made her way to the back of the mission building. The sobering quiet, broken only by the tap of her soles and the beat of her heart, made her think of walking through a museum. Or a church.

Or a mausoleum.

Kelsey's nervous sigh added another sound to the silence. She didn't have to touch the polished stone walls to feel cold. She shivered beneath her sweater and apron. As warm and vibrant as this place had been at dinner time, full of people responding to the reverend's generosity and hearty laugh, it felt like a tomb when it was empty. Despite its high, arching ceilings, Kelsey felt more than alone. She felt trapped.

"Ho, boy." She was really letting her imagination get the better of her this time. The stone walls blocked the cold air; they didn't transmit it. And she wasn't alone. There were at least a hundred other people in the building. They just weren't out here in the hallway where she was. All by herself.

Thankfully, her fingers throbbed, diverting her attention to more practical, less fanciful notions. She stopped outside the carved walnut door marked *Clinic,* with a chipped, white plastic plaque that read, *Marlon Siegel, M.D.* A glance at her feet revealed no light shining beneath the door. "I hope it's not locked."

Rapping lightly on the door, Kelsey leaned in. "Hello?" No answer.

She tested the doorknob, and when it gave, she breathed a sigh of relief. "Thank goodness."

The interior was dark beyond dark. At night, with no windows, no lights and little illumination from the hallway, the furniture inside the clinic looked like big, monolithic shadows in the blackness. Leaving the door open, she felt along the wall for a switch. "Victory."

When the room flooded with light, she turned.

And screamed.

One startled yelp. She clutched her good hand over her thudding heart and backed against the doorjamb. "Doc. I'm sorry." Her irregular breathing seemed to get in the way of coherent speech. "I knocked. It was dark. I didn't know. Sorry."

As her heart rate slowed toward normal, her startled senses cleared and details registered. Doc Siegel, sitting at his desk in the dark. A black-labeled, half-empty whiskey bottle in one hand. A sleek, black, powerful-looking gun in the other.

For one wild, crazy moment, she thought he was dead. His dark eyes stared deep into nothing. His stringy, shoulder-length hair fell across his gaunt face. "Doc?"

But then he blinked. His eyes closed slowly, and when they opened again, he moved. He bolted back a long swallow of the golden-brown liquid, screwed the white plastic lid back on, then opened a drawer and placed both the gun and the bottle inside.

"I didn't mean to interrupt. I'll come back at a better time." That was a lie. She was creeped out enough to know she never wanted to come back to this room. Kelsey turned for the door. She'd wear the towel home and strap it on with shipping tape if she had to.

"What do you need?" A chair scraped across the floor behind her.

"I cut myself. I was just looking for some first-aid supplies. But I'm disturbing you. Good night."

For a man who looked half drunk and twice deranged, Doc Siegel could move surprisingly fast. And he wasn't any ninety-eight pound weakling, despite his Ichabod Crane-like build.

An arm reached past her and shut the door, and five bony fingers closed around her wrist and pulled her wounded hand up toward the overhead light to view. "You're bleeding."

You think? She idly wondered what kind of test he had to pass in med school before he could make that in-depth diagnosis.

She kept her sarcasm to herself, though, and tugged against him. "I'm sure it's stopped by now. It's nothing you need to worry your time with."

But the skeletal grip didn't budge. "You're here. I'm here. We might as well check."

"Doc—"

"Can't be too careful. Might need sutures or a teta-nus shot."

Oh, no. No cutting, no poking. Not by Dr. Personal-ity, especially after half a bottle of whiskey. And she was sure he'd downed it all tonight. The bitter tang of alco-hol burned her sinuses with every word he spoke.

"I need to go. T…Detective Banning will be looking for me."

But the doctor wasn't intimidated.

He dragged Kelsey across the room and pushed her into a seat on the edge of a long white hospital cot that looked like something cast off from a 1940s war movie. Ho, boy, she didn't want to be here.

The doc released her just long enough to pull up a stool and a rolling tray. Kelsey leaped to her feet at the first sign of freedom. But his hand clamped around her wrist again before she could escape. He tipped his face up to hers and the greasy strings of his hair fell back to reveal every line cruelly carved by life and years of al-cohol abuse. As quickly as he moved, his speech was agonizingly slow. "Is there some reason you don't want me to look at your hand, Ms. Ryan?"

Because you're drunk? Mad? Scaring the hell out of me?

"I just needed a bandage," she explained evenly. "I feel guilty about wasting your time on such a little thing."

Doc Siegel smiled. At least she thought that's what that crooked line across the middle of his face was sup-posed to be. He pulled her back to her seat, unwrapping the towel before she could voice another protest.

"We don't get anybody pretty in here. Or anybody

young and clean." He pulled the tray beneath her hand and adjusted the lamp to inspect her wound. "It'll be a treat to doctor something that isn't transmitted by sex or gang violence or destitution."

The bleak cynicism in his tone almost tugged at her heartstrings. Almost. Kelsey pulled her hand away and tugged her sleeves as far down her wrists as they would go. "Aren't you going to wash your hands first?"

When he got up to go to the sink, she'd run for the door. But the doctor didn't get up. He pulled a pair of latex gloves from a box on his tray and slipped them on, all the while watching her. He might be smiling at his oversight, but his bleary black eyes didn't seem amused that she'd pointed out the mistake. "Now let's see what we have."

With the last of the towel peeled away in the trash can beside him, Doc Siegel grasped Kelsey's hand and examined it. She swallowed hard, bracing herself for a bombardment of sensations. The doctor's gloves muted his impressions. But the gloves themselves carried images that distracted her.

He'd used the gloves before. On another patient. While the conscious side of Kelsey's brain cringed, the intuitive side worked to process what she felt.

When the doctor wore the gloves, he thought of money—how much he needed for his clinic, how much he wanted for himself. Regret and contempt were equally strong emotions. The gloves had been worn by a man who wanted escape. A man whose reality was worse than the nothingness he found at the bottom of a bottle of whiskey.

He pulled out a pair of tiny scissors and trimmed a ragged flap of skin on her pinkie. Kelsey wanted to pull away. Her breathing quickened as panic sparked in her veins. His nothingness, his dire emptiness tried to work its way into her psyche and consume her.

"I heard that that woman who got murdered—Delilah—came to see you Christmas Eve." It was the first thing she could think of, the first that could distract her from the depressing emotions.

The doctor nodded as he worked. "Got herself beat up on the job. Nearly got her arm twisted off because her latest sugar daddy didn't treat her right. You know, if you stay with one man, he'll take care of you. You go selling yourself to everything in pants, you're bound to get beat up—or murdered—somewhere along the way."

What a morbid, depressing philosophy. It triggered painful memories of her own.

She'd tried to stay with Jeb. But the verbal abuse only got worse. And when she finally called him on it, when she threatened to leave, he'd slapped her. Her ears still rang with the memory of that smack. But she'd made good on her word. She'd left. She moved to Kansas City and never looked back.

"Sometimes, the man you're with is the man who hurts you."

Wrong. Why did she choose now to play devil's advocate? How did she think disagreeing with the doctor would accomplish anything? The man had scissors in his hand, for God's sake. He had a gun in his desk. She had...

"Just soak it here for a few minutes. Make sure we get out all the glass fragments before I wrap it up." He pushed her fingers into a small bowl of saline and got up to go to the supply cabinet.

Kelsey breathed deeply, using the brief respite to debate whether sneaking out now and possibly incurring the doctor's wrath was a safer alternative than sitting here and letting him finish his unsanitary work.

Again, the man moved quickly. He'd already turned around with the gauze and tape he needed before she could decide.

"I can do that part," she offered.

"Like I said. My treat." He wavered as he sat down, but there was nothing tentative about his touch when he placed the gauze on her fingers. "Besides, it's hard to doctor your own hands."

Figuring cooperation would be the quickest way to get herself out of there, Kelsey merely nodded. She closed her eyes against the revisit of such dreary depressive thoughts and rested her free hand on the mattress beside her thigh.

The pain crept in first. Not the pain in her fingers, the sting of pressure on her raw skin. Pain. Bone deep.

Her lungs felt deprived of oxygen and the pressure around her heart swelled, squeezed, crushed.

"No." She breathed a word that might have been another's protest, might have been her own.

The pain buffeted her and Kelsey shook. She grabbed on to the metal frame of the bed to pull herself away from the encroaching nightmare. "No." Louder this time. Her voice.

"Is that too tight?"

Doc Siegel's voice slurred against her ear. But was it real? Or remembered?

Fear overrode the pain. "No. Why?"

Kelsey cried. Someone else's tears became her own.

All was lost. All was lost. Her trust was shattered. Her heart broken. It hurt too much to consider how she'd been betrayed. It hurt too much to know she would never be free of this hole. Never leave no-man's land. Never see her son again.

"*No!*"

The scream was real. Inside her. All around her.

"*Hey. Stop it. You're all right. You ain't hurt bad. You're all right.*" *Real? Dream?*

Didn't matter.

"*No! Let me go. Please, let me go.*"

He stood in front of her, looming over her. A shadow amongst the shadows.

She sat up in the bed. Screamed.

A hand clamped over her mouth. Smelly. Filthy. Hard. "*I said I'd take care of you. Why are you making me do this?*"

She screamed beneath the hand. Fought.

"*I tried to help you.*"

"*No!*" *Get away. Run. Fight.*

"*Stop it, bitch!*

The hand pressed her down into the bed, cut her mouth with its cruel pressure.

"*I wanted to treat you right. I wanted to be nice.*" *He whipped a long yellow scarf from his pocket. Looped it around her neck. Once. Twice. He released her mouth but pulled the scarf tight, turning her scream into a helpless gurgle.* "*I said I'd take care of you.*"

She twisted, her hips jerking in the bed. She clawed at his wrists, but her hand was too weak.

She had to get out. She had to escape. She had to make it stop.

Kelsey screamed. "T!"

She clawed at the hands that covered her mouth and cupped the back of her neck. "What are you doing? You stop it." The hands shook her. "Stop it!"

Memories blurred with reality, but the panic remained.

"T!" She was on her feet. Her hip hit something hard. Metal scraped against metal and crashed to the floor.

"Are you crazy?"

"T!"

The clinic door burst open. She saw a flash of gray and white. Something wrenched against her arm, but then she was free.

"What the hell are you doing?"

"Is she all right? Ms. Ryan?"

Kelsey blinked her savior into focus. Golden hair. Broad shoulders. Precise hands pinning Doc Siegel to the floor.

T. Merle Banning to the rescue. Again.

She squeezed his shoulder to see if he was real. Solid. Warm. "T?"

He angled his head up to hers. Clear, moss-green eyes, pinpoint in focus and dark with concern, looked up at her. "Are you all right, Kels? Did he hurt you?"

"I didn't do anything to her!" Stringy brown hair. Doctor on the floor. Protesting. "All of a sudden she just wigged out on me. I was trying to subdue her."

The green eyes looked away. "You had your hands around her neck."

"She fought me. Look at these scratches on me. I was just trying to help."

Kelsey recognized reality clearly now. But the past was still with her, just as strong.

The death had been here. Right here in this room.

The woman had come in alive, battered, afraid. She'd expected help, comfort, caring.

She found death.

Two more hands touched her arm, gently this time. A

gruff, fatherly voice spoke. "Are you all right, Ms. Ryan? Whatever happened, I'll take care of it. I promise."

Reverend Wingate. She brushed her fingertips along the edge of his beard. Curly. Prickly. Real.

As real as the cold imprint of death on her soul.

Kelsey withdrew. She pulled her hands to her stomach, felt for the pendant against her chest and clutched it tight.

"I can't do this anymore." She backed away from the three men, with variations of shock, anger and concern etched on their faces. She turned for the door and ran. "I can't do this."

She ran down the long hall, past the curious onlookers gathered in doorways and arches. She stripped off her apron and ran out the door into the Arctic blast of the night.

"KELSEY!"

What was T supposed to do? The cop in him wanted to stay here and grill Marlon Siegel. Read him his rights and book him for drunk and disorderly, maybe assault, maybe something more—something Kelsey had seen. But, hell, he had no proof.

The man in him needed to go after her. Bring her out of the cold. Find out about the stark white bandage on her hand. Rekindle the warmth and life in her terror-blanked eyes.

"I swear to God, man. I didn't hurt her. She cut herself. I fixed her up." The doctor's pleas babbled like white noise inside his ears. "She's the one who freaked out. Not me."

T looked at the scratches on Siegel's neck, the turned-over lamp and cart, the rumpled bed. Good. Whatever had happened, she'd gotten her licks in against the creep. But she'd been scared. When he'd dumped out his coffee, he'd seen the blood in the sink where she'd been working. A chill had gripped him. When she'd screamed for him, he thought he might be too late.

T tightened his hold and Siegel moaned. "If I find out you hurt her in any way—"

"I didn't. I swear."

"And she's not a freak." T shook him loose and pushed to his feet. The twinge in his knee was nominal, an annoyance he could overlook.

Siegel got up, walked straight to his desk and pulled out a flask of whiskey.

Was he a cop? Or a man?

"You'd better go find her, Detective." Reverend Wingate sounded concerned. "Make sure she's okay. After that murder on Christmas, I imagine it's easy for any of us to get spooked." He nodded toward Siegel, who was taking his second drink. "I'll take care of him."

"He doesn't leave the premises," T warned.

The reverend nodded. "At the rate he's going, he'll pass out in his bed before midnight. Go."

T was already on his way out the door. The man in him had already made the choice.

"Kelsey?"

He checked the hall. No fire-red hair.

A few helpful points from the staring crowd and an apron on the floor by the front door sent him running.

He shoved open the door. "Kelsey!"

Squinting against the bitter wind, he rolled down the sleeves of his shirt and searched up and down the street for her. As cold as it was, this wasn't just a matter of finding her to comfort her. If she got lost, if she got stopped… He refused to think about exposure to the elements or getting mugged or raped or… "Kelsey!"

"That way, man." His gaze connected with Zero's across the street. He couldn't make out the black man's expression. But the jewelry glistening in the pool of streetlight pointed east. "Toward The Underground."

T spared a nod for the man who had been his nemesis earlier in the day and prayed the pimp was trying to get on his good side.

Dashing down the steps, he jogged to the east, scanning ahead as far as he could see. He spotted a woman, with spiky hair, silhouetted up ahead. "Kelsey!"

She didn't answer. The cold air constricted his lungs and stiffened his knee. That had to be her, huddled up against the cold, walking so fast. Her hand shook as she raised her arm to flag down a cab two blocks away. "Taxi!"

Bingo.

"Kelsey." Ignoring the pounding on his knee, he broke into a run. "Kels!" He was closing in on her. She wouldn't stop. Twenty feet. Ten. He could hear her crying now, sniffing back tears. Five. "Kelsey."

"Go away."

"Kelsey. Sweetheart. Stop. It's me." He latched onto her sweater, blocked her with his chest, wrapped her up in his arms and crushed her against him. "It's me, Kels." He buried his nose in her hair and held her shaking body as tightly as he could. "It's me."

"I can't do this anymore." Her half-frozen tears soaked into the front of his shirt. Her fists bunched between them. "My head hurts and I want to go home."

"I know, sweetheart. I know." He glanced up and down the street, made sure they were safe. Then he pressed his lips against her temple and rubbed deep, warming circles against her back. She was so cold. Shivering. He wondered how much was from winter, and how much was from the mystical, amazing stuff that went on inside her head. "I'll take you."

She sniffed and he thought maybe she breathed a little easier. "Your mother's going to get on your case. You don't have your coat."

T smiled. She was going to be okay. "I have you. You feel better."

Kelsey's heavy sigh vibrated through them both. Then her arms reached around his waist and she moved closer. Those full, heavy breasts pillowed against his harder chest and T felt a calming, masculine power seep through him, blotting out the cold, strengthening him.

He needed his strength.

"I saw Delilah's death. In Doc Siegel's clinic."

His arms tightened convulsively around her, absorbing some of her pain and terror. He'd let the bastard go. "You saw him kill her?"

She shook her head, rubbing her cheek against him. "I couldn't see his face. I didn't want to. But he had to be the one, T. Delilah went to him for help that night. She trusted the man who killed her. She thought he was going to make everything all right for her. But he…he…"

"Shh." He rocked her gently, back and forth. "You don't have to go to that mission ever again. You never have to see him again. He can't hurt you." When the tears were done, he turned her toward his car. He wrapped his arm around her shoulders and hugged her to his side. "I'm going to take you home now."

"I can take a cab," she insisted, though she fell into step beside him. "I can take care of myself."

"I know you can. But you don't have to."

He stopped, hesitating a moment, remembering those sexually charged minutes in Reverend Wingate's office when he'd been dying to taste her lips, and she'd informed him that kissing *her* wasn't what he'd really wanted to do. But he was a man who learned from his mistakes. He just hoped she was a woman who could learn, too.

He took her hand, touching her chilly skin with his own, and placed it against his cheek. "If you're going to read something, read this. You are the only woman, the only person I'm thinking about right now."

He watched the struggle to believe in those soft brown eyes. "I can't read minds," she whispered. But she didn't pull away.

T smiled. "Then listen to my words. I need you to be safe. I find it very stressful when you're screaming my name and I'm not there." She almost smiled at that. "I intend to stay with you tonight."

She nodded and dropped her hand down to the placket of his shirt, but he got the idea she was letting go more from fatigue and headache than from revulsion or distrust. "Take me home, T."

When they reached his Jeep, he tucked her inside beneath the blanket and cranked up the heat. Placing the portable red-and-white siren light on the top of his car to dissuade any curiosity seekers from paying her a visit, he locked the doors and hurried back inside the mission to retrieve their coats and her purse. He found Siegel and Wingate still sitting in the clinic, sharing a drink and talking. T warned Siegel that he'd be back tomorrow to follow up on whatever harm might have come to Kelsey.

On the way out, he took note of every parked car, a couple with people sitting inside. He checked every window facing the street and lost count of all the people interested in his and Kelsey's business. He eyed Zero and his buddies hanging beneath the streetlight. And he caught a glimpse of a light going out in an upstairs window of the mission.

Someone in this neighborhood knew more than they were telling. Maybe a lot of someones. But they held tight to their secrets with the same tenacity with which they held on to life here in no-man's land.

Someone knew he was closing in on a killer.

Someone knew Kelsey might be the key.

And he knew that someone was watching.

THE DRIVE TO KELSEY'S HOME was long and silent. She wanted to hold his hand—glove free—all the way, and T didn't mind a bit.

By the time he turned into her driveway, he realized that exhaustion had claimed her. Breaking one of his mother's cardinal rules, he got into her purse without permission and retrieved her keys. He unlocked the house first, convinced the dog he was a friend, then went back and pulled Kelsey into his arms.

The run and the cold and the scuffle with Siegel had turned his knee into a swollen throb of pain. But he limped along and slowly but surely carried her to her bed. He removed her boots and her belt and unsnapped her jeans. He tucked the quilts up to her chin and bent low to press a kiss to her forehead.

"Good night, Kels. Sweet dreams."

She stirred beneath him when his lips touched her skin.

"Can you feel that?" he wondered aloud.

Even in her sleep, could she sense how scared he'd been when he'd heard her cry for help? How desperate he'd been when he couldn't immediately find her out in the frigid night? Or was she sensing other things? Like being shot? Being abandoned by his father?

Feeling strangely intuitive for a man who functioned in a world of facts, T kicked off his shoes and belt, and unbuttoned his shirt. He climbed onto the bed beside Kelsey and gathered her into his arms, quilts and all, and held her until she settled quietly against him.

"Feel this, sweetheart." He concentrated on every laugh they'd shared, every moment they'd touched, every time they'd butted heads and come out stronger for it. He thought of his friends at the precinct and his mother's unfailing support. He considered the questionable wisdom of a man like him falling for a woman like Kelsey. "Feel this," he whispered.

And he held her tight until he drifted off to sleep.

Chapter Eight

"All right, ladies and gentlemen, let's get this meeting started."

Captain Mitch Taylor's imposing presence had always been enough to capture T's attention. But this morning, he had to hear the booming voice that needed no microphone in order to turn his focus from the early breakfast he'd shared with Kelsey to the Fourth Precinct's morning roll call meeting.

"First up, it's New Year's Eve in the big city. Most of this will fall onto C shift, but let's try to stave off any problems before they start. We can plan on a few parties getting too loud, a few drunks celebrating too hard. I especially want you to keep an eye…"

The routine warnings and sobriety sweeps became background noise as T returned to the bright music of Kelsey's voice over breakfast. She wasn't back to full sass, but she was able to laugh and tease Frosty, and comment on what a great chef T was for fixing them cereal, coffee and peanut-butter toast.

T had gotten up early, knowing he needed to get back to his own apartment to change before driving into work. But he'd almost been willing to forgo clean clothes and stay the extra minutes. After her morning shower, Kelsey had look refreshed, except for the light shadows beneath her eyes. Remnants of her headache, she'd explained. She'd come out to eat before gelling her hair in its rock-star do, and it fell in soft natural waves that framed her face and kissed her nape.

And she didn't have to worry about the comfy gray sweats she'd put on being any kind of turnoff. He'd spent most of the night memorizing her lush curves and wishing his mother hadn't raised him to be such a noble guy. Every time he'd woken up through the night—to identify a noise, to shift positions, to check on Kelsey—he'd been happily aroused. But instead of climbing under the covers with her, he'd snuggled her tight, imagined gentle, positive thoughts and fallen back to sleep.

He had a dizzying feeling that once he kissed her—and he fully intended to cast aside her doubts and do it—there'd be no turning back. He and Kelsey were flint and stone, and once the spark was struck…

"Detective Banning." T had to be nudged in the arm to realize that the front-desk sergeant, Maggie Wheeler, had whispered his name. "Sorry to interrupt." She slid him a sealed manila folder across the long, narrow conference desk. "It's the lab report from CSI."

"Thanks."

He sat up to open the envelope and scan the contents while tuning a closer ear to Captain Taylor's morning briefing.

"…so that's an official no-progress on the Baby Jane Doe murder." The captain flipped a page on his clipboard. "Next up are the Holiday Hooker murders. Banning, you've been busy on this one. Any updates?"

With the rejuvenating thrill of answers finally starting to fall into place, he read off the highlights of the report. "I've got the Susan Cooper, aka Delilah, murder weapon. A silk scarf. Apparently, epithelial cells on the scarf match samples taken from the victim."

Kelsey had known that before any scientific data could prove it. His departmental consultant was turning out to be a compass, guiding him through this investigation. Leading him in a direction toward suspects he might not have considered before.

"They're running further tests to see if they can match it to any of the other victims. All roads seem to lead back to the Wingate Mission," he reported. "Reverend Wingate offered up his lodging records voluntarily. Each of the victims stayed at the mission the night before she died."

"So you're looking at someone who works at the mission?"

A vivid image of Marlon Siegel's hands clutched around Kelsey's throat distracted him for a moment. But he blinked it aside and answered the captain. "Right." He did have to be fair, since he currently lacked the hard evidence to accuse Siegel of anything more than being a drunk who lacked a gentle healing touch. "The departmental consultant is pointing me toward an employee or someone with regular access to the building."

"The consultant." A low voice laughed at the table behind him. But not so low that T couldn't hear it. That was probably the point. "You're actually listening to what that Flake is telling you? Oh, sorry, boss man. *Ms. Ryan.*"

T gripped the edges of the table, keeping his fists from forming. Josh Taylor sat beside him. He leaned his big shoulder closer and whispered. "I can reach him from here if you want me to."

T had to grin at the offer. Slow, pudgy, over-the-hill Watkins wouldn't stand a chance against big, bad, buff Josh Taylor. Still, there was personal satisfaction at stake. Amusing as it might be to see those two go head-to-head, T had other plans. "I'm waiting for the right moment when I can lay him flat myself—and not get a reprimand in my file. Or better yet, I'll let Kelsey have the fun. She could take him."

Josh chuckled out loud and the tension was broken.

Captain Taylor continued. "So the next step is running records and profiles on employees and neighborhood regulars?"

T nodded. "I've already got the programs set up to run."

"Good work. Sounds like you've made more headway in a week than we have in a decade." He marked something on his clipboard. "Josh and A. J., you just wrapped up that meth lab sting—why don't you work with Banning on the background checks."

"Will do." A. J. nodded and jotted the assignment in his notebook.

Josh gave a thumbs-up and leaned over to whisper. "This way I can find out why you paid my wife a visit yesterday."

"I was there to see Kelsey, not Dr. Livesay."

Josh gave him one of those wink, wink grins, as if he'd just revealed something he shouldn't. "Yeah, Rache wants me to find out about that, too."

"And Watkins." Captain Taylor's voice was bringing the meeting to a close. T should have known that Mitch Taylor's keen observation skills hadn't missed the ribbing exchanged a few moments earlier. "You worked the Jezebel case. Hit a stone wall. Since you're familiar with the mission district, I want you to report to Banning and give him whatever assistance he needs. Look at it as the chance to get the one who got away."

T assumed, from the groan and grumble behind him, that Watkins was a little irked that his failure to solve that crime—and prevent others like it—just got broadcast.

For some reason, he just couldn't help but smile. Payback didn't always require a fist in the mouth to be satisfying.

"The last thing," Captain Taylor went on, knowing his decision wouldn't be questioned, "is that Commissioner Cartwright has taken a personal interest in the Holiday Hooker murders. With the homicide on the twenty-fifth all over the news, she intends to put out some counterpublicity to highlight progress being made on that investigation and others. So everybody needs to be aware that the press is going to be a bigger presence in our lives for the next few days or even weeks." T added his own moan to the murmur of groans and curses across the room. "Be prepared for phone calls and cameras when you least expect it. Be polite. Be honest. But make us look good. If you question anything, run it by me first."

When Captain Taylor closed his clipboard, everyone in the room followed suit and put away notepads, pens and PalmPilots. The shuffle of noise crescendoed with scraping chairs and moving bodies once the captain called out, "Dismissed. Let's go get 'em."

Josh and A. J. touched base with T, divvied up assignments and headed for the break room. Putting his glasses back on, T scanned the rest of the lab report and joined the migration from the conference room back to desks, offices and elevators.

"T?"

He imagined the sound more than he actually heard it. Peeling off his glasses, he stopped and looked up. Kelsey was sitting at his desk, just like that first meeting, waiting for him. The same alertness energized her posture. The same black-and-white coat and fire-red hair snagged at least a passing glance from everyone on the floor.

Anticipation suffused him. He almost smiled.

Almost.

He frowned. There was something different today. This time, when he made contact with those soft brown eyes, she translated an urgent, personal message. Everything inside him tightened with concern.

"T."

He heard her now. He was already closing the distance between them when she shot out of the chair and zigzagged through the desks to meet him. She was almost running. Running to him.

"Kelsey?" He reached out and caught her beneath the elbow as she barreled to a halt and snatched up a handful of his lapel. "What's wrong? Did you see something else?"

He could feel her shaking. Her mouth dropped open, but instead of answering, she caught a shallow breath and glanced to the side. Her chin dropped. She released him as quickly as she had first grabbed him and retreated a step.

"I'm sorry." What was she apologizing for?

"What is—?" He followed her line of sight and nailed Ed Watkins's odious leer. A bolt of white-hot anger charged through T's system. Making jokes behind Kelsey's back was one thing; being rude to her face wasn't gonna happen. "You son of a—"

"Hey, Watkins." A. J. Rodriguez had spotted the same trouble. Whatever that sixth sense of his had detected, he silently offered T the backup he needed. With an I'll-handle-this nod, the dark-haired detective turned to Ed Watkins and smiled. "Over here. You're going to sit down and tell me everything you know about Jezebel's murder."

"Now?"

A. J. never blinked. "Now."

With a curse beneath his breath, the sergeant followed A. J. over to his desk and took a seat. Not waiting for any more interruptions, not wanting Kelsey to feel like a spectacle any longer, T took her by the arm and guided her to an empty interrogation room.

"I'm sorry about that," he apologized, closing the door for privacy and offering her a seat. "A. J. will set him straight for being so damn rude."

"Sergeant Watkins isn't the first person to gawk at me." She'd chosen to stand. She was rubbing her grandmother's pendant through the lime-green sweater and striped blouse she wore. Bad sign. She was really agitated about something. "But he creeps me out because he never blinks when he stares. It's like those beady little eyes can see right through this stuff—" she fluffed her fingers through her hair and plucked at her sweater "—and see what a freak I really am."

"Hey." He circled the table but she put up her hand and warned him off. He respected her wish and halted a few feet away, but he wouldn't give up the argument. "You are not a freak."

"You thought so a few days ago."

"I know you…better," he amended, thinking there were probably mysteries about this complicated woman he might never understand. "It bothers me to hear you talk that way about yourself. You're smart, intuitive, caring, feisty, stubborn, brave."

She cocked one eyebrow and almost smiled. "Is that supposed to be a compliment?" He shrugged. Eloquence wasn't his strong suit, but Kelsey saved him. "You sounded a lot like Lucy Belle just now."

"Yeah? Well, then I think I would have liked her."

"She would have liked you." Letting the pendant go, she gripped the back of one of the chairs and glanced at the door. "I think Sergeant Watkins reminds me of my ex-fiancé." She glanced back. "Lucy Belle didn't like him."

"You were engaged?" Why did he find that so surprising? Why did it bother him that she'd had a serious relationship with another man?

"Can you believe it? Not the smartest six months of my life." She hunched her shoulders and shivered, as if the experience had left a bitter taste in her mouth.

The unexpected stab of jealousy eased. "Why didn't it work out?"

"Mostly because he called me things like *freak* and *witch* and worse."

"Son of a bitch."

Kelsey grinned. "He was."

But T's anger hadn't fully abated, and a lot of it was directed at himself. "I apologize for ever labeling you. You'd think I'd have been a little more accepting. I've had a few stigmas of my own to outgrow. I should have understood."

Kelsey reached out and took his hand. She wore her gloves this morning and he missed the skin-on-skin contact. But he wrapped his fingers around hers and squeezed back, appreciating the forgiveness and comfort she offered. "The difference with you, T. Merle Banning, is that you learn from your mistakes. You keep trying to make yourself a smarter, better person. Men like Watkins and my ex never see the world through anyone's eyes but their own."

"And you see it through everyone's."

His compassionate statement filled the room with quiet. Kelsey pulled her hand away and hugged her arms around her waist, reaching for the pendant again.

T pulled back from his emotional reactions to this woman and tried to focus on being a cop. "What's wrong? What made you come in this morning? I said I'd finish the investigation without getting you any further involved."

Kelsey pulled out a chair and sank into it. "Somebody else might not be giving me that same choice."

"What do you mean? Did something happen?" He unbuttoned his camel tweed blazer and sat in the chair beside her.

She worked those turquoise-gloved fingers together on top of the table. "First of all, thank you for staying the night with me. You are one amazing gentleman. But you could have sent me home in a cab."

"A cabbie wouldn't tuck you in."

Her cheeks warmed with color. "You did more than just tuck me in. You made me feel…secure. Like it was okay to let things go while you were there. That's the best night's sleep I've had in months."

So she'd been snoozing in the land of Nod, completely oblivious to the fact that he'd been horny as a son of a gun all night. The compliment flattered him, frustrated him—made him feel potent all over again. But this wasn't about him.

"But something this morning made you feel *in*secure?"

She nervously glanced at her hands, then looked him straight in the eye and answered. "Someone was watching the house this morning."

His protective instincts flared; he'd had the feeling someone had been watching them last night at the mission. But his cop instincts kept him from overreacting. "Explain."

"There was a car parked in front of the house. They pulled up and parked just a few minutes after you left."

He pulled out his notepad and pen. "What kind of car?"

"Gray SUV. I'm bad with makes and models, but it wasn't new. There was rust around the wheel wells."

He jotted the description, wracking his brain, trying to recall if he'd seen one parked in no-man's land last night. "You said *they*. How many? Man? Woman?"

"Actually there was just one. The driver was slender. Had dark brown hair and wore a cap pulled low over her eyes."

"Her?"

Kelsey considered her assessment. "Yes. It was a woman. She had smooth skin, no beard. And her lips were too pretty."

Definitely not Marlon Siegel. Not anyone near the top of his suspect list if she was a female. "And what makes you think she was watching you?"

"When I took Frosty for a walk, she followed us. Followed my cab to the police station, too."

A few questions later and he was steaming. Rebecca Page, crime reporter, was apparently working overtime, trying to make a story he didn't want told. She might justify her spying as some sort of necessity to complete her father's journalistic legacy, but to T's way of thinking, she was just going to bring Kelsey a lot of publicity she didn't want or deserve.

›   "I'll handle it," he promised, escorting Kelsey back to his desk. "Captain Taylor said the press was going to start hounding us. But that shouldn't include private citizens like you. In the meantime, make yourself comfortable. The one place Rebecca Page, or anyone else, can't get to you is right here."

EVEN WITH EARPHONES to muffle the sound, Kelsey flinched every time T's gun went off. The K.C.P.D. indoor firing range was deserted by late afternoon on New Year's Eve, so she and T were the only ones occupying a booth. After a hectic day, bumping into people in the break room and being introduced to every well-meaning friend on the force curious about the woman who wasn't his partner sitting at Detective Banning's desk, he'd suggested coming here for the solitude.

True to his word, not a single reporter had invaded her privacy all day. But she'd been antsy with boredom, having little to do but sit back and observe the bustle around her. She'd finally given herself a task and had borrowed a legal pad to start a list of everything she could remember from her impressions of the two murders. She had pages now, of images, sounds, smells. The more she wrote, the more real they became. The more agitated she became. The cruel taunts. The betrayal. The sheer, helpless terror.

Finally, at about three in the afternoon, T had tapped her on the shoulder to ask something about coffee. When she jumped in her chair and sent an entire mug full of pens and pencils scattering across the floor, he'd turned off his computer, picked up their coats and said they were taking an elevator ride to someplace more private.

For a few brief moments, Kelsey had imagined something warm and romantic—a tropical beach, a hot tub, his arms.

But then she remembered his partner, Ginny—the woman he fantasized warm, romantic thoughts about.

T was her friend. Her partner. Her protector.

To imagine him as anything more would surely get her heart into bigger trouble than the nightmarish mess she was already a part of.

When he walked her down to the basement and turned on the lights, she'd laughed out loud with amusement and relief. This was where he came to blow off steam when life got too tense to bear. It was as private as he'd promised, yet she didn't have to worry about getting any romantic notions. The concussive repetition of noise keeping her nerves on edge would see to that.

"Any questions?"

She set down the notepad where she'd been scribbling out her stress and took a deep breath. He set the gun down on the counter and invited her to take his place at the rail. "I don't know, T. Maybe I don't want to actually shoot it."

He nodded with a sage, teacherly expression on his face and pulled her into position. "You don't want to be afraid of guns. You want to respect them. To do that, you have to learn about them."

"What if I have terrible aim and hit the target in the next lane? Or blow out the gearbox that moves the targets?"

He grinned. "Relax, Calamity. We don't give real bullets to someone who's never fired a gun before."

"I've never even held one."

"Then let's change that." He reached for her right hand and picked up the gun and placed it into position in her palm. Then he guided her left hand to the base of the grip and let her take the weight of the gun.

Kelsey gasped in surprise. "It's heavy."

He shrugged, indicating what she found amazing was no big deal to him. "That's a standard police issue. A Glock 9 mm."

She spread her feet in the same position he had used, one foot slightly behind the other. "I hold it out straight, lock this arm, and…" The gun slipped in her hands when she tried to stick her finger through the trigger keeper. "I can't get a good grip with wool gloves."

"Besides the impact-resistant lining, that's one reason we wear the leather gloves. Better traction. They'll be big, but—"

"It's okay." She snagged him by the arm when he went back toward the coat-rack at the firing range door to retrieve his gloves for her. "I can do this."

She set the gun down, debated for a moment, then tugged off her turquoise gloves.

"You don't have to."

"It wouldn't be much of a lesson if I didn't finish, now would it?"

Kelsey wiggled her fingers as she blew out a steadying breath. Then, just as he'd shown her, she picked up the gun and braced herself.

The images came, but she focused her energy in the here and now and blurred them like a watercolor painting. The gun butt felt warm between her palms, the trigger, cold. She extended her arms, closed one eye and sighted the target.

T wrapped his hand around both of hers and lifted the gun to the proper level. The instant fire of his skin touching hers scattered the hazy images. "Just squeeze gently."

But she was no longer in the firing range. No longer in that booth with T. The gun had its own story to tell, and, adding the contact with T's hand, the impression became startlingly clear.

"My gun."

T clawed at the ground, trying to reach their only means of protection. His chest felt like a deflated tire. His leg burned so bad, he was sure he'd pass out from the pain. He couldn't keep his eyes open.

Urgent hands scrambled, placed the gun in his hand. He curled his fingers around the familiar, solid steel.

The big man was coming. That jackass son of a bitch was coming back to finish what he'd started. Kill Mac Taylor. He was going to kill them all.

Bleeding from the wound in his own shoulder, the big man panted. "I'm sorry, Mr. Taylor."

He raised his gun, but T was faster. The shot exploded in the air and the big man went down.

He'd saved his friends. For now. But he couldn't help them anymore.

"Go." His chest heaved with the effort to speak that one word. He just needed to rest. He needed to close his eyes and sleep so the pain would go away.

Kelsey squeezed her eyes shut and struggled to inhale. But the huge weight on her chest made it impossible to breathe.

"…all right, sweetheart. Let it go." A strong hand pried the gun from her grip. Stronger arms folded around her. "Kelsey. Come back to me."

The scratch of soft wool abraded her cheek. The smells of crisp, pressed cotton and warm, musky man filled her nose. T's smells. It was such a good place, such a safe place, that Kelsey wrapped her arms around his waist and burrowed against his strength and warmth.

Kelsey shuddered as the image left her and she gasped for air. T held her tight and whispered sweet, gentle things against her hair. "Oh, T. It was awful." She slid her hands beneath his jacket and clutched at the back of his shirt, needing to be even closer to his warmth. "You had to kill a man."

His lips brushed her ear, but the touch was so light, so loving, she didn't feel anything but the shiver of awareness that tingled beneath the sensitive spot. "I'm so sorry. I should have thought of that. I never should have asked you to—"

"You were shot." She leaned back, keeping her hand at his belt to anchor herself. That was the image she'd seen when they'd touched at lunch that first day. Bleeding on the ground after a drive-by shooting. When the attacker returned to polish off the wounded, T had fired first.

"Here." In her mind she could see the exact spot. She pushed her hand beneath the left side of his jacket and splayed her fingers over the puckered circle of scar tissue she could feel through the cotton. "And your leg. You were shot in the knee."

He laid his hand over the top of hers and pressed it to the spot he'd been wounded. "Don't think about that. It's over." He dropped his chin to capture her gaze. "I'm healthy as a horse now. I'm okay."

"But you hurt." Tears burned in her eyes as she re-lived his pain, as she took solace in the knowledge that he'd saved lives that day, including his own. "I didn't know how much you'd lost. How much you hurt."

Pinching her chin between his thumb and finger, he tilted her face to his. "I don't hurt like that anymore."

She blinked the mist from her eyes and focused on the acceptance and the promise she saw in those wise green eyes. "The body heals, the brain learns from it, the instincts are a little sharper the next time."

He wiped a tear from her cheek with the pad of his thumb. Her skin burned beneath his touch. "If any of these are for me, don't. I'm tougher than I look."

"You've always had to be tough, haven't you." She wasn't sure if she sensed that through the caress of his thumb, or if she'd just spent enough time with him to learn that he'd been misjudged by others throughout his life. But that persecution had made him stronger and more determined inside than most other men ever had to be. "Just like me."

She boldly reached up and brushed her fingers along either side of his jaw. The sensations that seeped in were a mix of physical and metaphysical. Tenderness. Strength. The erotic prickle of beard stubble that tickled her sensitive fingertips. Warm skin. Lips melding. Bodies mating.

Kelsey's lips parted as an overheated breath escaped. He wanted to kiss her. He'd wanted to before. He wanted…

Something hot and feminine clenched inside her, pouring liquid heat into her veins. Warm honey pooled between her legs, gathered in her breasts and made them heavy.

She could picture herself in bed with T. Naked shoulders. Bare butt. Climbing over her body, sinking inside. Filling her with a slow, torturous heat. His fantasy or hers? And then…

The sensations were blotted out by the very real pressure of T's mouth against hers. Her breath caught in her chest. Time and images seemed to stand still.

Her lips softened and surrendered to his gentle, probing lips. Her fingers felt his strong jaw, and the precision dance of muscles and pulse moving beneath the skin as he angled his mouth to deepen the kiss. Her lips parted and she tasted rich coffee and deep, uneven breaths that matched her own. She sighed with contentment and longing, filling her head with his clean, masculine scent.

His hands were at her hips and in her hair. They slipped beneath the weight of her sweater and blouse, and skimmed along the silk of her camisole, examining every curve and contour with exacting precision.

The heat in her body ignited, fed by the abundant warmth and sensual assault of his hands and mouth. She slipped her arms around his neck, rubbed her tingling palms against the short silk of his hair and pulled herself up on tiptoe to lose herself in the inexplicable reality of this kiss.

There were no images to distract her. No impressions to confuse her or cause her pain. It was just T. Kissing her. Holding her. Backing her against the counter and dragging her primed, needy body against his to give her a very real imprint of his desire for her.

It was two world-weary souls coming alive in each other's embrace. Two outcasts who found acceptance in each other's kiss. Two hearts joining that had never been able to give all they wanted before.

A bird chirped inside T's pants, and, at first, Kelsey wanted to laugh. Her body was singing, too.

But then she felt the tension in him, the sudden stilling of his hands inside her shirt. He tore his mouth away and rested his cheek against hers. His deep, ragged breath and frustrated curse scorched her neck.

She knew now it was his phone. And the damn thing kept ringing.

"I should get this," he gasped, pulling his hands to a more neutral location outside her sweater. He cupped her shoulders and backed away. "I'm expecting calls…" He nodded jerkily, as if needing the affirmation that leaving her stunned and shaky was the right thing to do. "…on the case."

"I'm okay." Kelsey straightened the tie and lapels she'd smushed in her greedy hands and gave him the smile he needed to go back to work.

She should take a step back from this, anyway, and consider the magic of what had just passed between them. She'd never kissed a man before without seeing bits of his past, without being inundated by thoughts and words and symbols. But she'd been so overwhelmed by T's kiss, so into it, so on fire, that they'd just been a man and a woman together. In this place. In this now.

He pulled his phone from his pocket and flipped it open. "Banning."

His face blanched. He frowned an apology then he turned away.

"Ginny. Happy New Year to you, too."

Kelsey's ego crashed and burned. *Ginny.*

She hooked her bag over her arm, grabbed her gloves and notepad and walked away.

It was just a kiss.

Hot bodies coming together at a mutually needy moment. Nothing more than a physical outlet for simmering fears and frustrations. She shouldn't read anything life altering into that.

"Hey." She felt his hand on her arm, stopping her. But it didn't mean anything. He mouthed the words, *Stay close,* then let her go and continued the conversation. "Yeah, Gin. What did you find out?"

She shouldn't feel angry or hurt. She shouldn't hold anything against Ginny Rafferty-Taylor. She was probably a very nice woman, deserving of T's loyalty and devotion.

This was actually a step up for Kelsey in the relationship department. T had shown her she was a woman he *could* want…as long as the woman he *did* want wasn't around.

But her raw lips and hopeless heart didn't seem to believe this was anything but a huge step back into loneliness.

He tried to hold her gaze as he retreated into the booth. But he was too busy listening to Ginny. Kelsey thumbed over her shoulder toward the exit. "I'm just going to visit the ladies' room."

He nodded and disappeared.

A splash of cold water on her face might clear her thoughts. Maybe she should douse her whole head. Kelsey shoved open the metal door, leaving T and his phone call and that kiss behind. She paused and squinted a few moments to let her eyes adjust to the brighter light in the hallway.

She heard the sound first. An ominous shuffle of footsteps on a supposedly deserted floor. Kelsey froze. Was someone following her again?

Hugging her notepad and bag to her chest, she quickly scanned the hallway. She saw the open entryways into the men's and women's locker rooms on the opposite wall. The closed elevator at the far end of the hall. The door to the stairway.

Just a few yards away, the door to the supply closet clicked shut.

Kelsey whirled around to face the creepy sound. There was nothing suspicious about someone hiding in a supply closet. Yeah, right.

Reporter? Camera? Killer?

"Hello?" Kelsey retreated a few cautious steps.

She'd thought she needed her space from T, but suddenly, she felt way too far away. "Good-bye."

Half a step toward the firing-range door, rough, black-gloved hands grabbed her from behind and dragged her into the ladies' room.

Kelsey's scream rang inside her head. She bit into the hand covering her mouth, but something hard and wiry inside the glove kept her from doing any damage. A hard arm cinched her around the waist and lifted her off the floor, crushing her against leather and padding and something hard that poked her in the hip.

"Stop it! Get your hands off me!"

She kicked her feet, beat with her hands, tried to grab the door frame. But the hands were too strong, the hot breath and curses against her neck too angry. Her assailant yanked her loose and carried her inside, behind a concrete-block wall that hid her from the hallway opening.

He twisted her in his grasp and threw her up against the wall hard enough to smack her head against the concrete. Pain radiated through her skull and made her dizzy. *"No. Stop. Please. T!"*

By the time she shook her aching head clear, the gloved hands had muffled her mouth and the weight of a man's heavy body pinned her. He was already talking, whispering vile, filthy things right in her face.

"…making me look bad, you freaky bitch." She knew those beady, hateful eyes. "At the station house and on my own turf." Ed Watkins's hands tightened painfully on her mouth and neck. Her eyes widened at the blame and contempt in his expression, so like Jeb's had been. A man who refused to understand anything *different* that he couldn't control.

Her protests vibrated in her throat and rang in her ears.

"I've had to deal with your kind before. I've seen how you work. You're casting a spell over everybody, and that ain't right. I know how you can turn a man's head and make him think things. You make my people very uncomfortable."

Her kind? His people?

The sergeant's spittle sprayed her face, but he seemed more desperate than angry. Wild and insistent in his grip and his eyes. "You have to stop telling people you see stuff in your head. Do you understand? I can help you if you listen to me. But I won't be able to protect you if you keep talkin' crazy like that."

He thought *she* was talking crazy?

"It's gonna happen all over again, and I won't have that. I can't keep you safe. I couldn't keep Jezebel safe. But I tried. You don't know how hard I tried. But you are gonna stay out of trouble. Understand?" He tugged at the pocket of her jeans. "If you won't listen to me, you listen to Jezebel."

What?

With a monumental heave, Kelsey twisted her body. Her bag slipped off her elbow and she caught it in her hand.

But that poke she'd felt had been Watkins's nightstick, and he shoved it into her chest now, pinning her arms, squeezing her breath and igniting her anger.

"Everything was nice and quiet down in no-man's land until you and Banning showed up. I couldn't figure out why another cop would stick his nose into my business. But now I know why he's so interested in my territory. I saw you two in there." He flipped his nightstick to an obscene position against her thigh and smirked a filthy grin. "You're just like Jezebel with her wicked ways. You got his head all turned 'round. He wants to get in your pants."

Watkins's crudeness cost him. With her arm free, Kelsey swung her purse and clocked him in the side of the head. It wasn't enough to free herself, but it was enough to knock his hand loose.

Kelsey screamed.

Chapter Nine

"T-eeee!"

Every confused, frustrated nerve still racing inside Banning slammed to a halt. Fear jolted through him. "Gotta go, Gin."

"What about the rest of the info I found on the doll? It's a registered collectible and I have owner names."

"And I have a problem." He grabbed his gun off the counter, ejected the blanks and slipped in a magazine of the real thing. "I'll call you later."

"Be safe."

T ended the call and pocketed his phone, already running to the door. "Kelsey!"

They were in the subbasement of precinct headquarters. What kind of trouble could find her here?

Didn't matter. He'd vowed to keep her safe, whether the threat came from inside her head or from someplace decidedly more sinister.

"Kels!" He threw open the door and flattened himself against the wall. With his Glock gripped between his hands he tuned his eyes and ears and heart toward the source of the danger.

The empty hall didn't throw him. The closed access

doors didn't distract him. He heard the struggle, the low-voiced curses, the stifled protests.

"Hang on." He ran into the ladies' locker room and ducked around the concrete wall, leading with his gun.

"What the hell?"

He'd faced down bullies on playgrounds and men with guns. But nothing had ever scared him the way seeing Ed Watkins's nightstick rammed up against Kelsey's throat did.

"This woman's trouble, Banning." Watkins puffed the warning out on a wheezing breath. "I'm glad you're here to back me up. Who knows what kind of hocus-pocus stunt she's gonna pull on us next."

"You're a cop. She's on our side."

"I didn't do anything." Kelsey coughed against the pressure of the stick at her throat.

This was crazy. "Let her go."

Kelsey's eyes darted to him, but Watkins was too angry to listen to T or see him coming up behind him.

But he felt him.

T pressed the nose of his Glock into the side of Watkins's neck. Cold steel got the older cop's attention. Except for the stout man's labored breathing, Watkins froze. "I said, let her go."

"What are you doing?" Watkins seemed stunned. "I'm trying to help you."

"Drop it, Sergeant." It was the most succinct command Detective Banning had ever given. He removed Watkins's service pistol and tucked it into the back of his own belt as the nightstick clattered to the floor. "Get out of there, Kels."

She scrambled away from the wall, picked up her bag and hid behind him. Good girl.

"You're on her side? Of course you are. She's just like Jezebel. She's got you under her spell. I'm too late."

"Shut up." The sergeant wasn't making any sense. "Against the wall."

Watkins knew the drill. He raised his hands slowly into the air and pressed them against the very space Kelsey had just vacated. He knew the excuses, too. "You're making a big mistake, Banning."

T ignored his rambling. "Where's your spare?" Almost every cop he knew, especially the ones who walked a beat, kept an extra sidearm hidden somewhere.

Watkins was no exception. "Right ankle holster. I'm telling ya, man, you gotta listen to me."

T kept his gun trained on the target, ignoring the explanation as he knelt down and retrieved the second weapon.

"I didn't hurt her," Watkins protested. "I just wanted her to understand that they're on to her. She can't go back there. We can't keep her safe."

T straightened. "You hurt, Kels?"

"I hit my head on the wall. He just…spooked me. He said something about Jezebel and my kind causing trouble. He's not making any sense."

She sounded a little shaken, but strong. He thanked her stubborn, red-haired temperament, whether the hair color itself was real or fake. "On the floor, Watkins."

"What are you gonna do? Arrest me?" He started to turn.

"On the floor!"

Once he'd assumed the prone position, T gladly put a knee in the middle of Watkins's back to hold him down while he handcuffed him. Then he rolled to his feet, called for backup, and eyed Kelsey to make sure everything was unharmed and in one place. "How's your head?"

"I'm okay." She was hugging herself, squeezing that pendant.

Not as okay as he'd like.

But he couldn't reach for her now. Watkins was squirming like a beached fish and blathering like a crazy man. "You can't do this to me, Banning. You have to let me go. Let me go back to no-man's land and get everything back to normal. You can't take me off the street. He'll find her. Just like he found Jezebel."

"Who'll find her? What are you talking about?" T traded a confused glance with Kelsey, then tried to force Watkins to make sense. "Who are you talking about? Siegel? Zero? Who's looking for Kelsey?"

"He'll find her."

T knelt down and jerked Watkins up by the collar to look into those beady, cowardly eyes. "Who?"

"T." Kelsey's soft hands on his shoulders warned him off the violence. "Something's wrong. I don't think he understands you."

"He understands enough to track you down and rough you up." He turned his focus back on Watkins. "What do you want from Ms. Ryan?"

"Don't lock me up." The pitiful pudge of a man pleaded. "Word on the street is that she's talking about stuff no one's supposed to know about. She makes people nervous. Draws too much attention to folks who don't want anyone to know who or what they are."

"Give me a name."

"I don't know."

T heard the ding of the elevator, heard the footsteps in the hall and knew backup was on its way. He stood, linked his hand with Kelsey's stiff grip and backed her to a safer position.

"Sergeant. Ed." He tried a more personal appeal. "Who wants to hurt Ms. Ryan?"

"Jezebel can explain. I loved her. I tried to help her, but I couldn't. He knew she was different. That's why her husband threw her out. That's why she was all alone."

"Who is *he?* Who was Jezebel's husband? If we knew that, we could identify her real name. C'mon, Ed. I need answers that make sense. Why would he throw her out? Why would he kill her?"

Was that a sob? What the—? The man was crying. "I don't know who he is. She never said his name. I've looked all these years. If I'd found him, I could have saved all those girls. Poor Jezebel."

T knelt down beside the whimpering man. "Do you know who killed them?"

Watkins shook his head back and forth. "But I know why."

T squeezed the sergeant's quaking shoulder, urging an answer as much as offering comfort. "Why?"

The sergeant tilted his bald head and looked up at Kelsey. He looked more frightened than frightening.

"That one'll understand. Jezebel can explain."

"WHAT DID HE MEAN—*Jezebel can explain?*"

Kelsey had her pendant out now, openly worrying the blue crystal between her palms.

"Don't let Watkins get to you. The police psychologist seemed to think he was having some sort of breakdown."

"Yeah. And I'm the freak who sent him over the edge."

"Don't." T took his eyes off the road long enough to

reach across the front seats of the Jeep and squeeze her knee. He wanted to offer some friendly reassurance. But judging by the stiff way Kelsey held herself—as if it required a great deal of will not to jerk away from his touch—he suspected he was only adding to her stress.

Respecting whatever space she thought she needed right now, he reluctantly put both hands back on the wheel.

He hated seeing her like this. The way she'd been when they'd first met—aloof, closed off, suspicious.

He was still keyed up from that kiss at the firing range—how close they'd gotten. How fast they'd gotten there. At first, he'd just needed to hold her, to take back some of the pain she'd absorbed from his past. She'd understood how much it hurt to have his body ripped apart by bullets. How afraid he'd been to think he would die before he could see his friends to safety. How hard it was to turn off his emotions, raise his gun and take another man's life.

She'd felt all that. She'd hurt for all of that. And so he'd held her. But then he wasn't comforting her. He was finding comfort for them both. Acceptance. Healing. He'd been dying to kiss those lips, dying to feel the curves beneath those colorful clothes, dying to taste a little of that fire burning inside her.

So he'd kissed her. And when she didn't stop him, he'd kissed her more.

He hadn't expected Kelsey's uninhibited response. But he'd reveled in it. She was always so careful about how she touched. And whom. But she'd grabbed on to him, bare-handed, and wouldn't let go.

It was the truest passion, the deepest connection to another person he'd ever known.

Then the phone rang and the connection with Kelsey

had been lost. It had been lost long before Ed Watkins ever got his crazy, pudgy paws on her.

Maybe he could reassure her from a distance. "Don't put stock in anything Watkins said. Apparently, he had feelings for Jezebel. Tried to look out for her after her husband kicked her out on the streets. And then she was murdered. He couldn't save her, and he couldn't find her killer. That kind of guilt could break a man."

"But what's the connection to me? Sergeant Watkins can't stand to be around me. Why did he think I would understand?" Kelsey stared out into the night as they drove through the lights and parties and people getting ready to ring in the new year. But she wasn't seeing the festivities outside. "A man has to hate his wife an awful lot to throw her out without any money or any way to support herself. Thank God there are places like the mission, shelters and crisis centers. But, why not just divorce her? It feels as if her husband was punishing her."

Maybe, in some gruesome plan that required no cash and no hit man, Jezebel's husband had been hoping she wouldn't survive. It was a damn coldhearted way to save on alimony. The mysterious husband might even qualify as an accessory to murder because of his reckless indifference to his wife's safety.

But T didn't share his dark thoughts with Kelsey. She already had enough gloom hanging in a cloud around her.

"I wish Watkins could give us something on the husband," he said, opting to stick to business. "A description if not a name. If they really were close, Jezebel must have told him something."

Watkins had been booked for assault, and was now an official guest of K.C.P.D. until after the holiday when he could post bail. Though chances were, he'd be spending his time in a hospital ward instead of a jail cell.

"He seemed to think she was going to tell me." Kelsey tucked the lap blanket more securely around her legs, even though he'd already cranked the heat up to maximum. "One minute Watkins is accusing me of hocus-pocus and warning me not to use my gift again. The next, he's looking at me as if I'm the only one who can help his dead girlfriend." Her heavy sigh fogged up the passenger-side window. "I just wanted to put those women's spirits to rest and get them out of my head. I didn't mean to cause all this trouble."

"*You* haven't done anything," T insisted, slowing the Jeep as they neared a stoplight. "We've stirred things up by asking questions and paying unexpected visits. A smart criminal is going to know we can't arrest or convict anybody except on hard facts. And while you've pointed me in some new directions that have paid off with legitimate leads, I don't have a case I can take to court yet."

"What if the murderer isn't that smart?" Her hesitant sigh burned into his compassion.

"He's gotten away with it for eleven years. And a whole neighborhood has kept quiet about it. I'm thinking our guy's pretty sharp."

"Funny how that doesn't seem like much of a reassurance."

Sarcasm. Was she coming back?

The light changed. He debated an idea for all of about two seconds. Then he wheeled the car around to the right.

Kelsey perked up in her seat. "This isn't the way to my house."

"It's New Year's Eve. I think we should do some celebrating."

Groaning, she turned in her seat. Good. Eye contact. "C'mon, T. The last thing I want to do is go to a party. Or sit in a bar with a bunch of strangers, waiting for a ball to drop."

He headed south toward the Plaza. "I don't want you home by yourself tonight, and I have a distinct feeling you wouldn't invite me in."

Now she was pointing a finger at him, getting herself a little riled up. "Do you have any idea what it's like for me in a crowd? Brushing against people? Especially if they're drunk and uninhibited? It's like having dozens of people shouting at me all at once. I can't push a mute button and make it go away. I'm too tired to deal with all that tonight."

"Trust me. I have something quieter in mind."

She sank back into her seat. "I'm not very good company tonight."

"Are you afraid I'm going to take up where that kiss left off?"

She shot him a startled look, then turned toward the window. There was enough light from the street and the dashboard to see the blush coloring her cheeks. But she didn't answer.

An unexpected anticipation lit in his veins. "Are you afraid I won't?"

"T." Her cheeks almost matched her hair now.

"Here." He twisted in his seat and fished a twenty-dollar bill from his pocket. He dropped it into her lap. "Take it."

"What's this for?"

He grinned. "Cab fare."

She held it out to him. "I don't want your money."

He curled his hand around her gloved fist and folded

the money inside. "Think of it as insurance. If you don't like my idea, if you decide you'd rather go home—you can call a cab anytime you like."

"YOUR MOTHER'S HOUSE?"

Kelsey had to hand it to him. When T had promised to take her someplace away from the crowds and partiers, he'd delivered.

"Won't she mind?"

"Nope." T wore a grin on his face that made her think they were getting away with something. Like sneaking in after curfew or skinny-dipping in the family pool. He dangled his keys in front of her face. "That's why she left me a spare key."

The two-story brick home south of the Plaza was small on the scale, compared to some of the wealthy old homes in the neighborhood. But it boasted a big yard behind its brick walls and wrought-iron gate. And the decor inside was elegantly homey, inviting guests to sit and relax.

Kelsey felt a sense of shelter and serenity from the moment she walked in. Still, "Why here?"

T closed the door behind them and locked the deadbolt before pocketing his keys and taking her coat to hang beside his own in the foyer. "One, I could guarantee that it would be quiet. Mom's visiting her aunt and uncle in Albuquerque thanks to a lovely Christmas present from her thoughtful son. Two, we're high enough on the hill that we can see the public fireworks display at midnight. And, most importantly, I know for a fact that she has champagne in the fridge."

He touched his hand to the small of her back and turned on lights as he guided her down a long oak parquet hallway to the spacious kitchen at the back of the house. Kelsey felt her mood lightening, and knew that had been T's intention. She was exhausted from fighting headaches and crazy men and the memories of two women who still needed her help.

There was something almost naughty about being in Moira Banning's beautiful home and raiding her fridge at 11 p.m. It felt juvenile and impulsive and fun—three things that had been missing from her life for longer than she cared to admit. "Your mom must be a really nice lady."

"She is. Of course, I'm a little biased. It's been just the two of us since I was eight." He opened the refrigerator door while he pulled off his tie and tossed it onto the center island counter. "So quit worrying. We're actually doing her a favor."

"How's that?"

"I promised to check the house while she's gone." He glanced over his shoulder and grinned. "So right now I'm checking the refrigerator." He pointed to the cabinets beside the sink. "And if you look up there, you can check out the plates and some champagne goblets."

Kelsey circled the island and opened the cupboard doors. "You're goofy, Banning."

"Yeah, but I'm awful cute. Just ask my mom."

She laughed. It was the first of many.

Bologna sandwiches with pickles and pretzels made a fine accompaniment to champagne bubbles. They toasted Moira Banning and the New Year. By the time she had licked the frosting off her fingers from the last of Moira's lemon bundt cake, Kelsey felt almost normal.

As normal as a psychic who relived murders in her head and fell in love with men who loved someone else could be, that is.

As she carried their plates to the sink and helped T load the dishwasher, she had to admit the truth. She'd gone and done the stupidest thing of her life with the squarest, nicest, smartest, most protective man she'd ever known.

Maybe Lucy Belle's guidance had opened her eyes to the possibility of having feelings for him. She'd known there was something different about T from the start.

He'd been skeptical about her talent, but he hadn't been afraid.

He'd argued with her, but he hadn't put her down.

He'd kissed her, and he hadn't run away.

She had.

Ho, boy.

Lucy Belle would have listened to her fears about getting hurt, given her a hug and told her to try again. *"Don't you be the one to give up on people, Kelsey."* She could hear her grandmother's twangy Ozark accent in her head, and almost smell the sweetly pungent aroma of the corncob pipe she used to smoke out on the porch on summer evenings. *"And I don't want to ever hear you givin' up on yourself and what makes you happy."*

So what made her happy?

Her work?

Her dog?

Helping others?

T?

"Deep thought alert." Kelsey had to blink her way back to the moment to see T standing right in front of her, crouching down a few inches to put him at eye level. "What's put a frown between those pretty brown eyes?"

She almost raised her fingers to ease the earnest concern from his quizzical expression. But she realized she wasn't wearing her gloves so she curled her fingers into her palms, resisting the urge. "I guess I'm making New Year's resolutions."

"And?" His sharp eyes hadn't missed the subtle withdrawal of her hand. He stood up straight but made no comment. "What did you resolve?"

Kelsey propped her hip against a stool beside the center island counter. "I'm going to take some of Grandma Lucy Belle's advice. I want to spend more time on the things that are important to me."

"Which are?"

She treated herself to touching his jacket. The sensations were vague and brief as she smoothed the nubby wool lapel. "I didn't get to the details yet. You interrupted me."

"My apologies." He checked his watch and caught a quick breath, energized like an adolescent again. "Just a few minutes till midnight."

He dashed out of the kitchen and Kelsey stood and turned in his wake. "What are you doing?"

He dashed back in with their coats, holding hers open for her to slip inside. "Hurry. We don't want to miss the countdown and the fireworks."

Kelsey barely pulled her gloves on before T ushered her out the arched French doors that led into the back yard. With their coats flying open in the brisk wind, he caught her hand and led her off the patio, knee-deep into the snow. Holding on with both hands, she followed in his footsteps as he crunched a path to the highest point in the yard.

"Right here." He stopped beside a dormant oak tree, its branches hanging with snow instead of leaves. He released her hands and gestured all around them. "Best view in the house."

Coldest view, too.

But Kelsey huddled inside her coat, not minding the chill or the promise of more snow as much as she expected. T's enthusiastic energy seemed to warm the air around them and seep into her.

The moist, cloudy sky hung low in the night, reflecting the glow of the city. Nonetheless, she could see some distance in nearly every direction while the high brick fence afforded them privacy from their closest neighbors. Kelsey grinned. The lights down on the Plaza sparkled with holiday intensity. But those million-plus lights couldn't match the boyish exuberance of T. Merle Banning. A grown man, checking his watch, counting down the time, stomping out a circle of snow with his flat, black shoes as they waited for the new year to begin.

What a wonderful antidote to gloomy thoughts, guilty second-guessing and fears about unsolved murders.

By the time church bells started tolling midnight in the distance, Kelsey was caught up in his silly, private celebration. Her heart pumped faster with anticipation, and her wind-whipped cheeks and nose were tingling with more than the cold.

Lucy Belle wanted her to do what made her happy? How about giving back some of the fun T was sharing with her?

He looked up into the frosty black sky, waiting for the fireworks. Kelsey squatted down.

T counted the chimes out loud. "...ten, eleven, twelve." Splat!

Kelsey nailed him square in the back with the first snowball she'd thrown since...well, hell. It might be the very first snowball she'd ever thrown.

"Oh, yeah?" When he whirled around, retribution

lined the grim set of his expression, but laughter sparkled in his eyes.

"T…" She raised her hands in placating surrender and slowly backed up.

He rolled a snowball in his hands and slowly advanced. "Now don't start something if you don't want me to finish it."

Kelsey's intuition tried to read a double meaning into that succinct statement. But when he cocked his arm, symbolism and deeper interpretations vanished. The game was on. "T!"

Scrambling for cover, Kelsey ducked behind the tree. T's snowball glanced off her arm, leaving a circle of white in the middle of one big, black check. She scooped up another handful of snow and packed it tight, circling around the trunk to keep T on the other side. His hands were behind his back, his coat hanging nonchalantly open, and he was whistling.

"I don't trust you for a minute," she warned.

"You shouldn't." He smiled. "Not in this."

She hurled the snowball. T ducked. And while hers sailed harmlessly past and plopped into a snowbank, he lobbed one behind his back that hit her in the middle of the chest.

"Aagh!" she cried, plucking her sweater away from her breasts as the freezing moisture instantly soaked in. "Cold. Cold."

"All's fair in love and war," he taunted.

"That is such a cliché." She charged down the hill toward him, scooping up an armful of snow and hurling it into the air above his head so that it cascaded down. She laughed as the flakes glistened in his hair and sank beneath his collar. "Take that."

Now he was the one squirming with melting snow against his skin. Kelsey dug into the snowbank beside the patio fence to gather ammunition and pummel him while he regrouped. Though she was laughing so hard, she ended up tossing golf-ball size clumps of snow that did little damage.

When she saw his arm go back, Kelsey ran, trudging up to her knees and pushing with her hands to get back to that tree and shelter. T pursued, tossing a barrage at her backside. One stung her tush.

"Ow!" She grabbed her bottom and spun around. She was breathing hard from laughter and exertion. "Don't throw so hard. I'm a girl."

"You certainly are." Was that a wink?

She backed up, blinking the moisture from her lashes to keep him in view as he advanced. Fireworks brightened the sky overhead, with rockets and whistles and colorful blossoms of falling light. Kelsey dove behind the tree, filling the inside of her coat with snow. But she came up with a handful, packed it tight. And when he tossed his, so did she.

One strikeout-worthy pitch hit T full in the chest.

In a fast-forward clip of images, she saw him startle, jerk his chin back in surprise, laugh another taunt and come down on his right leg. The leg buckled, slid out from under him and suddenly he was tumbling down the slope toward the fence.

"T!" Kelsey's buoyant mood vanished in a heartbeat, to be replaced by breath-catching fear. She scuttled down the hill behind him. "T!"

He thumped to a stop against the fence, and the bank of snow spilled down around his shoulders and chest. "Damn, damn, damn!"

He was hurt!

"T!" Kelsey sank to her knees in the snow and pushed against his chest as he tried to sit up, urging him to lie still while she probed his knee and inspected the rest of him for injury. "Are you okay? We should have been more careful."

"Gotcha."

Just like that, he folded his arms around her and rolled over, snugging her body beneath his in the snow. The cold bed acted as a cocoon now, melting and molding around her body as his long, strong frame covered her from breast to toe. He inhaled deep, steadying breaths that thrust his hard chest against hers as she, too, caught her breath. His eyes glinted wickedly above her. One hand cradled her head, the other made itself at home on the curve of her hip.

Kelsey swatted his chest, knocking loose snow that sprayed her bare face and neck. "I thought you were hurt."

"Easy, easy." She twisted once but froze at the grimace that crinkled his face. "I did jar the knee a bit. With the cold temps, it'll take me a minute or two to work out the kinks."

"Can I help?"

"Believe me, sweetheart, I'm feeling better and better all the time." The pain in his eyes lessened as something hot flared and took hold in its place.

The oddest mix of chill and heat consumed her. There was something about a man's weight—T's weight—pressing into the cradle of her hips that felt intimate, erotic. Right. Her lips burned beneath his hungry gaze and the tips of her breasts tingled with the need to be touched. A honey-sweet pressure gathered between her legs and drizzled its warmth throughout her body.

Should she feel this? Should she want this?

She searched his face for the sincerity and reassurance she needed. And with a resolute sigh, she dared to
offer some of her own in return.

"T." Was that drowsy, wanton sigh her own?

Frosty crystals clung to her cheek, but he brushed
them away. "Happy New Year, Kels."

As he lowered his head, her arms twined around his
neck. "Happy New Year, T."

She parted her lips to welcome his kiss, and moved
against his mouth to claim her own.

His hands moved along her body as his lips and
tongue slid against hers. His cold, wet gloves framed her
face, skimmed a breast and squeezed it through her
sweater. Kelsey moaned at the instant tendrils of desire
flooding to the spot and shifted, begging him to tease
the other with the same white-hot torture. He reached
down to drag up the hem of her sweater and blouse and
dipped his hand inside. Cold leather cupped her through
the silk of her camisole and lace of her bra, wetting the
material against her skin and erasing the initial chill
with his eager exploration.

Her legs parted ever so slightly, inviting his warmth
into the very heart of her. T moaned in his throat and
she trailed her fingertips across the vibrating sound. He
adjusted his hips, grinding against her. Through the layers separating them, the evidence of his response
pressed into her thigh, thrilling her, making her long to
have him even closer.

And all the while they kissed. The sensations she
glimpsed in her mind were as drugging and erotic as the
touches themselves. T had been thinking about her. Like
this. Wanting her in ways that no other man, not even

her fiancé, ever had. It was heady and humbling. Doubts were forgotten. Fears didn't exist. There was only passion, need, this man—and her fledgling trust.

Kelsey knew it wasn't just body heat thawing the snow. It was something more fiery, more potent blooming inside her.

T's lips, following a trickle of melting snow, scudded across her jaw and along her arching neck. Coming up for air, she inhaled the scents of wet wool and body heat. As his lips burned a path against her throat, she skimmed her hands across his shoulders and arms, squeezing the hard biceps and triceps that locked him into place above her. First from laughter, now from passion, Kelsey could barely catch her breath. "Is it too corny to say I see fireworks when you kiss me?"

With a mighty sigh, T lifted his mouth. His eyes looked as hooded and heavy as her own felt. But with a game smile he tilted his head and glanced up at the sparkles of purple and gold bursting against the backdrop of clouds above them. "They really light up the sky, don't they?"

He was so logical, so literal, so sweet. Kelsey palmed the back of his head and pulled his mouth down to hers. She'd never known she had a seductive bone in her body. But she couldn't resist. "What sky?"

T gladly did as the lady bid and kissed her again. He slipped his tongue inside and did the things to her mouth he wanted to do to the rest of her body. Her skin was icy to the touch, but she was pure fire underneath. She was hot, and hot for him, and he was beginning to think his untimely tumble into the snow was actually a very good thing.

Hearing her laughter had eased his guilt over letting

Watkins get to her. Seeing her play had touched his heart. Feeling her body open beneath his, and make demands he was more than willing to meet, practically sent him over the edge.

He'd never laughed like this, let loose like this—he'd certainly never kissed like this—with Ginny. Not even in his most private fantasies. His classic, Scandinavian ideal seemed far removed from this vulnerable, earthy, sexy, heart-on-her-sleeve woman he held in his arms right now. His feelings for Ginny had been a safe, unrealistic dream.

Everything about Kelsey Ryan felt real.

From her intoxicating scent to her lush body and busy mouth.

And he desperately needed something real to hold on to. To accept him, to want him—as he was—battle scarred and bookish, the product of a shame-filled past. A man who'd had to prove himself to his classmates, his colleagues, the world.

Kelsey made him feel as if none of that mattered. That she wanted him as is. As if he didn't have to prove a damn thing except that he wanted her.

But despite the fire pushing his body to the limits of its control, his knee was soaking up the cold and damp. He didn't want to risk the wrong achy body part short-circuiting this intensely personal celebration before it reached its hopeful conclusion.

With a surge of sheer will, T tore his mouth from hers and rolled to the side, letting fresh contact with the snow temper his libido. He sat up and awkwardly lurched to his feet, grabbing Kelsey's hand and pulling her up. He winced his way past the twinge in his knee and tucked her to his side.

"Help me inside."

He took the first limping step and felt her push herself into place beneath his arm and brace a hand at his stomach and back, fully prepared to take his weight.

"You *are* in pain."

Oh, yeah. But what a delicious kind of pain it was.

He hugged her close and kissed her temple. "My knee isn't what's killing me, sweetheart. But somehow, even with all the heat we're generating, I don't think we want to finish this out here. And unless you have any objections, I intend to finish it."

A lovely flush expanded the color of her chapped cheeks. With a graceful nod, she reached up and touched his jaw, angling his face to grant him full view of eyes as open and honest as the delicate fawn they reminded him of. "I have no objections."

T lowered his mouth and thanked her with a kiss. When her hand tightened around his neck and she went up on tiptoe to deepen the kiss, he nearly lost it again.

Suddenly, it was a race against time to get inside. They limped through the snow and across the patio. Once in the kitchen, he pushed her up against the door and stole a kiss as he locked it behind her. Then his hands were on her shoulders, peeling off her coat while she tugged at his.

He took her by the hand and led her through the house, up the stairs to his old room, stripping wet things along the way, snatching kisses and making contact whenever they could. They left their coats in the kitchen, his jacket in the foyer. Buttons were popping and shoes and boots were left behind.

Her blouse followed her sweater at the top of the stairs, and as his palms skidded against raw, warm silk, he sighed in frustration against her mouth. "How many layers do you have on, woman?"

"I'm always cold," was the excuse she offered, but he couldn't tell that she was anything but sizzling to the touch. She pulled her hands from beneath his shirt and reached for the hem of the camisole herself. "But I trust you'll keep me warm?"

If things got any hotter, there was going to be a serious explosion.

"I'll do my best," he promised. He cupped the bounty of her lace-covered breasts as she lifted the camisole off over her head.

She sank back against the wall and groaned in pleasure and he followed, squeezing the feminine mounds and teasing the hard nipples with his thumbs. He buried his face in the valley between and pressed his lips to the soft swelling above each lacy rim. Then her hands came down to frame his head and guide him exactly where he wanted to go.

He closed his mouth over one of the pebbly tips and licked her through the lace. She bucked beneath him and cried out his name. "I don't think I can... We better..."

Dropping his hands to the nip of her waist, he pulled her into the bedroom with him. "I'll hurry if you will."

By the time he'd set his gun and badge safely on the nightstand, grabbed a condom and shed his clothes, Kelsey had already climbed into bed beneath the comforter.

With her gloves on.

T frowned as he slipped in beside her. "What's this?"

He palmed her butt and pulled her against him, relieved to discover the rest of her satiny skin was as naked as the day she was born. And though his body fired in shameless response, he held himself still until she answered.

A skittish look in her eyes had her talking to his chin and kneading her fingers in the center of his chest. "I don't want to spoil this. I don't want to make you uncomfortable if…something happens."

Something fiercely protective and possessively male coursed through him from his heart on out. He nudged her chin up to look into her eyes and gently massaged his thumb across her swollen bottom lip. "I don't want you to ever think you can't touch me. That you have to hold something back because you think I'm going to freak out, or you think you're going to read something you shouldn't. I'll react however I react. Honestly. It won't be a judgment or a condemnation. I might be surprised. I might be curious. I might be turned on." He stilled his thumb against the tender softness. "But give me a chance to react to the real you. Always be yourself. Be real with me. Please."

He took her hands and stilled them against the eager beat of his heart. "May I?"

She nodded.

He tugged at one turquoise fingertip, then another. When he was done, he set her gloves beside his badge and gathered her back into his arms. She clasped her hands in the space between them. T kissed her fingers, then pulled them apart and pressed a kiss to each palm. Her eyes widened in surprise, darted back and forth, searching his face. Then her lids dropped to half mast and he had a feeling that whatever she was reading had something to do with the burning need that was about to bust through his pores.

"Touch me," he whispered, begging for her trust, offering his own.

With the gentlest of sighs, Kelsey lay her hands

against his chest and closed her eyes. T gritted his teeth and savored her timid exploration that grew bolder with each catch of heated breath, each moan of frustrated pleasure.

"Ah, sweetheart." She teased his nipples to attention and his groin danced in response against her hip. "Like that." She slicked her palms along his flanks and his skin tingled with greedy delight. "Yeah," he gasped, loving the confidence he could feel growing with each stroke. "Just like that."

"You want me." It was a silly statement, only slightly less amazing than the fact that she wanted him. She snuggled closer to kiss his neck and her breasts pillowed against his chest, branding him with their lush femininity. "You want me," she repeated.

He rolled her onto her back and nudged her apart with his knee, letting his thighs settle between hers and letting himself dance against her weeping heat. He smiled. She smiled. He slid inside her. "You don't have to be a psychic to know that."

Chapter Ten

Kelsey awoke to the dawning light of the new year, completely naked and deliciously warm.

It might be winter outside, but she felt cocooned in perpetual springtime, snuggled up to the hard wall of T's broad chest.

As her eyes drifted slowly open, she took note of the snow blowing outside the window. Even her drowsy brain could grasp the symbolism of the cold, harsh world outside, lying in wait for her to leave the warmth and security of T's bed.

Blinking aside the troublesome thought, she smiled at the details of the room she hadn't seen last night. T's bedroom was decorated in a gung-ho mix of black and gold and tiger prints, reflecting the spirit of a University of Missouri graduate. Apparently, Moira Banning had preserved her son's room from the last time he'd lived here. Though the detective had a boyish streak running through him, he had definitely matured beyond the collegiate obsession stage.

"Hey. You awake down there?"

T's teasing question made her realize that he sat half-propped up on several pillows stacked behind him against the headboard. "You're up early."

His hand rubbed slow, frictional circles against her bare back. "I got up while you were still sleeping and retrieved our clothes, some breakfast and some reading material."

Reading material? That would explain the glasses he wore. Though she was quite sure they were the only thing he was wearing this morning.

He must have felt the blush coloring her from tip to toe. "I guess wet clothes don't dry when they're left in clumps on the floor." Her blush intensified. He hugged his arm around her shoulders and didn't let her scoot away. "I hung things up since I didn't know what could go into the dryer. So we'll just have to tough it out for a few hours."

"If you insist." Impractical as it was, she didn't mind if he didn't.

Kelsey stretched against him, reliving every tender moment and thrilling release they'd shared the night before. Her body was unused to such strenuous activity— be it snowball fights or making love.

"I do." T dropped a kiss on the tip of her nose. "Happy New Year."

"Haven't we already celebrated?"

"Yeah, we did. Twice."

His green-eyed grin was wicked behind the glasses. Kelsey reached up and let the covers fall away, exposing the top half of her body as she stroked his lips and remembered his kisses. She loved the freedom of touching him, knowing she wasn't going to get zapped with anything unpleasant.

"It'll be three times if you don't stop that." T pulled her hand away and laced their fingers together, holding her against the wiry curls of golden chest hair and the warm skin underneath. "And I'm out of protection."

"Oh?" Kelsey sat up, fully awake, and dragged the comforter up to a more modest position. "Oh. Thanks."

"Try to sound a little disappointed."

"I do. I mean, I am." She combed her fingers through her hair, no doubt leaving a spiky mess in their wake. "I mean, I'm glad you thought of that. I sort of got carried away and forgot to even consider—"

"That's me. Always thinking." He grinned.

"But it's sexy when you do it."

"You don't think the glasses and the reading make me more nerdy than sexy?"

Kelsey turned herself to sit beside him, clutching the covers up over her breasts with both hands now. "T, I think Atticus Finch is sexy. You've got all his qualities, plus a little Dirty Harry mixed in. So you're downright hot."

Now it was his turn to blush.

Marveling at the confidence and security she felt around this man, Kelsey reached across and picked up one of the doughnuts he'd brought upstairs to nibble on. She took a bite and savored the sweet flavors of glaze and cake. "What are you reading?"

"Your notes. We need to talk."

The bite in her mouth turned bitter. She swallowed it past the self-conscious lump in her throat, her appetite instantly erased. "You shouldn't be reading that. It's private."

"It was sitting out beside your purse downstairs. You've seen all this?" A succinct tinge of investigative questioning colored the awed concern in his voice.

Kelsey felt a chill shimmy down her spine as she tried to withdraw to that sheltered place inside her. "They're the pertinent details of my impressions from Jezebel and Delilah."

T thumbed through several pages. "There are a lot of pertinent details here. I've read official police reports that weren't this thorough."

She put the unfinished doughnut back on the plate and reached for the notepad. "Thanks. I'll be sure to compliment my composition professor."

But the sarcasm didn't put him off any more than her outstretched hand.

"Explain this." He turned to the third page and pointed to the phrase she'd written over and over.

She clutched the covers in tight fists now and curled her knees up to her chest. She'd moved farther away from T and the winter was working its way into her bones now. "They're the words I heard, both times, with Jezebel and Delilah's murders." Somehow, while she slept, she'd lost a lover and regained a homicide detective. "I spelled them phonetically, then tried different variations to see if anything made sense."

"This one." He pointed to one version halfway down the page. "It's Latin."

"Let me guess, smarty-pants. You aced Latin class."

She made the effort to distract him from the topic, but he didn't bite. "All four years of high school." He read the words out loud. "The closest I can make out is *matrona*. That's 'wife.' Then *abi in malam rem*."

Kelsey shivered at the eerie accuracy of his pronunciation. She turned her head to face him. "That's it. He said that over and over while he was strangling them. Like a ceremonial chant." Her fingers slid to her throat, reliving the awful memory of silk drawing tight around her neck. "What does it mean?"

"Go to the devil."

"He's telling his *wife* to go to hell?" Kelsey sank

back into the pillows and huddled beneath the covers. Any lingering sense of warmth had fully dissipated. "And I thought I'd been verbally abused."

T squeezed her knee through the covers. "From what you told me about your ex, you were." He held up the notepad. "Ed Watkins might have been on to something. This crazy SOB thinks he's killing his wife."

"Every year for the holidays. What a lovely family tradition."

T slipped out of bed and picked up his slacks and boxer briefs. "I need you to do another reading for me today."

A reading? He was actually recruiting her help? It hadn't been that many days ago he'd been a skeptic. "I thought you needed facts to send a man to prison, not my hocus-pocus."

If he caught the derogatory quote from Ed Watkins, he didn't comment. He had his phone out now, checking messages. "Josh. A. J. Captain Taylor. Ginny. That's a lot of people working on a holiday." He turned on the phone and dropped it back into his pocket. He wasn't even looking at her. "The pieces are all there—I can feel it. But I need a name or a face from you to make them all fall into place."

His bold nudity in the bracing morning air gave her a clear view of his trim, muscular figure—reminding her clearly of the intimacy they'd shared last night. It also gave her a glimpse of the scars from bullet holes and surgeries that sliced across his knee and chest—broadcasting in graphic detail that he was a cop on a case. A man on a mission who needed her grim expertise more than he needed her.

She turned away instead of watching him dress and

latched on to her grandmother's pendant. "I don't remember any names. And I couldn't see any faces."

When she felt his weight on the side of the bed, she
knew he wasn't going to let her walk away from the
nightmares. He reached for her hand, but Kelsey tugged
it away, not ready to process any images beyond her own
turbulent, self-doubting thoughts. But those probing
green eyes demanded her attention, so she turned to
face him.

"At the university psych lab, you told me that if you
dropped your internal guards—if you really concentrated—you could see more, you could read deeper into
an object or a person." He eyed the silver chain around
her neck. "You said the crystal could help you focus
your perception."

She shook her head, hating this. "I've already felt
what the victims suffered through. I don't really want
to see inside the killer's mind."

"You don't have to go that far." He closed his hand
around her fist and the pendant inside. Kelsey tried to
ignore the image of a dead woman's beaten body, lying
in a pile of garbage bags. A life thrown away as if it was
so much trash. But that was what T had seen, that was
the life he was trying to find justice for. "I want you to
hold that doll again. The newspaper wrapped around it
puts it at the time of Jezebel's murder. And Ginny has
a list of owners for me."

Ginny, huh? She could bet Ginny dealt in facts and fig-
ures. The stab of jealousy she felt toward that pretty, normal woman he thought so highly of embarrassed her.
Lucy Belle would have been embarrassed, too. But Lucy
Belle was gone, and Kelsey had to deal with life and loneliness all on her own. "I already told you what I know."

"Not according to your notes. I had no idea of the complexity of your impressions. The subtle nuances of observation that a good crime-scene investigator would envy."

"You didn't want to listen to the subtle nuances."

"I'm listening now. If you can match a name or recognize a face on that list, I can open records, get warrants, find those facts that I need." He slipped his fingers inside hers and touched the pendant, intensifying the images of death he dealt with. "Your grandmother's spirit will be with you. I'll be with you. Will you do it?"

Tears burned in her eyes at the violence he'd seen—at the violence she saw through him.

But Kelsey blinked before they could fall and climbed out of bed, taking a pillow with her to keep herself modestly covered as she searched for her underwear. "That was some pretty heady persuasion you used last night. You know, you could have just asked me. I would have helped. I want to solve this case and get on with my life as much as you do."

She plucked up her bra, panties and camisole and headed down the hall toward the bathroom.

"What?" He snatched her by the wrist and hauled her around to face him. "What happened between us last night had nothing to do with this case."

That defensive sarcasm burned in her brain and leaked out her pores. "Cheering me up? Keeping me company? Clearing my head so I could finish the job for you today?"

"That's not fair. There were two of us in that bed last night." His eyes searched her face, looking for an explanation.

"Yeah, well one of us apparently had a hidden agenda."

He released her, stepped back and splayed his fingers at the waist of his navy slacks. "And one of us is scared we're moving too fast or we went too far. I know I over-stepped the boundaries of a partner relationship last night. I know that can make it a hell of a lot trickier to work together in the cold light of day. But I didn't step over that line all by myself, sweetie."

"No, you didn't." The tension eased beside his eyes as she admitted that much. "But you have to under-stand, I've only had one relationship with a man before in my life, T. One. And Jeb Adams wasn't a real smart choice for me. With men, I'm discovering it's always about my talent. They either abhor it, like Jeb. Or they make fun of it, like Randy at the psych lab. Or—"

"—they use it. Like me." Long moments of silence passed before he continued. "I wasn't thinking about the case when I made love to you last night. Not once. And the only time I worried about your talent was when you were holding back. I didn't want you to be afraid of me. Of us. But there is no us, is there?" A deep sigh set his stern, rueful expression into place. "I don't know how to prove myself to you. And just so *you'll* understand— I'm tired of having to prove myself to every damn per-son in my life." He shook his head. "With you, I didn't think I had to."

At that moment, T looked ancient. Older and tougher and harder than a man twice his age.

Okay. So she'd succeeded in inflicting as much pain and mistrust as she'd been feeling herself. Not her goal. But he didn't look as if an *I'm sorry* would make any difference right now.

Kelsey held on to her pillow as if it were a life pre-server. "Look. I'll do the reading. You can set up the sideshow and let anyone watch who wants to come." She slowly backed toward the bathroom, sticking to business since, with her insecurities, she'd royally screwed up anything personal between them. "But I have to go home first. Frosty's a good dog, but he's been in the house by himself all night. I need to check on him, get myself some warm, dry clothes, and then I'll meet you back at the precinct office."

He'd already pulled his phone from his pocket and opened it. "I'll drive you home."

"You obviously have phone calls to make, things to take care of. I've got your twenty dollars. I'll call a cab."

"But that money was for…" They locked stares, hers aching, his hard. "I will drive you home."

FREAK.

"Oh, my God."

T's response was decidedly more choice when he saw the bright red paint splattered across the snow in front of Kelsey's house.

He'd spotted the black-and-white police cruiser, cars and a van, along with A. J. Rodriguez's familiar black Trans Am, in front of her house the second he'd turned the corner. Suspicions flared. His hackles had kinked up. They'd gotten to somebody with all the questions they'd been asking.

What he didn't like was somebody getting to Kelsey.

Even if she had been safely tucked in at his mother's house last night, that somebody knew where she lived.

And that somebody knew her talent.

He parked his Jeep a house away, taking note of the neighbors standing at their windows, the open front door—the death grip Kelsey had on the dashboard and armrest.

The instant the Jeep stopped, she shot out her door and ran across her yard. "Frosty? Frosty!"

"Kels!" T killed the engine and hurried after her. "It's a crime scene. Don't—"

"Ma'am, you'll have to wait here." A. J. had slipped out of his car and wrapped a solid arm around her waist, stopping her. Josh Taylor was there to back him up in case she squirmed free.

She yanked at A. J.'s leather jacket. "My dog. Where is he? Is he hurt?"

Forgetting their argument and the raw gulf of past history and current fears looming between them, T wrapped his hands around Kelsey's shoulders to still her shaking. "Frosty's her pet and companion," he explained to A. J., whose golden eyes apologized for procedure taking precedence over compassion at the moment. "Do you know if he's still in the house?"

Lights flashed in their eyes, momentarily blinding T. The questions started even before the brunette woman came into focus. "Detective Banning, does this vandalism attack mean you're making progress on the prostitute Delilah's murder? Has anyone else on the investigative team been targeted? Do you have any facts to report, or is it all psychic conjecture at—"

"Not now, Ms. Page," T growled. He hugged his arm around Kelsey's shoulders and sandwiched her between himself and A. J., who'd also turned to block the next camera shot. "Somebody get rid of her."

"My pleasure." Josh Taylor stepped in. "Ms. Page. Rebecca, is it?" Using a lethal mix of charm and brawn, he moved the reporter back to the street, allowing Kelsey a chance to cope with the violation of her home. "It's my understanding you've written a whole series of…"

"T." Kelsey tugged at his coat. "What if somebody hurt him? He'd try to guard the place if somebody broke in. I've heard about burglars just shooting a dog who gives them trouble or makes too much noise."

"There were no reports of gunshots, ma'am," A. J. reassured her.

The fear T read in her eyes nearly made him forgo procedure himself to ease her concern. He hugged her tight against his chest, wishing she'd take more than comfort from him. "C'mon. He's built like a little bear. I'm sure he's fine."

Her fingers clutched the back of his coat. This was killing her, not knowing the fate of her pet. "Oh, God, T, this is my fault. If anything's happened to him…"

He rocked her back and forth, feeling the restless urge to take action jolting through his own legs. He looked over the top of her head. "How much longer, A. J.?"

"The crime scene team's been in there an hour now. One of the neighbors called in the spray-painted snow. Must have been done last night before the new snow started to cover it up. Apparently, the intruder entered through a back window. He trashed up the house pretty good, came out the front. Doesn't look like anything was taken."

Kelsey pulled away and turned to A. J. "Why?" She hugged her arms around her waist and reached inside her coat, no doubt to find the pendant to hold on to. "This is like something my ex would do, serving no point but to torment me. When can I go in?"

A. J.'s gaze bypassed Kelsey to meet T's. "We figured this was related to the hooker murders. She's got an ex who could be responsible?"

She answered before T could even speculate. "No. Jeb's too lazy to leave his hometown to cause this much trouble here. He's a big fish in a small pond back there. That was one of the attractions of moving to the city. It wouldn't be as easy to single me out for being different."

Her voice trailed off before she finished. She knew what they all did. She'd already been singled out. Neither the big city nor T. Merle Banning had kept her out of the spotlight.

"Rodriguez?" A man and a woman, wearing fluorescent orange vests identifying them as the crime scene team, walked out the front door. "We're clear."

"Now?" Kelsey prodded.

"Go on. I'll—" she took off before T could promise any support "—be right behind you."

A firm hand on his arm stopped T from following her. "At least now I understand why your phone was off the hook." A. J.'s expression refused to reveal whether that was a teasing congratulations or a reprimand. "You should have checked your messages. I agree that it's not likely an ex-boyfriend or husband did this. Did you see this morning's paper?"

T's entire world had been Kelsey Ryan for the past twelve hours. Building to something great, then crashing to pieces when she second-guessed his motives. He hadn't seen anything beyond that. He followed A. J. to the Trans Am and brushed off the light dusting of snow on the roof to spread open the paper A. J. pulled from the front seat.

It wasn't a very big article, and it was buried in the middle of the newspaper. But the two pictures and the headlines were very clear. One was a stock photo of Kelsey from the paper's archives. Her hair was longer and a nondescript mousy color. But the soft, intelligent eyes were the same. The second picture showed the current version of Kelsey—spiked red hair and wild coat—walking Frosty along this very street.

Psychic Unravels Connection In Decade-Old Murder Case.

"Son of a bitch." He crumpled the paper in his fist and sought out the skinny brunette with dangerous ideas about breaking a big story. "Why don't they just paint a target on Kelsey's back? I'm going to strangle Rebecca Page."

"No, you're not, my friend. Josh'll sweet-talk her into killing the story and pics for a few days. Right now, you need to go be with Kelsey. Figure this one out for us, Banning. And we'll all rest easier tonight." Even with a case like this one that stumped the department, T had never heard A. J. lose his cool. That calm sense of duty and responsibility grounded him now. "Go. We'll give you whatever backup you need. Whenever you need it." A. J. shared a hint of a smile. "So keep your phone turned on."

T nodded, a bit stunned to hear the confidence that a veteran like Detective Rodriguez had in him. Along with that crazy line about being a mixture of Atticus Finch and Dirty Harry that Kelsey had fed him in bed that morning, A. J.'s plain words might have finally put to rest any lingering qualms T had about his computer geek reputation at the precinct.

He was more than the son of a criminal who'd taken the coward's way out. He was a friend, an equal. A good cop.

Maybe he had nothing left to prove, after all.

Not to anyone but Kelsey. And while it bruised his ego and humbled his heart to think she didn't believe the depth of all he felt for her, he understood. He hadn't given her a real warm welcome when they'd first met. She'd been through hells vastly different, but no less painful than his own. Unflinching faith in another human being wasn't an easy commodity for a woman like her to buy. But he could be patient. He could be persistent.

It was how he'd achieved everything else that mattered in his life.

He jogged up the driveway to Kelsey's front door. He was going to solve the damn case, and then he was going to burrow away someplace private with Kelsey and do whatever it took to convince her that they were meant to be partners in the most loving, trusting way imaginable.

"Kels? Did you find him?" Half of him hoped that she hadn't, in case the pooch had met with a gruesome end defending his territory.

"In here." Following the sounds of scuffling and scratching, T picked his way across her living room to her bedroom.

T cursed the pointless wreck the intruder or intruders had made. The television and CD systems sat untouched, but the sofa cushions had been shredded along with two of her antique quilts. Almost every book had been pulled off its shelf. And the dolls that she'd placed so neatly around in cubbyholes and a display case had been tossed into a heap in the middle of the floor.

"There you go, ma'am." T recognized the man's voice. A member of the CSI team was still here.

"Come here, baby. Come here." Kelsey's joyful cry

quickened his steps. He entered the room just in time to see a silver ball of fur launch itself into Kelsey's arms and tumble them both onto the bed. "Frosty! Good boy, good boy. Mama loves you."

Judging by the furious wag of the poodle's tail, he hadn't been too traumatized. "That's terrific news, Kels. I told you he was a little bear."

He took in a quick view of the scene, including a wooden camp box, the tumble of furniture and debris that had been barricaded in front of the closet door, and the tall blond man standing in the middle of it all.

"Mac." T shook hands with his best friend, Mac Taylor. "Looks like you saved the day."

"Banning." Mac centered his glasses on the bridge of his nose. "I was actually packing up when Ms. Ryan came in. We'd cleared the closet but hadn't looked inside the camp box. She thought of that." T looked over to see the hugging and petting and happy licking that had completely changed Kelsey's mood. "Fortunately, she'd drilled some holes in the box or he'd have suffocated. He was still pretty drowsy when we opened it up. He'd been muzzled with this."

Mac handed him a clear plastic evidence bag. Inside was a long, thin silk scarf, similar in design but newer than the one Kelsey had found in the mission's giveaway box. Attached to it was a typed note that must have been tied to Frosty's neck, a macabre gift if the intruder hadn't planned for the dog to survive. *Next time it'll be you.*

T checked his curse and whispered. "Did she see this?"

Mac nodded. "But I don't think it registered. She was too caught up in the dog's welfare."

"Mr. Taylor?" T and Mac both turned at the concern

in her voice. "There's blood on Frosty's leg. But I don't see anyplace where he's been hurt."

"Let's check it out." Mac grabbed a pair of scissors and a bag and knelt in front of the dog in Kelsey's lap to inspect the splotch of red matting Frosty's fur. "I think you got a chunk of your attacker, boy." He trimmed the fur and dropped it into the bag to label it. He stood and turned to T. "That's DNA evidence I can match if you bring me the perp."

T nodded. "It's also a wound we can look for to identify our man."

"Good boy, Frosty." Kelsey hugged the poodle again. "We'll get that bad guy."

Was that renewed determination he heard in her voice?

Mac dropped the bags into his kit and closed it. "Ms. Ryan. Banning." He shook hands and let the conversation take a friendlier turn. "Sorry to run into you this way. But Happy New Year. Jules swears she's going to name the baby after you when he comes in March."

"I appreciate the honor, but don't torture the kid like that."

"Thomas," Kelsey interrupted. Then she hesitated, as if realizing she'd revealed a deep, dark secret. "Call him Thomas. Not Merle. Sorry."

But Mac could be trusted with the truth about his name. "Tom Taylor. I like it. My wife will love it. Take care, buddy."

"You, too."

After Mac left, T debated the urge to sit down next to Kelsey. That's when he realized she'd taken off her gloves to stroke the dog's soft, curly fur.

"He's the friend you saved," she announced before he could ask. "The man you took two bullets for."

"I wondered if you'd sense that."

"He thinks of you like a brother."

"It's mutual. The Taylors have been good to me. I've learned a lot about being a cop…about being a man from them." He pulled back the front of his coat and splayed his hands at his hips. "When you're an only child, it's good to have somebody you can look up to."

Kelsey understood. "Yes, it is. I had Lucy Belle."

"Maybe you and I are luckier than we thought we were."

She hugged the dog and he wished it was him. Pitiful. This longing. This desperate need to reconnect with her, to heal wounds and distrusts that, too late, he realized went as deep as his own. But he had to get the investigation out of the way first. Or she'd question his motives.

"Find something warm and dry to change into," he ordered, hating to bully her about this. "I'll have Josh and A. J. secure the house. We need to get to the station and find out what that doll can tell us."

Kelsey nodded and stood. "I can take Frosty with me to the precinct offices, can't I?"

"Sure." He'd clear it with Captain Taylor later.

Right now, he didn't think *he* was the security she'd want to put her arms around to help her look into the eyes of a murderer.

Chapter Eleven

The clean, bright walls of the Fourth Precinct's interrogation room faded into a place much darker, more sinister—and all too familiar.

"I beg you. Please. Don't."

She backed away as far as she could go, giving a soft, startled yelp when she hit the hard, dark wall. Trapped.

Kelsey stroked the doll's silky hair, touched its face, cradled it between her hands and hugged it to her shoulder. She laid her cheek against its soft body and focused through the pale blue light, seeking out the images in her mind.

"Most men bring cash. I didn't understand. I'm surprised, that's all. It doesn't mean I don't like it. I can learn to appreciate it."

He'd given her the doll as a gift. A fine prize for a real lady. She'd laughed and asked if it was some kind of fetish for him.

He caressed her face. She jerked her head to the side, hating his touch.

"Oh, God." A fist constricted around her lungs and Kelsey cried out. Now she understood why the impression of Jezebel's murder had been so clear. Why Ed Watkins had insisted that Jezebel could talk to her and explain her death.

Hating his touch.

Hypocrite! He'd taken an oath to help those in need. It was his job to be kind. But there were strings attached. Unknown dangers awaited anyone who accepted his help.

He wanted to clean her. Fix her. Heal her.

"Oh, God, no."

"Kels." She heard her name through the distance, muffled by the clouds and snow and bone-deep chill that shivered through her body.

But she forced herself to stay with Jezebel. To see everything that Jezebel saw. To feel everything she felt. To fear everything she feared.

He reached into his pocket and pulled out a scarf. It was long and narrow, tattered as if it had come from an old woman's attic or a flea market. Its mustard-yellow trim and fuschia dots were the only colors that registered in the darkness.

Kelsey snatched at her pendant, trying to hold on to the blue light that made everything so clear.

Rotted wood. The slats of an unfinished wall.

Slanted ceiling. The room was long and narrow and sparsely furnished. A white metal cot, more like a hospital bed than a place to earn her keep.

Yellow scarf with fuschia dots, so tight around her throat. She was dying. She couldn't breathe. She was so cold.

"Kelsey!"

"No."

She forced her mind back to Jezebel, settled inside her body. Looked through her eyes.

As the oxygen left her body, the horrific images finally began to fade. The hate. The rage.

She was the one who'd been betrayed. First by her husband, and now by this man she'd trusted.

Blackness crept in. Her knees buckled. Her hair tangled in the wood's coarse texture and ripped from her scalp.

Help me.

She was calling to Kelsey. Calling across time. Calling from one cursed mind to another.

"Open your eyes, Jezebel. Tell me your name."

"I'm Mary."

"Open your eyes!"

Fear dragged her down into its frigid grasp. Her screams gurgled in her throat.

Like raising ironclad doors, Jezebel opened her eyes. But everything was fading to black and white. Her eyes slammed shut.

No more pain.

Kelsey slumped in her chair. She let her arm fall to her side and the doll tumble to the floor.

"Kelsey! Kels, are you all right?"

She heard a bark.

She was cold as the dead. But a warm cloak wrapped around her shoulders and she was pulled up tight against a hard wall of pure heat. Rough hands rubbed urgent circles along her back and arms and her nose was buried against the clean, tangible scents of cotton and damp wool.

She recognized those scents, recognized the heat. She opened her eyes, rooting herself in the familiar chairs and walls of the tiny precinct room. "T?"

"I'm here." His voice drizzled against her ear. Real. Live. Now. "I'm right here. I'm so sorry you had to do that. I'm so—"

Kelsey pushed back against his arms enough to press two fingers to his mouth. His green eyes blazed with emotions she was too weak to identify. But his coat was warm and snug around her, his body a solid anchor to cling to.

"Let me talk," she whispered. "Before the headache gets worse and I have to lie down."

"I'm listening."

She talked to the familiar green eyes that never looked away. "I saw the place where it happened. I saw the room. The walls were open slats, without any drywall or paneling. The ceiling sloped down at an angle."

"An attic."

She nodded. "I think it's the top floor of the mission. It's a place to start, at any rate."

"What else?"

She invited Frosty up into her lap and ran her fingers through his soft, warm fur. T kept rubbing circles; she kept talking. "If you find the room, you'll find strands of Mary's hair stuck in the wood. That's Jezebel's real name. If DNA lasts eleven years, that's a fact that'll place her at the scene of the crime."

"And his face?"

She curled her fingers into the lapel of T's jacket. "She wouldn't let me see. But it was someone she thought was there to help her. A doctor, a cop, a boyfriend."

"Her husband?"

"No. She said she'd been betrayed by her husband *and* this man."

"You're doing great, Kels. Anything else you can tell us?"

Us? When had her audience expanded?

Frosty stood in her lap, propping his feet on the table

and making the same curious survey of the people sitting around the meeting table as she did. A. J., T's detective friend with the unusual eyes and soft accent. Josh, without a smile for the first time since she'd known him. She'd known they'd be present. But there was also Mitch Taylor, the precinct captain. Another big, dark-haired man who was almost his twin sat beside him. Then a petite, pregnant blonde in a wheelchair.

Kelsey had seen her a number of times through T's psychic residue. Ginny Rafferty-Taylor. The big brute must be her husband, the man who'd won Ginny's love and sealed off T's heart.

"Ho, boy." She breathed the phrase without realizing she'd said it out loud. She *was* a sideshow.

"These are all cops, helping with the investigation," he explained in his succinct, logical way. "Except for Brett there."

Ginny squeezed her husband's hand and spoke gently, as to a child. "He wouldn't let me out of the house without him. Not in my condition. Thank you for letting us share in your gift. We hope we haven't made you too uncomfortable. But we wanted to give you and Merle every bit of help we can."

Ginny was nice? That would put a crimp in the hating-her department.

T went on. "We all need to be on the same page with this, so we can close in on this guy."

Instinctively, Kelsey groped at the front of her sweater, searching for her pendant. T's fingers were already there.

He pressed the crystal into her hand and folded his fingers around hers. She wearily braced herself for the images to start—Ginny at the altar, him being shot. But she saw none of that, only sadness and—oh, geez—rolling on top of her in the snow.

Her memories must be getting mixed up with his. She was well beyond tired. Kelsey pushed away from T's comforting touch. "The doll was a gift. Something pricey and nice that her killer thought a real lady would appreciate. He was trying to help her turn her life around."

"Like Ed Watkins."

"Maybe. But I couldn't say it was him." Adrenaline seeped into her system and tried to revitalize her. A subconscious image tried show itself. "Black and white," she whispered

"Black and white?" T questioned.

She tried to focus. It hadn't been just a fading image. Mary's last thoughts were of colors—or the absence thereof. Black. White. But Kelsey was so tired. Her mind was shutting down and she just couldn't make a connection. Her thoughts scattered, surrendering to the fatigue. "I never saw the killer's face."

An intense pain pierced her brain like a hot knife. She buried her face in her hands and groaned. Frosty's warm tongue licked at her wrist and T gathered her up against his chest. "I can't do this anymore," she whispered. "I have to rest."

"It's okay, sweetheart. It's okay. You did great." T helped her up out of the chair, picking up Frosty's leash and guiding them both out the door. "There are some cots in the locker room. You can rest there while we sort out everything we know."

"I know why Sergeant Watkins said Jezebel would talk to me." She stopped moving in an effort to get T to listen. He caught her when she stumbled, held her up when her feet refused to work. "She was a psychic, too."

"What?"

"That's why her impression was so strong. Even after all these years. That's why her husband threw her out." She latched on to his jacket, reliving Jezebel's shame. "He called her a freak. Like that word in the snow. Like m—"

"Dammit, Kelsey, don't even say it."

T palmed the back of her head and pulled her close to his chest. He was so strong in his defense of her, so angry on her behalf. Maybe she'd been wrong to doubt him. Wrong to think he saw her as a tool instead of a person. Wrong to think she was a substitute for the woman he couldn't have.

"I have to help her, T. That could have been me." Her words sounded drowsy, even to her own ears. She pushed at his chest, but she didn't feel any budging. "I have to help her."

"You have already."

"But—"

"No buts."

"I can do more." She tapped at her temples. "There's more here. I just need a little time to recover."

"No." The word was kind but firm. She wasn't going to win this argument. "You need to rest. We'll handle it from here."

Her led her and the dog inside the locker room to an even smaller room with a pair of bunk beds along each wall. She was embarrassed by how weak and vulnerable she felt. Even though it didn't take much urging for her to lie down and let T remove his coat and cover her with a blanket, her tongue still worked.

"Okay," she agreed, her eyes drifting shut. T set Frosty on the lower bunk with her, and she rolled onto her side and curled the dog into her arms. "But just for a few minutes. Then I'll be back. I want you to tell me everything you figure out. Everything, T…" She yawned. "I have to help those women myself. I need to so I…get them out…my head."

As her voice trailed off into slumber, she heard his answer. "I'll fill you in on everything, I promise. Your bag's on the floor beside you. Rest for a bit, then freshen up and come back in when you're ready."

As she drifted into deeper sleep, Kelsey was aware of two things: T's gentle kiss at her temple, and the fact she'd left her turquoise gloves back in the room with the doll.

T UNBUTTONED HIS COLLAR and leaned back in the chair at the end of the conference table. He studied the charts he'd drawn on the dry-erase board and the pictures and reports on the table, willing his logical mind to click it all into place.

The Taylors and A. J. had taken off a few minutes ago, but he'd wanted to stay behind to take care of Kelsey. Beyond the skeleton crew manning the office and the redhead sleeping away in the staff locker room, T was alone with his thoughts. He replayed snippets of the brainstorming session in his head.

"Does Siegel have an alibi for the time of Jezebel's death?" Captain Taylor had asked.

Ginny answered. "He says he was attending Christmas morning service at the mission with Reverend Wingate."

"Can he verify that? Is there a way to track which guests were there at the service eleven years ago?" The captain had been playing devil's advocate, making sure every piece was in place before they ran with this theory. "If we could find any of them, would they speak out against the doctor who provides them with the only health care they ever see?"

"Reverend Wingate would be a reliable source." Ginny thumbed through the original case file. "Sergeant Watkins's report says Siegel's the one he talked to to vouch for the reverend's whereabouts that morning." She glanced up at T. "It's entirely possible he said that to establish his own alibi."

"Nobody followed up?" T asked.

"Siegel wasn't a suspect then."

He was at the top of T's list now.

A woman would trust a doctor, expect him to help her.

Kelsey's impression of Delilah's murder was that it had taken place in Siegel's clinic.

Siegel had been at the mission when every one of the victims had checked in.

The doctor would know Latin. *Matrona. Abi in malam rem.*

Records showed that he'd turned to the bottle twelve years ago, shortly after his divorce. Was it grief or guilt that kept him in that alcohol-fogged state?

Ginny's investigation into the doll's history revealed that an *M. Siegel* had pawned the doll at The Underground shortly after the holidays a year ago. Probably for booze. Possibly to fund his clinic. Perhaps to finally rid himself of the rejected gift.

"It's too much." The clues were too pat, too convenient. After eleven years of searching for the truth, this was too easy.

He scratched behind the ears of the poodle camped beside him. His fingers stilled as he looked down into those dark, round eyes. There was one piece of irrefutable proof that would convince him Siegel was his man.

A dog bite.

"Who'd you sink your teeth into, buddy?" he asked.

Of course, the dog didn't answer. But he did turn his head, reminding T that nearly an hour had passed since tucking in Kelsey, and she still hadn't awakened from her nap.

"Think we better check on her?"

Frosty responded as if he understood the words, hopping to his feet and trotting out of the conference room. T grinned and followed the little dog, who wound through the maze of desks as if he was some big police dog who owned the place.

That unquestioning devotion to his mistress sparked an answering chord inside him. Kelsey had had so little reason to trust people's motives throughout her life. Maybe he shouldn't be so surprised—or hurt—that she'd doubted his motives for getting closer to her.

She'd sensed his feelings for Ginny, his reluctance to give his heart to a woman who was anything less than his ideal. Though he'd opened his mind over the past few days, his skepticism of her talents had been obvious when they'd first met. Why had he expected her to accept him and love him and trust him, when he hadn't been completely willing to do the same for her?

It was a guilty admission that burdened his heart and quickened his steps. Proving himself took on a whole different meaning when it came to Kelsey. This wasn't about pride or respect, this was about love.

And if she'd give him the chance to prove the depth of everything she'd awakened in his heart, everything she'd healed in his soul, everything she'd added to his life—he was going to take it.

He'd protect her. Listen to her. Love her. Make love to her... "Kels?"

T pushed open the door to the bunk room. The tapping of Frosty's claws against the tile floor made the only sound in the empty room.

"Kelsey?"

Good feelings, hopes, resolutions—all plummeted through his system, leaving dread in their wake. Alarm buzzed along every nerve, putting him instantly on hyperalert. She didn't. She wouldn't. "Oh, no, sweetheart. No, no."

He picked up the dog, backed out of the room and hurried to the front desk. T didn't for one minute think she'd ducked out to go to the ladies' room. She'd taken her coat and her purse.

But she hadn't come back to see him or pick up her gloves.

She'd snuck out. Despite his reassurance that she'd done more than enough to help those murdered women, she'd snuck out to handle some damn dumb thing all on her own. Putting herself at risk. Putting his heart at risk.

"Maggie." He set Frosty on top of the sergeant's desk and grabbed his coat from the coatrack.

"Hey, poochie." The tall blond Amazon cooed and cuddled the silver dog. "Whatcha doin—?"

"Have you seen Ms. Ryan?" He didn't give Maggie time to get acquainted or answer his question. "Did you see her leave? Did she say where she was headed?"

Maggie nodded. "She got on the elevator about half an hour ago. She said she had an errand to run. You and the captain were still in your meeting." She reached for something beneath the desk. "Here. She said to give you this when you were done."

T snatched the folded note from Maggie's hand and opened it. "Hell." He crammed the paper into his pocket. "Can you dog-sit for a while?"

"I—"

"—I owe you one."

"Sure."

He was already at the elevator. T didn't waste much time speculating where Kelsey might have gone.

Though their approaches to solving a case were decidedly different, her determination to uncover the murderer's identity was as strong as his. Maybe even more so, since she'd been inside the victims' heads and had been victimized herself.

T entered the parking garage and ran to his Jeep. He could call the cab companies or check the city bus routes to see if anyone had picked up a sexy redhead with rock-star hair. But he knew where she was going already.

T—If you want my help on this case, you have to let me do what I do best. Sgt. Watkins was right. Jezebel is telling me what happened. But I need to find something else that belonged to her, something else she touched. As a cop, you'd need a search warrant for what I intend to do. I'm not a cop. I'll call as soon as I know anything. K

Once behind the wheel of his Jeep, he started the engine and jerked it into gear. The wheels spun for a moment as he gunned it up the ramp out of the parking garage.

And turned toward the Wingate Mission.

THE FIRST THING she noticed was the smell.

Damp and rotting. Like winter and death.

Kelsey swallowed hard, curling her toes inside her boots to keep from running back down the stairs to the bustle and crowd of the dining room.

Reverend Wingate had been delighted to see her. Volunteers were in short supply on the holiday. He'd given her a big hug, pointed her toward the kitchen, then gone back to greeting and blessing his guests off the street. Lines in the hallway led to bed check-in's, Doc Siegel's office and the dining room. Everyone—staff and guest alike—was busily occupied, giving her the opportunity she needed to slip up the stairs unseen.

Kelsey pulled the flashlight from her bag and squinted into the dusty air of the mission's attic. The air was almost as cold up here as it was outside, thanks to the unfinished walls and crumbling insulation. Without her coat or gloves to warm her, she hugged her arms around her waist to ward off the shivers that had as much to do with atmosphere as they did temperature.

"Ho, boy." She twisted her fingers around Lucy Belle's pendant and walked over the threshold. "Let's do this."

T needed facts. She intended to find a few, then get the hell out of this creepy place.

The floorboards creaked beneath her footsteps and she paused and held her breath, wondering if anyone could hear her. She was three stories up, with the empty residence floor between her and the people down below. She trained her ear to the distant mumble of voices, and finally decided that if she could barely detect the sounds of over a hundred people, then none of them could hear one lone woman sneaking around in the attic.

Kelsey breathed in, trying to calm herself, but the moldy scents in the air tickled her nose. She covered her mouth to stifle a sound that was half sneeze, half startled yelp as she stumbled into a small, white wooden stool.

"Calm down, girl." She looked around, verifying that she was alone with her imagination and the rotten air. "Might as well start now."

With one last anxious glance over her shoulder toward the empty doorway and dark hall beyond, she reached down and flattened her palm against the stool's flat top. The painted wood was clammy to the touch, and sticky with dust and age. But, using the warmth of her grandmother's crystal to center her, she sorted through the images attached to the stool.

A man sitting. Nothing helpful there.

Kelsey tilted the beam to the sloping ceiling and traced it all the way down to the far wall. Her light was too dim to make out the bulky shapes in the distance. She wished she could turn on the light switch, but with two windows and no curtains, she didn't dare, for fear someone outside would see and either phone the police or warn the mission staff they had an intruder.

With no choice but to feel her way through the dim, damp air, Kelsey slowly moved forward. At the far end, she stopped, feeling a chill so cold it felt as if an unseen hand had dropped an ice cube down her back. Instinctively, she reached for the pendant and clung tightly to the warmth of her grandmother's spirit.

"You're here, Mary," she whispered. "I can feel you. Talk to me."

She inched closer, shining the light so that the bulky objects took shape. This far corner was designed like a little bedroom—with a chipped, white dresser and row of empty hooks lining one wall. A tattered throw rug covered a small section of floor beside a bed. A bed she'd seen before in her mind. A white metal hospital cot, just like the one down in Doc Siegel's office. But this one had a bare ticking mattress.

Solid walls and a coat of paint might have turned the furniture into a cozy alcove. But in this sparse, unadorned condition, it bore closer resemblance to a prison cell.

Kelsey walked over and poked the mattress, wanting answers yet not wanting to touch it. After a few shaky moments, she gritted her teeth and laid her hand in the center of the mattress. Tears welled up almost instantly. Such degradation. Such confusion. Such fear. She sank to her knees as the past revealed itself in a barrage of images.

A naked woman.

"Isn't this what you want?"

"You filthy slut. Haven't you learned anything? Can't you remember a thing I've tried to teach you? You're supposed to be a wife and mother. That's what a lady would do."

He tossed a blanket at her. It was itchy, grubby against her skin. She quickly scrambled onto her knees and wrapped herself inside its abrasive cover. "I can be a lady. I was a lady. Until Patrick threw me out. He left me no choice. I have to survive."

The man sat beside her. He stroked her hair and gentled his voice. This was the kind man she knew. The man she could turn to for comfort. "I want to help you."

"I don't want to live like this."

His soft caress became a clinical grasp of her chin. He turned her face from side to side, shaking his head.

"I can save you from this life."

This is wrong. This feels wrong!

"I can cure your problem."

"What?"

Soft gentle words became damning lectures. Damning lectures became unnerving silence.

"*I thought your gift— I thought this was how I was supposed to pay you back.*"

"*Shut up, you crazy freak!*"

Get up. Move. Go. Get out.

"*Abi in malam rem. Abi in malam rem.*"

The man slapped her. Hard across the face.

Kelsey flinched, her head ringing with the memory of Jeb's final good-bye. She jerked her hand off the mattress and tumbled back onto her bottom.

Her heart raced in her chest. Her lungs couldn't seem to find enough oxygen in the stale air.

Mary had been punished the same way she had. Ridiculed for being different. Singled out.

But Jeb had merely mocked and abused.

This man cleansed, purified, killed.

"Oh, God, Mary." Kelsey picked up her flashlight and scrambled to her feet. "Oh, God."

Mary had died in this room. It wasn't a crime of passion. Or a business transaction gone horribly wrong.

It was an exorcism.

Kelsey lurched across the room to the far wall. She swept the light back and forth across the rough slats of rotting wood, searching for something too tiny to find by vision alone. Shaking so hard that the batteries rattled inside the flashlight, she squeezed her eyes shut and turned around.

Slowly, ever so slowly, dreading the coming sensation the way she'd dread a knife to the heart, she pressed her back into the wall. "Oh, God." *Matrona. Abi in malam rem.* "Mary!"

Kelsey clutched at her throat. *Scratches flayed open as he shoved her brutally against the wall.* Kelsey forced her eyes open. *Her hair tangled in the wood's coarse texture and ripped from her scalp.* Black and white.

Not a metaphor of fading vision.

Not a liquor bottle.

Not a police car.

A collar.

Kelsey spun around. She shone her light on the rotting remnants of wood. There. Facts.

A handful of hairs, torn from a woman's scalp.

The rush of relief and triumph almost made her giddy.

If T needed facts…

A hard, bruising hand muffled her mouth and dragged her back against a stout, unyielding chest.

"I knew you were one of those freaks the second I laid eyes on you." The hate-filled voice spit the condemnation against her ear. "I'll teach you how to be a good woman. Or you'll die trying."

The pungent cloth he held over her mouth and nose muffled her screams until she passed out.

Chapter Twelve

T ignored the pain in his knee and took the steps two at a time. He pushed his way through the crowded hallway and prayed to God he wasn't too late.

"Excuse me," he said to the last startled man waiting in line for the clinic.

He burst in on Doc Siegel, sitting in front of a patient on the bed, administering some kind of shot. "What the…?"

"Where is she?"

The skinny son of a bitch shot to his feet. "You can't barge in here—"

T got right in his face, articulating every word with a biting threat. "Where is she?"

Siegel was plastered, judging by the bleary focus in his eyes, but he wasn't stupid. But there was no need to identify *she*. "I haven't seen your crazy girlfriend. Not since she wigged out on me a couple of nights ago."

"Um, Doc?" The small, grizzled man on the bed wheezed and interrupted. "Is this a bad time?"

T tore his gaze away from Siegel's beady black eyes to spare the old man an explanation. He pulled back his coat and jacket, exposing his gun. The old man gasped.

T pulled his badge from his belt and flashed it. "K.C.P.D., sir. This is police business. You'd better get out."

The old man rose. Siegel pushed him back to his seat. "I'm treating this man for pneumonia. Who knows how many other cases are waiting out there? I'm the only treatment they get—you can't toss him out."

"I'm not tossing him." T took the older man by the arm and helped him up. "I'm strongly suggesting that he might not want to stick around while I'm talking to you."

"Do you have a warrant? I'll sue you for harassment."

"I have probable cause to ask you anything I want. I'm looking for a missing woman." He stepped closer to the grungy doctor. "I have probable cause to throw you across that desk if I find out anything's happened to her."

The old man tugged on T's grip. "Are you talking about that red-haired lady from the newspaper picture?"

T glanced down at the old man's rheumy, yet lucid eyes. "Have you seen her?"

"She came in before dinner. I haven't seen her since."

Siegel turned and shuffled toward his desk. "And I haven't seen her period. Now get the hell out of my office."

Toward his desk. Something Kelsey had warned him about flashed in his mind. Shoving the old man behind him, T pulled out his gun and pointed it straight at Siegel. "Move away from the desk."

"What are you going to do? Put me out of my stinkin' misery?" Ignoring T's warning, Siegel reached into the open desk drawer...

"Don't do it."

...and pulled out a bottle of booze.

Without wasting a breath on a curse, T strode to the desk and pushed Siegel aside, checking the drawer for himself. He quickly opened the other drawers and found papers and supplies and more bottles. But no gun.

"Kelsey said you kept a gun in here," T prompted. "Where is it?"

Siegel wavered back and forth as he inspected the open drawers himself. "I guess it's gone."

"And you didn't report it?"

"This is no-man's land, Detective. Things get stolen here all the time."

"Like that doll you pawned last year?" Siegel's gaze darted to T's and tried to focus for a moment. "You don't seem like the doll collecting type, and yet here you are down at The Underground with an antique worth almost a grand. Where'd you get the doll?"

Siegel's sallow skin blanched and he sank into his chair. "Clinic's closed, Mr. Amos." The old man nodded and left. "I want a lawyer."

"You'll get a lawyer when you tell me where Kelsey Ryan is."

Siegel shook his head. "I pawned the doll because I needed supplies for the clinic."

When he lifted the bottle to his mouth once more, T snatched it from his hand. "What did you do to Kelsey?"

"Nothing, I swear." He dropped his face into his hands and his shoulders shook as if he was crying. "I only killed that first girl, I swear. And I don't even remember doing it. I must have been so wasted. I swear to God, I didn't hurt anybody else."

T frowned. Only one? "You killed Jezebel?"

Siegel raised his head and looked at the bottle in T's hand as if it was a lifeline denied him. "That's what he told me. When he found me with the body, I guess it was easy to see that I'd done it."

Too pat. Too easy. The facts had added up too easily at the precinct office. The confession came too easily now.

"Who found you with the body, Doc?"

Lifting his gaze to T's, the bleary drunk answered. "Ulysses."

Reverend Wingate. "And he didn't report the murder to the police?"

"He said I could atone for my sin by staying on at the mission and taking care of these people. He lied and said I was at the morning church service with him so I'd have an alibi. Then we took the body out to the trash and called it in."

"He covered for *you.*" T worked his brain around everything he'd read, everything Siegel was telling him. Everything Kelsey had seen.

Black and white.

"Son of a bitch."

The pieces finally fell into place.

T set the bottle on the desk and pulled out his handcuffs. When Siegel reached for the whiskey, T snatched his wrist and cuffed him to his chair. "I hate to say this, Siegel. But I don't think you killed those women." He pulled his cell phone from his pocket and punched in a number. "I don't even think you killed Jezebel. But you did cover up a murder and hinder a police investigation. And I know there's got to be some law about practicing medicine in your condition. Stay put."

The phone picked up as he headed out the door. "Ginny. Get Josh and A. J. on the line and get them down to the Wingate Mission. I've got a lot of civilians on the premises I need to clear out. I think all hell's about to break loose."

KELSEY'S HEAD felt like a ton of bricks as she drifted back toward consciousness. It pounded as if those bricks were shifting inside her skull when she tried to open her eyes.

"Abi in malam rem. Abi in malam rem."

The chant grated against her ears and abraded her soul with fear. She could barely breathe beneath the pressure in her chest.

"You…are one heck of a lot of trouble, Ms. Ryan."

Her eyes snapped open at the grimly solicitous voice. "Reverend Wingate."

Her head wasn't just throbbing from whatever drug he'd used to knock her out. The bearded reverend with the black-and-white collar pressed his heavy hand against her forehead, filling her with chilling impressions of ten deaths. Ten cleansings. Innocent women judged unfit to be wives and mothers and friends and contributing members of society.

Judge, jury and executioner. Like all his other victims, Ulysses Wingate had found Kelsey guilty. "I tried to help you." His smile turned her stomach. She tried to pull away from his touch, but her hands were bound with a long silk scarf and his hands were heavy on her forehead and heart. "I invited you into my sanctuary. To cast aside your affliction and become a better person. And how do you repay me?"

"By finding out the truth. By finally laying those women's innocent souls to rest."

His hand fisted in her sweater. He jerked her up to a sitting position. "Don't you talk to me about innocent souls!"

His face was so close to hers, she could feel his beard scratching her skin in a repulsive caress.

"I know your kind." While his hot breath damned her, Kelsey looked beyond his shoulder to take note of her surroundings. He was sitting on the bed beside her up in the attic. Still dark, still dusty, still rotten with mold and decay. "You're abominations of nature. Possessed with unholy powers. I thought you could learn a better way. But you can't be taught."

She spotted the gun on the dresser behind him. He hadn't used a gun in any of the other murders.

He shoved her onto her back and wedged his hand against her throat. "See? You're doing it now!" Kelsey spluttered for breath. He stood over her, increasing the pressure. She beat at his arm with her bound fists and twisted her hips, trying to escape. "Don't fight me. It'll be so much easier to help you if you don't fight."

His grip lessened enough for a gasping breath, but no more, as he leaned back toward the bowl beside the gun. She blinked as he splashed water into her face and chanted something in Latin. Her lungs burned. Her thoughts clouded.

She couldn't pass out. She had to find a way to stay conscious and try to escape.

"Every year, I take on a project." Target a victim, he meant. "I take her in. Treat her kindly. Give her mean-ingful work and try to teach her the way to be a good wife, a good mother, a good woman. But if she refuses to learn…" He eyed Kelsey up and down, clicking his tongue as if he loathed what he saw. "I suppose New Year's is another holiday."

Kelsey turned her head to the side as he splashed her again. *"Stop it!"* she wanted to scream. *T!*

A new surge of hope energized her, dampened the fear. T would come for her. She'd left him that note, and he was too smart not to figure it out. *Find me, T,* she prayed. *Find me.*

As if he could somehow read her mind, Ulysses Wingate eased his grip and laughed. She sucked in a reviving breath of air and scrambled to a sitting position, with her back against the rough, slatted wall. "Detective Banning is coming for you. He'll figure this out. We're partners. We work together. He knows everything I know."

He shook his head and slipped the gun into the waistband of his black slacks. "That detective friend of yours is so blinded by lust that he's chasing the wrong clues. Clues that I've carefully set up over so many years. Doc thinks he got drunk one night and killed a woman. I let him think that—all these years. Even made him believe I'd conducted a church service. I did. Later in the day. But that morning, Jezebel and I were the only two taking part in the ceremony. In return he's done whatever I've asked of him, incriminating himself time and again."

He pulled another scarf out of the dresser's top drawer. Could she overpower him? With her hands tied together? Could she outrun him? Only if she got past him. She had to stall for time. She had to get that gun. She had to think. "You gave Doc the doll to pawn."

"Yes. He needed money for the clinic. He had no idea where it came from." Wingate twisted the ends of the scarf around his fists. "He's been too drunk with guilt and booze all these years to ever question my instructions."

Curling her knees up to her chest, Kelsey backed to the farthest corner of the bed. "What does Patrick Halliwell have to do with all this?"

He paused, as if surprised to hear the name. "Our benefactor?"

Kelsey watched his hands snap the scarf tight. Her aching throat suddenly felt parched at the thought of being strangled to death. "I know he was Jezebel's husband. Mary's husband. You've been blackmailing him, too, haven't you."

The reverend laughed, shaking his head. "Well, aren't you just the clever little thing." Kelsey flinched as he pulled the scarf taut and advanced.

"No." She tried to work her feet beneath her so she could have leverage and stand. "No!"

He slipped the scarf between her lips, pulling them hard against her teeth and cutting the sides of her mouth. "Finding out that Mary was Patrick Halliwell's wife was an unexpected bonus. Do you have any idea what guilt can do to a man? Imagine, sending your wife to a hellhole like no-man's land. And she dies." He tied a knot at the base of her skull, plucking out hairs, bruising her scalp. "He's been atoning for his cruelty ever since."

Kelsey jerked away when he caressed her face. Her cheek caught the wall, raising a welt. He tried to touch that, too. She screamed behind the gag and knocked his hand away.

The reverend cursed and grabbed at his forearm. "You freak!" He pushed up his sleeve and inspected a small, bloody gash on his forearm. About the size of a poodle bite.

Inspired by Frosty's ferocity, Kelsey pushed to her feet and lunged at Ulysses. She managed to knock him back a step and leaped to the floor.

But she was dizzy. With her hands bound, her balance was off. She veered toward the door, but she could hear him behind her. She grabbed the stool, swung around and aimed it at his head. But he put up an arm and batted it aside. It crashed to the floor and careened into the shadows.

He didn't even give her time to turn around. Kelsey's cries were gobbled up in silk and violence. He grabbed her around the neck, fisted her grandmother's necklace between his fingers and flung her to the floor. The chain popped and he slung the pendant away. *"No!"*

Pain ratcheted through her skull as every bruising touch—dragging her kicking and twisting across the floor, throwing her onto the bed, pinning her hip with his knee and yanking her arms above her head to tie them to the headboard—was intensified by horrific images of the same abuse he'd used on ten other women.

"I do good work here." He whispered the words like a damning curse. "I need a doctor and I need money to make this happen. To help these people. To save them when society forgets them and they're too evil to save themselves.

"Now you are going to sit here and shut up like a good little girl until I can take care of you later."

He raised his arm. Kelsey braced for the backhanded slap that would send her into oblivion.

"Touch her and you're dead."

T HIT THE SWITCH, flooding the sadistic scene with light. *Son of a bitch.* Kelsey was bound and gagged. Her face was bleeding. That bastard had a gun and he was going to hit her again.

Anger—distilled by pure, adrenaline-pumping fear—poured through his veins, sharpening his senses and making his aim crystal clear. He cradled his Glock between hands that were rock steady and motivated to do some damage of their own.

"Move away from her, Wingate, or I will shoot you right between those smug little eyes."

The preacher froze, one hand on Kelsey's throat, the other poised to strike.

For a big man, he moved surprisingly fast. For a man of the cloth, he had surprisingly little compunction about endangering another human being's life.

Wingate rolled to his feet, hauling Kelsey with him. In one smooth maneuver, he had her braced in front of him with the gun at her temple. "I don't think so."

"You can't get away." T held his ground, not risking an advance, refusing to retreat. "Your accomplice is already under arrest downstairs and backup is in the building."

"My accomplice is a weak, drunken man. Anything he told you about me will never stand up in court."

He allowed himself a brief glance into Kelsey's eyes. They were frightened, but clear and strong. "Let her go and I'll let you live to take your chances in court."

Wingate shook his head. "She's twisted your mind

all around with her sinful ways. She's got the devil in her head, Banning. Let me take care of her and I'll put us both out of our misery."

T was tempted beyond sane, rational sense to take his chances in this Mexican standoff and put a bullet through Wingate's head.

But Kelsey was there. Too close. The woman he loved.

She couldn't read minds, but he let everything he felt for her shine through his eyes. *Be strong, sweetheart. Give me a chance. Give us a chance.*

What? Was that a nod? Was she thinking…?

Oh, no. No, no!

Kelsey shoved her fists into Wingate's forearm. The reverend cursed in pain, the gun shifted.

"Get down!" he hollered, ready to fire.

But Wingate jerked her off her feet, right into his line of sight. She kicked the reverend's shins, elbowed, screamed.

"No!"

T charged. He lowered his shoulder and rammed full force into Wingate's gut. The two men tumbled to the floor with a thud. Kelsey rolled free, but the fight was on.

KELSEY RIPPED the gag from her mouth and forced her aching jaw and raw throat to form a single letter. "T!"

Oh, God, what had she done? He was supposed to take a shot, like Dirty Harry on the firing range. But now both men had guns. Both were so angry. She was so afraid.

Ulysses Wingate was a bigger man. But T was younger, stronger. The reverend's foot connected with T's bad knee and she cried out.

She heard their pants, their curses. They smashed into

furniture, screeching it across the floor. Grunts and oofs mixed with the chilling sounds of fist on bone.

A gun skittered across the floor.

What should she do? How could she help?

He'd said backup was in the building. Of course. Get help. She ran to the door and screamed, "Help!"

But she was so hoarse. Her throat was so sore. The weak sound echoed back up the empty stairwell. The gun.

She'd never fired one in her life. She'd only held T's once. But it had been deafening in her ears.

"Give it up, Wingate," T ordered. He'd pulled his opponent up to his feet. Four hands on one gun.

"I'll die first," the reverend promised.

Kelsey scrambled for the discarded weapon. She ignored the smattering of deadly images. She held it up over her head, closed her eyes and aimed at the ceiling. She squeezed the trigger and…

Boom!

Kelsey jerked. Her eyes popped open.

She hadn't fired.

"T?"

The two men stood locked together, frozen in a split second of time. Oh. My. God.

Reverend Wingate's eyes stared, wide-open with fury and surprise. T stared right back.

"T?" Kelsey lowered her own weapon. The others would hear it.

Why didn't Wingate fall?

T took a step back, fisted his hand and smashed it into the middle of the preacher's face, driving him to his knees. "Don't you ever…touch her again." He pushed the big man to the floor, where his head lolled back, unconscious.

Kelsey shook as hours of fear and frustration worked the final sparks of energy out of her body. T tucked the gun into his belt and glanced over his shoulder at her. A cut bled over his left eye; his skin was pale. "We caught him, partner."

She offered him a weak smile. "We sure did, smart guy."

She dropped her gaze to the fallen man, needing to make sure for ten other women and herself that the threat was finally over.

Kelsey frowned.

Where was the blood?

"T?" A whole new sense of dread suffused her. He turned to face her, took a step toward her. "T!"

He'd been shot. A bright crimson stain slowly seeped across the front of his crisp, white shirt.

T FELT HIS KNEES buckle before he could get across the room to Kelsey. "Are you all right?" he asked, going down to the floor. "Are you hurt?"

He needed to know. His twisted-up heart needed to know.

She ran to him, caught his shoulders in her arms and sank to the floor with him. "Shut up. Just shut up."

"Is that a yes or a no?" Damn, it burned. Worse than the chest wound, but not as bad as the knee.

Kelsey had him in her lap, his cheek pillowed against one of those beautiful breasts. She ripped open his shirt, placed her cool, bare hand against his belly. Oh, Lord, she was crying. He tried to reach up and brush the tears away from those soft brown eyes.

But she was groping around his pockets now. "Where's your phone?"

"Backup's downstairs. They'll have heard the shot." He grabbed her hand and brought it back to his heart. For the third time in his career, he'd been in a shoot-out. He knew the drill by now. Take out the bad guy, save the girl. But this was the first time he'd gotten the second part of that equation right. "It hurts like hell, believe me." He idly wondered if she could sense everything he felt through the tips of his fingers. His relief, his love. His physical pain. T cringed. Oh, man, he didn't want her to feel that. "It's not life threatening, sweetheart. I'll be okay."

"Dammit, T, this is not okay." She moved her hand back to the wound and pressed. Ow. Hell. The images she must be seeing. "Where's your backup?"

"Jeesh. I'm running out of places to get shot, you know. One of these times, I'm going to stop—"

Kelsey cradled his jaw in her hand and smothered his complaining with a heart-deep kiss. Automatically, his arms went around her.

Hmm. The pain seemed to recede exponentially when she showered her attention on him like this.

"I love you, T," she whispered against his mouth. "Don't you ever joke about getting hurt again. I love you."

She kissed him again.

What did she say?

T found the reserves of strength to wrap her up and take over the embrace as best he could. He barely remembered the pain of being shot. He did remember the fear of losing her feeling a hell of a lot worse than the bullet in his belly.

Hmm again. When she'd said that love stuff, he couldn't seem to think of anything much but her—and how good, how right, how perfect it made him feel to hear those words come out of her mouth.

"Oh, yeah. Banning's hurtin' real bad."

As soon as Kelsey heard Josh Taylor's voice, she pulled away, demanding medical attention immediately. "He's hurt. He's been shot. You have to help him."

T nodded an okay to the two armed detectives standing in the doorway, waiting for an all clear to enter. "You'd better cuff Wingate before he comes to. And get a crime-lab team up here. I'm sure you'll find plenty of circumstantial evidence to go along with Siegel and Halliwell's testimony." He glanced up at Kelsey. "Right?"

"You figured it out, too?"

He reached up to finger a strand of that bright red hair, that didn't detract for one moment from what a beautiful, brilliant, special woman she was. "*We* figured it out, sweetheart. We're a team, remember?"

Kelsey nodded. He truly hoped she believed in what he was saying.

Before the paramedics swarmed in to separate them and treat their respective injuries, T palmed the back of her head and insisted on one more kiss. "I love you, Kelsey Ryan. Put your hands on me and feel that. Put your faith in me and know that my heart is yours."

He clutched her hand, lacing their naked hands together, skin to skin. "Can you feel what I feel? Do you believe me?"

She brushed her fingers across his jaw and smiled. "I'm sorry I ever doubted you. You don't have to prove a thing to me, T. Just love me."

He smiled back as her sure acceptance made him whole again.

"Yes, ma'am."

Epilogue

"Are we really snowed in?"

Kelsey cinched her robe around her waist as she dashed to the window and pulled the curtain aside to peek through the lacy crystals of ice that clung to the panes of glass. The early-morning sunlight was bright and magical, reflecting off the coat of ice that turned the bare branches and rolling hills of southwest Missouri into a winter wonderland.

Two strong arms wrapped around her waist and snuggled her back against the warm wall of T's bare chest. "More like iced over. Great way to celebrate the New Year, hmm?" For a moment, Kelsey relaxed in the security of his embrace. But muscles began to tighten and nerves started to tingle when he dipped his head to nuzzle along the side of her neck, punctuating every point with a sensual kiss. "We could have gone for some fun in the sun. Florida, the Bahamas. But you insisted on a lake cabin in the Ozarks. In the off-season. During the worst December storm they've had in a decade."

When the drizzling sensations of warmth seeping through her body made her knees weak, Kelsey turned and wrapped her arms around T's neck. "I find this much more cozy than lying on a beach. Don't you?"

The heat in his green eyes seemed to agree. "This is the second time we've celebrated New Year's Eve like this. It's a holiday tradition I could get used to."

"Me, too." Kelsey feathered her fingers across his lips and was delighted as he kissed each one. The images that crossed her mind were happy, positive, hopeful—and she owed that to the faith and acceptance this man had in her.

It had been a hell of a year since that awful night in the attic of the Wingate Mission.

As if sensing the darker turn of her thoughts, T's hands began rubbing slow, comforting circles against her back. And the patience in his handsome expression was every bit as evident as the desire inside his jeans.

He gave her a moment to touch and explore and re-flect. Kelsey brushed her fingers across his shoulders and felt his strength. She touched the old scar on his chest and gently caressed the newer, pinker scar on his flat belly. A knot tightened inside her chest as her mind replayed that horrible moment when she knew T had been shot. That he was bleeding, maybe dying, for her.

"Don't." T's voice—in the here and now—whispered against her ear. He framed her face between his hands and tilted her gaze back up to his. "Feel the good things, too. Feel the love."

Kelsey flattened her palms against the scorching planes of his chest and nodded. "I do."

And as his mouth closed over hers in the tenderest

of kisses, Kelsey's mind filled with other images. Memories of her own. T's memories. T's love.

Ulysses Wingate could preach in prison to his heart's content—until his death penalty appeals ran out. But thoughts of the trial and sentencing hearing, of T's recovery in the hospital and at home, were quickly pushed aside by images like the welcome-back party at the precinct office—where Captain Taylor had laughingly presented T with an engraved plaque that read *Bullet Magnet,* and Kelsey had traded a hug and kindled a genuine friendship with Ginny Rafferty-Taylor. She saw the private celebration she and T had had at his apartment later that night.

Then, of course, there was the wedding. This one happy and full of pride and hope—and *she* was the bride standing beside T at the altar. And now, with T's precision hands inside her robe and her senses stirring with much more than psychic impressions, they were making new memories—new images she could see in her mind and treasure.

Kelsey was ready to thank him in the way he liked best. But she had to give credit where it was due. "It was awfully nice of your mother to watch Frosty for the weekend so we could finally have some kind of honeymoon."

"Are you kidding? The way she spoils that dog, you'd think we'd already given her a grandchild."

Reluctantly pushing his lips from the dip at the base of her throat, Kelsey demanded that he look at her. "Is that something you want to work on? A grandchild for Moira?"

His answering smile was pure seduction.

Though her body leaped in eager response, she felt compelled to warn him. "You understand that my psychic abilities are an inherited trait? Lucy Belle had them. I do. A child of ours might, too."

Detective Logic's eyes narrowed and she knew he had more than one way to convince her that they really did have a future together. "What are you saying? That I couldn't handle a special child?"

"No. You can handle anything the world throws at you."

"Because I'm that unique mix of Atticus Finch and Dirty Harry?"

"Because you're Thomas Merle Banning. A damn good detective. An intelligent, caring man. And my husband."

"Husband. I like that." He kissed her. Firmly. She liked *that.* "Any child we have would be special to me." His arms tightened around her and he kissed her again, teasing her in a way that would never hurt. "Besides, I'm sure there are numerous books I could read on raising a psychic child, Web sites I could check—" he zeroed in for a kiss that would seal the argument "—personal interviews I could conduct."

In a matter of minutes, they were on top of the cabin's down-filled comforter, well on their way to making that special baby.

Kelsey was no longer afraid to touch, no longer afraid to ask for what she wanted, no longer afraid. Because of this man who loved her. This cop. This skeptic. This hero.

"Partners?" She pulled him down on top of her, invited him inside, welcomed him home.

T smiled. "In the very best way."

* * * * *

Coming in April 2005 from Harlequin Intrigue...
Watch for POLICE BUSINESS by Julie Miller,
the next gripping installment in **THE PRECINCT!**

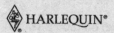

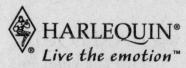

Like a phantom in the night
comes an exciting promotion from

HARLEQUIN®

INTRIGUE®

ECLIPSE

GOTHIC ROMANCE

Look for a provocative
gothic-themed thriller each month
by your favorite Intrigue authors!
Once you surrender to the classic
blend of chilling suspense and
electrifying romance in these
gripping page-turners, there will
be no turning back....

Available wherever Harlequin books are sold.

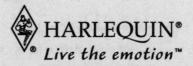

HARLEQUIN®
Live the emotion™

www.eHarlequin.com

HIE3

SPOTLIGHT

Dying To Play
Debra Webb

When FBI agent Trace Callahan arrives in Atlanta to investigate a baffling series of multiple homicides, deputy chief of detectives Elaine Jentzen isn't prepared for the immediate attraction between them. And as they hunt to find the killer known as the Gamekeeper, it seems that Trace is singled out as his next victim...unless Elaine can stop the Gamekeeper before it's too late.

Available January 2005.

Exclusive Bonus Features:
Author Interview
Sneak Preview...
and more!

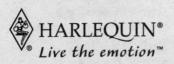

HARLEQUIN®
Live the emotion™

If you enjoyed what you just read,
then we've got an offer you can't resist!

Take 2 bestselling love stories FREE!

Plus get a FREE surprise gift!

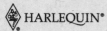

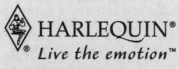

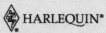

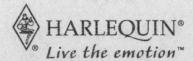